THE UNHOLY

PAUL DeBLASSIE III

HALLOWED REALMS
PRESS

Cover Design and Formatting by The Book Khaleesi
Editing by The Editing Hall

Published by Hallowed Realms Press
Albuquerque, NM

ISBN: 978-0-578-57875-0
Library of Congress Control Number: 2018903217

Printed in the United States of America

ALSO BY PAUL DEBLASSIE III

Goddess of Everything

Goddess of the Wild Thing

WHAT READERS ARE SAYING

"Paul DeBlassie III has brought us a richly imagined super-natural thriller set in the high mountain desert of Aztlan, where Claire Sanchez, an herbalist and medicine woman, has come to reclaim her healing heritage and uncover the secrets of her mother's death. The book digs deep into legend, folk-lore, and the author's own imagination to paint a stirring picture of a traditional curanderismo pitted against the oppressive forces of institutional religious power. Make sure you have lots of time; once you start reading this book, it will be hard to put down."

**- Stephan V. Beyer, author of Singing to the Plants:
A Guide to Mestizo Shamanism in the Upper Amazon**

"The Unholy, an excellent novel by Paul DeBlassie III, keeps the reader engaged throughout in mystery, suspense, and church politics. In addition to vividly depicting the beautiful landscape and culture of New Mexico, it exposes and strengthens the traditional work of the medicine women of the Southwest. I am looking forward to Dr. DeBlassie's next book."

**- Eliseo "Cheo" Torres, author of Curandero:
A Life In Mexican Folk Healing
Professor and University Administrator**

"Paul DeBlassie III has captured the energy and challenges of shamanic healing practices in a book that will keep people reading long into the night. Many speak or write about shamanic experiences or skills with no real understanding; Paul, on the other hand, is the real deal. Enjoy a great read!"

- **Jim Graywolf Petruzzi,**
Author of White Man, Red Road, Five Colors

TO KATE

*T*here are sacraments of evil as well as of good about us, and we live and move to my belief in an unknown world, a place where there are caves and shadows and dwellers in twilight.

~ Arthur Machen ~

PROLOGUE

L ightning streaked across a midnight dark sky, making the neck hairs of a five-year-old girl crouched beneath a cluster of twenty-foot pines in the Turquoise Mountains of Aztlan stand on end. The long wavy strands of her auburn mane floated outward with the static charge. It felt as though the world was about to end.

Seconds later, lightning struck a lone tree nearby and a crash of thunder shook the ground. Her body rocked back and forth, trembling with terror. She lost her footing, sandstone crumbling beneath her feet, and then regained it; still, she did not feel safe. There appeared to be reddish eyes watching from behind scrub oaks and mountain pines, scanning her every movement and watching her quick breaths. Then everything became silent.

The girl leaned against the trunk of the nearest tree. The night air wrapped its frigid arms tightly around her, and she wondered if she would freeze to death or, even worse, stay there through the night and by morning be nothing but the blood and bones left by hungry animals. Her breaths became quicker and were so shallow that no air seemed to reach her lungs. The dusty earth gave up quick bursts of sand from gusts of northerly winds that blew so fiercely into her nostrils that she coughed but tried to stifle the sounds because she didn't want to be noticed.

As she squeezed her arms around the trunk of the pine tree, the scent of sap was soothing. Finally, the wind died down and sand stopped blowing into her face. She slowly opened her eyes, hoping she would be in another place, but she was not; in fact, the reality of her waking nightmare was more obvious than ever.

Wide-eyed with fear at the nightmarish scene playing out before her, she clung to the tree. In the distance, she saw her mother raising a staff with both hands, her arm muscles bulging underneath her soaked blouse. Directed straight ahead, her mother's gaze was like that of an eagle, her power as mighty as the winds and the lightning. The girl loved her mother and, through her mind, sent her strength so that she would win this battle and the two of them could safely go away from this scary place.

The girl turned to follow as her mother's gaze shifted to an area farther away and so dark that only shadows seemed to abide there. To and fro, her mother's eyes darted before fixing on a black-cloaked figure who emerged from behind a huge boulder surrounded by tall trees whose branches crisscrossed the sky. He was much bigger than her mother, at least by a foot, and his cloak flapped wildly as winds once again ripped through the mountains.

Swinging a long, hooked pole, the man bounded toward her mother like a hungry beast toward its prey. His black cloak looked like the wings of a huge bat as they reflected the eerie light of the full moon. As his pole caught the moonlight and a golden glow bounced back onto the figure, the girl saw his face with its cold blue eyes that pierced the nighttime chill. He seemed to grow bigger with each step, and the girl's heart pounded so loudly that she was sure he would be able to hear it.

The stranger stopped a short distance from the girl. Crouched low between rows of trees, trying to make herself disappear, she saw him clearly as he threw his head back and let out a high-pitched cry like a rabid coyote. The air crackled. Thunder struck. Lightning flashed. She was blinded and then could see again.

Quick as a crazed coyote jumps and bites, the man struck her mother, his black cape flapping wildly in the wind.

The girl leapt to her feet, her legs trembling, her knees buckling. Straining to see through the branches, she was terrified.

The moon vanished behind dark clouds rolling overhead. Then came a scream of terror that cut to the bone. Now the night was lit up again by lightning flashing across the mountain range, and the girl could see the black-hooded man hit her mother again and again.

Her mother crumpled to the ground and stopped moving.

The girl's hand flew to her open mouth, stifling a scream.

The man stood over her mother, his long pole poised in the air, ready to strike again.

A twig snapped in the forest, and the girl spun toward the sound, holding her breath. Then she saw three gray forms slowly creeping toward her through the darkness and recognized them as wolves. She was not afraid as they encircled her, their warm fur brushing her skin. One after another, the wolves lifted their snouts and looked into her eyes, each silently communicating that she would be protected.

Her mother cried out again. The girl turned and saw her rising to her feet, then striking the man's chest with her staff.

As he batted his pole against her shoulders, her staff flew out of her hands, landing yards away in a thicket of scrub oak.

Her mother screamed and blindly groped for it.

The girl jumped up, then stopped when the black-hooded figure looked her way. Tears clouded her vision, and all she saw was darkness. Tears rolled down her cheeks, dropping into the tiny stream of water running beneath the tree she was clutching. She looked down and saw the dim reflection of her frightened self.

As she peered through the trees to catch sight of her mother, a wailing wind blew the man's cloak into the air, making him again look like a monstrous bat. Once more he swung his rod high and smashed it against the back of her mother's head. She saw and heard her mother's body thump against the hollowed trunk of the lightning-struck tree and slump to the ground. The evil man bent over her mother's limp body and howled.

Suddenly, the girl felt arms encircle her waist, and she was swept away, deeper into the forest. She sobbed and at first let herself be taken because she had no strength. But then she became angry and started pushing against the arms carrying her, trying to escape and run back to her mother. She wanted to make her mother well, and then this nightmare would stop and they could go away.

"Hush now, child," said a voice she recognized as that of her mother's closest friend. "The man cannot harm you, *mijita*, as long as you are with us. We will make him think you are dead. But you must be very quiet. *Ya no llores*," the woman warned, raising a finger to her lips.

The woman then carried her into a dark cave illuminated

by the light of a single candle. The cave was frightening, with shadows of what appeared to be goblins and demons dancing on the red sandstone walls. "I will return for you soon. You will be safe here," the woman said. The girl watched the woman walk away, shivering as a breeze blew through the cave's narrow passages.

Closing her eyes, she rocked back and forth—imagining herself safe in her mother's arms—then opened her eyes to the light of the full moon shining through the mouth of the cave. The shadows on the walls were just shadows now, no longer goblins and demons. As she slipped into a trance, images flickered in her mind. She saw the woman who had brought her to this place scattering pieces of raw meat around the open mesa where her mother had struggled, helped by two other women the girl could not identify.

Suddenly, the scene shifted to a stone ledge jutting over the mesa, and she heard the pounding footsteps of a man running toward the women. The girl felt her heart race and her breathing quicken, afraid that the bad man would spot them and kill them. Then the image shifted again, and she now saw on the mesa three gray wolves circling the raw meat and the man walking away from the granite ledge. As he left, she heard his thought: *The child is dead.*

1

A chilly autumn morning wind swept over the grounds of the Ecclesia Dei Psychiatric Hospital. Claire Sanchez walked along the red brick path to her office in the administration building, where she had worked as the director of Mental Health Workers and Natural Therapeutic Services. She stopped for a moment to gaze over the more than two thousand acres of high-mountain desert three miles south of the plaza in the region of Aztlan. Homeland to generations of peoples whose ancestors once crossed the Mesoamerican border to settle what is now the American Southwest, Aztlan was considered by natives to be the *axis mundi*, navel of the world. Aztlan was the Land of Herons, of the Seven Caves, of the mystic beauty of horizon-to-horizon turquoise blue skies, arid desert mountain air, and great swells of earth like reclining nude goddesses. Aztlan was home to the *katsinas*, rain spirits, Tlaloc, the lightning god, and the feathered serpent deity Quetzalcoatl, who unites earth and sky, eternity and the death-defined world.

The turquoise blue sky arching overhead was an ocean of

delight and refreshment for Claire. She enjoyed the sight of eagles as they glided effortlessly across the cloudless expanse, the piñon and aspen trees, with clusters of loping sagebrush dotting the arroyos and mesas, the rolling hills sprinkled with Indian paintbrush, columbine, and cornflower leading the way to the base of the Sagrado Mountains that encircled the city.

Claire glanced at the granite megalith rooted in the middle of the courtyard with an inscription that read, "Dedicated to the Faithful Hispanic and Native Americans of the Ecclesia Dei." The Ecclesia Dei was a wealthy, centuries-old church in Aztlan that prided itself on charitable care for its members, particularly the natives that populated Ecclesia Dei Hospital. Few, if any, of those admitted due to mental distress were ever discharged from it, remaining ministered to for the rest of their lives. Claire's passion was to alleviate people's physical and mental suffering, which she had the chance to do during the last two years at Ecclesia Dei Psychiatric Hospital. The hospital was full, the patient need great, Claire single-minded, intent.

That morning, after her regular four-mile run and shower, Claire had looked into her bedroom mirror and noted that her five-foot-three, one- hundred-ten-pound body appeared healthy and strong, inspiring her to get to the hospital to try to help her first patient's health. On some days, the sadness pervading the hospital seemed overwhelming to her. But when Claire felt most worn out and discouraged, she'd remember the reason she had taken this job—her dedication to her people, the natives of Aztlan.

A month prior to her graduation the hospital's administrator, Karl Himmel, had written to the School of Natural Therapeutics. As there was a shortage of health-care practitioners in Aztlan, especially those qualified to treat psychiatric patients, Himmel hoped the school would assist him in placing suitable practitioners with the hospital. The letter announced an opening for a licensed natural therapist with a background in mental health services to work with Hispanic and Native American patients. This was an unusual combination of skills to request since few natural therapists were trained in psychology, focusing instead on healing the body through massage as the primary course of therapeutic intervention. The fact that Claire had supported herself during her professional training in natural therapeutics by being a mental health worker at the Turquoise County Mental Health Center and also was a *mestiza*—Hispanic and Native American—prompted her to immediately inquire about the position. Her teachers' glowing letters of recommendation, along with her personal and professional qualifications, made her competitive for the position.

Claire anxiously waited a number of weeks before finally hearing from the hospital's administration. After driving to the hospital to be interviewed by Mr. Himmel, she was promptly offered the job at a higher salary than expected. Although she had been surprised by the immediacy of his decision, she didn't hesitate to accept his offer, even though her colleagues and teachers had cautioned her about taking on too much too soon. Mr. Himmel had made clear from the outset that the patients in the Ecclesia Dei Psychiatric Hospital were "the worst of the worst," many dangerously psychotic. But something about their helplessness and hopelessness stirred Claire, making her want to work with them. And this passion and drive had never left her since her first day on the job.

Arriving at the door of the brown stucco building, Claire took one last breath of the crisp mountain air, then opened the door, prepared for the pungent odor of disinfectant that she knew would assault her senses the moment she stepped inside. It never failed to momentarily daze her. Even though she'd been traversing this corridor with its dull green linoleum and sterile white walls every morning five days a week for the past two years, she was never prepared for the stench. Each of the compound's four pueblo-style structures—the administration building, the locked ward, the open ward, and the cafeteria and gymnasium facility—smelled the same, like an overturned bucket of ammonia and water. After the initial shock, she always had to shake her head and steel herself before moving on down the corridor to her office.

Approaching her office at the end of the hallway, she unlocked her door and stepped inside the room, which, although small, met the requirements of her patients and her own need for privacy. A year after being hired, she'd been promoted to her current position, the chief attending physician, believing she was the perfect employee to bridge the gap between mental health workers and natural therapists. Without hesitation, she had accepted the position since it would permit her to more effectively care for patients. She directed clinicians to engage in more clinical services, to minimize meetings, committees, and bureaucratic dealings. Her leadership skills were noted and respected throughout the hospital.

Claire hung her wool cloak on an antique brass coat rack next to her old pine desk. The scent of piñon, from incense she'd burned the afternoon before, lingered in the air, a soothing scent that she associated with her childhood. Raised in the culture of the medicine women of northern Aztlan, Claire understood the healing properties of natural fragrances such as pine, cedar, piñon, sage, and wild chamomile. To the Aztlan medicine women, the comforting smells of the earth cleansed people and places of bad temper and foul energy. The evils of life, the medicine women taught, often caused the best of people to go down a bad path and need help. Medicine women in this tradition were said to be Women of Lozen—the name of a renowned nineteenth-century Apache woman warrior and healer who had fought with Geronimo and healed with intuition and caring. These healers had helped raise Claire when she had become a *huerfana*, a child orphaned by a mother's untimely death.

After pulling the charts for the day from the steel file cabinet in the closet and laying them on her desk, Claire went to the storage bin where she kept sealed bags of *yerba buena*, the healing tea she offered each of her patients. She had been instructed as a child to give *yerba buena* to those in need of healing, for the drink of steaming mint leaves settled the stomach and opened the rest of the body to healing.

Opening one of the bags, she inhaled the bouquet of damp earth and mint. As she pressed the herb into a tea strainer, memories of her mother, Lucia, the great woman who had loved her for the first five years of her life before she had been killed, flashed through her mind. Tears welled as Claire remembered her mother placing the delicate leaves into a ceramic pot of boiling water, stroking her head, and telling her that medicine women used the herb to soothe the stomach and heal the nerves but that the true healing came from within the heart. After drinking her mother's tea, and sharing their dreams and nightmares to ease their burdens, people inevitably left her childhood home looking younger and happier.

Recalling those days also reminded Claire of how she used to nestle close to her mother's warm body, and how helpless she felt when she saw her from a distance being struck without being able to do anything. Shaking her head, she quietly brought herself back to the present, filled a glass decanter from the small sink next to the closet, and in less than five minutes had a steaming pot of water. After dunking the strainer in, she opened the file of her first patient, Elizabeth Gonzales, a severe woman made so by a life riddled with disappointments and secrets. Claire read her notes from the session with Elizabeth two days before, a depressing reminder of how draining Elizabeth could be:

Elizabeth yelled and accused me of being a sellout, a mestiza *made white by the "man." Her hatred was intense. I needed to find a way to help her to talk about her anger and work through it rather than acting it out through outbursts of temper. As I remained calm and listened to her, she eventually stopped yelling and sat quietly for the last five minutes of the session, rocking back and forth with her arms wrapped around herself. I was careful not to say anything or make any move to touch her. She would have found either far too threatening. At the end of the session, she stood up, glared at me, then, without saying another word, walked out, slamming the door behind her.*

Claire closed the file and looked at her watch. Elizabeth was due in five minutes, at 9:00. She was always on time and did not tolerate Claire being even a minute late.

Claire took a deep breath, closed her eyes, and quieted her mind so she could focus on the day's work ahead. She noticed the unease that came with anticipating Elizabeth's grating voice and demanding presence, knowing it was a signal that the work with Elizabeth would be demanding. Soon, a mild sense of heat went up her spine to the center of her forehead, the place of the mystic third eye, and into her hands and fingertips. Claire meditated on this feeling, which gradually became stronger, softer, and kindled empathy, an ability to feel what her patients felt, to understand their pain, to help them to heal. She had learned about the mystic third eye as a young child when her mother had taught her to respect the world of invisible realities. After her mother's death, Claire had continued to learn from the medicine women who had been friends of her mother, one in particular who had assumed responsibility for her care and instructed her well in the art of healing and natural magic.

Seconds later, Claire was startled by a sharp, demanding knock at the door. Silently and slowly, she removed two ceramic tea mugs from a nearby shelf. There was another, more demanding knock accompanied by Elizabeth's harsh voice saying, "Hurry up, Claire. I know you're in there. I saw you walk in."

"Good morning, Elizabeth," Claire said, smiling as she opened the door and motioned her patient in, grateful for the morning's brief meditation and its grounding effect. It helped now, as it had many times before, to keep Elizabeth's grating manner from getting under her skin before the session had even begun. "How are you doing this morning, Elizabeth?" Claire asked, feeling a surge of concern for the woman, who seemed more anxious than usual.

Elizabeth, a brown-skinned woman in her early fifties with shoulder-length graying brown hair and at least a hundred pounds of excess weight, scowled and walked to the massage table, sitting down on the edge. "I don't want to be here, Claire," she said, her voice aggressive but also betraying a faint plea for help.

"You don't want to be here for your session?" asked Claire.

"You know what I mean," answered Elizabeth, her eyes sharpened with irritation. "I don't want to be here in the hospital."

"But you are, Elizabeth. So, let's put your session to good use. Besides having to be here, what else is angering you?" Claire inched her way in. She had to be especially sensitive with Elizabeth since she could retreat into silence for sessions on end if she in any way felt pressured. Work with Elizabeth was demanding. A misstep here or there meant therapeutic disaster, at least for a time.

Elizabeth's countenance darkened as she added, "I don't want to talk anymore."

Claire remained quiet, trying to sense what it was in Elizabeth's voice that concerned her. After a few moments, Claire recognized that Elizabeth's voice had the quality of a suicidal person standing on a ledge. Softening her own voice, she said, "It's all right, Elizabeth. We don't have to talk right now." Elizabeth stayed sitting near the end of the massage table as Claire fixed two cups of tea. She put Elizabeth's on a small wooden stand next to the massage table. The warm glow of the morning's meditation stayed with Claire as she took a sip of tea and stood near Elizabeth, silently, patiently waiting.

Elizabeth cradled the cup in her hands as she sipped. Claire had just begun to feel settled into the session as Elizabeth finished her tea, set her eyes hard on Claire, and threw a poison dart, in her gravelly voice, asserting, "You are a medicine woman—of Lozen—like your mother, Claire." The words were hate-filled, meant to wound. Despite the culture in which she had been raised, Claire considered herself a natural therapist not a medicine woman, the distinction a matter of life and death. In her mind, she had long ago made the decision that being a medicine woman like her mother meant exposing herself to evil and injury and, potentially, death. Years ago, when handed the five-foot oak staff that had belonged to her mother, Claire had angrily rejected it, refusing initiation into the way of the medicine woman. Back then, she had often had fearsome memories of being a young child in the forest, an ominous black-cloaked man assaulting her mother and hearing her mother's screams—a child's nightmare.

The words of her adoptive mother, her mother's closest friend, reverberated in her mind: "You are of Lozen—a medicine woman. A time may come when only the staff can save you."

Claire's stomach churned. None of her patients had ever attacked her so personally. She felt the blood draining from her head and a sharp pain shooting through her eyes.

Elizabeth was trying to stop her from asking anymore prying questions. "Are you all right, Claire?" she asked after a minute, her tone laced with sarcasm and a sneer on her face, expressions Claire was sad to see.

"You did what you wanted to do, Elizabeth. You shut me down," Claire replied evenly, holding her gaze. She felt compassion for Elizabeth, realizing that all that she had locked inside of her must be nothing short of terrifying.

Elizabeth didn't let it go, though, saying, "You are of Lozen just like she was." This time her sneer was even more etched into the sunbaked lines that streaked across her face.

"I'm a natural therapist, Elizabeth, not a medicine woman," Claire replied firmly.

"If you say so," said Elizabeth, snickering as she slipped off her shoes to prepare for her massage.

Despite Claire's assertion, she continued to feel the assault of having been thought of as a medicine woman, which caused a lingering fear. In her experience, medicine women ended up dead. She was seized by the memory of her mother falling to the ground as quickly as a tall ponderosa struck by lightning. Dread bore into her as though she were a child again. She flashed on the image of an evil man hidden in the darkness of the forest howling and looking her way, his blue eyes cutting through the midnight dark like lasers. Claire shuddered. She hoped Elizabeth hadn't noticed.

Elizabeth, face down on the massage table, turned and ordered tauntingly, "Well, let's get on with it. Unless you're not up to it."

Claire struggled to keep her professional distance, calming herself by closing her eyes, taking a deep breath, and briskly rubbing her hands together, generating heat in her palms to ensure a warm touch for Elizabeth's tense and aching body. Elizabeth had regularly complained that her body was racked with unimaginable pain, and Claire had no doubt about this since the muscular tension over her frame seemed like mounds of stone.

Claire felt her mind clearing, energy moving through her hands, and was ready to begin treatment. As her warm hands touched Elizabeth's back, Elizabeth let out a sigh, an obvious expression of relief. There was no resistance coming from her, no sense of meanness, her tension dissipating by the second. For the next thirty minutes, Claire massaged Elizabeth's neck, back, and legs, enjoying the silence between them. Silence allowed the patient to drift into a timeless realm and the natural therapist to focus undisturbed so that maximum energy was directed to the healing process.

As she massaged Elizabeth, Claire's thoughts drifted back to her childhood, when her mother was still alive and the three of them would sit at the kitchen table eating red chile, beans, and warm tortillas. She would listen while Lucia and Elizabeth talked about people in the village, their aches and pains, their rages and fights, and how herbs and their dreams could be used to heal them. Elizabeth had visited regularly, and Claire remembered anticipating with great enthusiasm the conversation she would hear between the two, their words seeping into deep places of her being and their friendship nourishing her.

When Claire had asked her mother why she and Elizabeth spoke so much about so many things, Lucia had explained that because Elizabeth knew the way of the medicine woman; they could help each other by discussing their patients who came seeking healing. Lucia had also told Claire that Elizabeth was a seer who knew how to heal through the voices that spoke in the deep mind. This did not seem strange to Claire, since from a young age, she had experienced both visual and auditory psychic impressions that informed her about people, situations, and problems. Lucia had instructed her to listen to and follow deep feelings and instincts, visions and dreams, for through them she would gain wisdom and guidance during dire times.

As the massage went on, Claire wondered what tragic experience had turned Elizabeth into the disturbed woman she was today. She had become a woman as different from the one young Claire had known as day was from night. Yet Claire felt *cariño* for Elizabeth, a deep affection for the woman who, in her right mind, had been her mother's friend.

Claire moved her fingers over Elizabeth's neck and said, "You're finally relaxing." The effects of the massage were not always so evident. The knotted muscles in Elizabeth's back that sometimes created grotesque formations seemed like demons that had buried themselves within her. Now it was evident she had less tension and that the real Elizabeth, beneath the anger, was nearer and closer.

Elizabeth sighed and agreed, "Yeah, I guess so." Her voice

had lost its hostility, sounding more like the Elizabeth of Claire's childhood. Now the closeness between them seemed palpable to Claire.

Wrapped in the warmth of the therapeutic mood, Claire closed her eyes as she continued stroking Elizabeth's body from head to toe with the tips of her fingers before gently finishing the massage. The ending of a treatment was as important as its beginning, drawing together its healing benefits.

"Feeling better?" Claire asked, sensing the ease and openness in her patient.

Elizabeth hesitated, as though reluctant to break the spell, then said in a hushed tone, "There are things I have to tell you, Claire." Her voice, even though almost a whisper, still was that of the sincere woman of years past. Suddenly, images flashed into Claire's mind of Elizabeth, a few years younger than her present age, screaming with pain as a man cloaked by shadows, a rogue with occult powers sanctified by the masses, forced himself on her, then grazed her face with his fingers, shattering her mind, leaving her desperate and crazed by a long-held secret.

Claire's heart raced so quickly that her breaths became shallow and every muscle in her body tensed. She felt the room spinning, and she reached out to the edge of the table to steady herself and regain her composure. Elizabeth looked at her knowingly. Her pallor was ashen gray. All light was gone from her eyes.

At that moment, a howling wind came up. Through the window, Claire saw dust devils swirling outside, their dance frenzied, grit and grime spewing every which way as they crisscrossed an endless expanse of desert. As the window began rattling like a bag of old bones, both women looked up and saw a large black crow perched on the ledge outside. It stared at them, then cawed defiantly, unaffected by the winds.

Elizabeth bolted upright, eyes wide. "I have to go," she said, fingers trembling as she slipped on her shoes, more frightened than Claire had ever seen her. Claire thought of trying to help her settle down, but held herself back, not wanting to risk upsetting her further.

"What's wrong?" Claire asked, trying to disguise her own sense of unease. Her words went unanswered.

As Elizabeth reached the door, she glanced back at the window where the crow had been. The wind had died down, and the crow had vanished; yet the dark force of moments past crackled through the atmosphere like sparks of electricity jumping wildly from shorted wires.

The hairs on the back of Claire's neck stood on end. She clenched her teeth in anticipation of something worse about to happen. A chill swept through the room as if a ghostly presence had made itself known. Involuntarily, Claire shook her head as though waking herself from a bad dream.

"Get out of here while you can, Claire," Elizabeth stammered. Her eyes were wide as the full moon sitting low across a midnight desert landscape.

"What are you so afraid of, Elizabeth?" Claire asked, moving forward to calm her. "Please, talk to me about what's going on with you." Carefully, she placed a hand on her patient's taut shoulder.

Elizabeth shrugged it away, saying, "Let go of me." Claire knew that Elizabeth could turn on her, becoming violent.

Still, Claire inched a little closer and said, "Elizabeth, I could help if you'd let me." But the words seemed futile.

"Help me? Help yourself! Face what is yours to face," Elizabeth hissed. She yanked the door open, then forced it to slam behind her.

Claire stood still for a moment, feeling as if a tornado had swept through the room. Elizabeth's demand had left her shaken. She drew a deep breath, then went to her desk and picked up her tea, noticing her trembling hands. Turning toward the window, Claire saw a muscular orderly accompanying Elizabeth to the locked ward at the far end of the hospital compound. A flock of crows circled high overhead, seeming to follow the two receding figures. As they arrived at the outer doors of the locked unit, the orderly reached for his keys. The crows circled while the two crossed the threshold of the unit, Elizabeth suddenly pausing, turning, and looking outside, her gaze riveted on the flock of birds.

All but two flew off, disappearing into the piñon-covered hills. The two that remained came to rest on the red brick wall adjacent to the locked unit, their black eyes boring into Elizabeth. She looked panicked then enraged and, shaking a finger at the creatures, yelled something. Her frantic gestures told Claire that she was screeching curses to ward off evil.

Claire took a step back from the window, from the impact of Elizabeth's rage.

The orderly grabbed Elizabeth roughly by the arm and pulled her inside.

The crows waited, watched, and then flew away.

Late that afternoon, after a day of report writing and meetings, Claire caught a glimpse of herself in the small mirror hanging over the old porcelain sink in her office. Shocked to see herself looking haggard, her shoulder-length auburn hair disheveled, her usually sparkling brown eyes dull, Claire couldn't help but think that she appeared twenty-five going on forty-five. The session with Elizabeth had taken its toll. Not for a while had a patient been that demanding of Claire's inner resources.

She sensed that there was more to Elizabeth and their therapeutic relationship than she could yet fathom. Claire wanted to help Elizabeth, but there was too much Elizabeth kept locked up inside. And Claire knew that revelation of secrets was the only path to healing.

She bent down over the stained white porcelain sink and splashed cold water on her face. As she straightened up, a fleeting image crossed the mirror, the face of a little girl abandoned in the forest, crying for her mother, angry that she had been taken from her. Claire grasped the lip of the sink and tried to steady herself, forcing herself not to look again at the haunting image.

Soon after, she hurried out of her office, eager for dinner with Francesca, her spiritual guide and foster parent, the person to whom Claire turned during times of crisis. The thought of Francesca's cozy adobe home nestled in a forest of piñons brought her some peace. She longed to sit and talk to Francesca, her ever-present source of wisdom, guidance, and loving assurance. Since Claire's childhood, Francesca had always listened to her concerns calmly, from her rocking chair beside the fireplace, the cedar and piñon fire providing warmth and soothing fragrance.

Claire whisked by the night guard at the front of the administration building as images and memories continued to flash through her mind like lightning across a mesa: a funeral pyre; herself at age seven watching the cremation of Alejándra, one of the last medicine women; Francesca touching Claire's shoulder, whispering, "You are the last in the lineage." Black wings flapping wildly in the night; evil eyes searing aspens and ponderosas; a child, anger buried deep, frozen by fear.

Quickly walking across the gravel parking lot to her car, Claire glanced over at the locked ward and saw Elizabeth's face in a second-floor window. Motionless, Elizabeth stared at Claire, the windowpane reflecting the desert darkness, lit candles in Elizabeth's room flickering like spirits on the watch. Yet Elizabeth exuded a familiar sense of warmth and sincerity that seemed to cut through the chilly desert night.

As Elizabeth waved, Claire shuddered, spotting a flock of crows cawing and circling overhead, then flapping their wings erratically and flying at the window, Elizabeth motioning them away to no avail. Finally, they left the window, scattering into the night sky, their distant cawing sending an eerie message.

Elizabeth glanced at the window ledge and startled as she noticed, lying there, a white dove, bloodied and dead.

2

Heavy raindrops splashed against the windshield as Claire drove to Francesca Mirabal's humble adobe home, about seven miles from the hospital. Its finely cracked brown earthen walls acted as insulation against the cold during the severe winters and kept the house cool during the parched summers. Despite its humble nature, it had been a fortress to Claire as a child.

As the miles quickly passed, Claire began feeling anxious remembering the dead white dove. The windshield wipers flicked furiously back and forth, keeping rhythm with the pounding of her heart. Her tension triggered the recollection of a nightmare she'd had earlier that week about her liver not expelling bile and bad health coming from bad living. The thought of death caused her muscles to tighten, her breaths to become short and quick, her knuckles to turn white as she gripped the steering wheel tightly. She tried to let her mind wander and relax.

Lately, deep sleep had escaped her. She was tired and feared not being able to adequately tend to her patients.

Perhaps the nights of light sleep would cease, but, if not, she feared her mind might not withstand the strain.

She tried to shake off the worry by remembering the comfort of being held in Francesca's arms as a child. The loss of her mother had hurt Claire badly then, and sometimes even now as an adult, anxiety and sleep loss were symptoms of unresolved emotions. Francesca's warmth and guidance were soothing in the midst of what Claire knew was unfinished emotional business. A rush of cold air made Claire shiver. Checking the ambient temperature on her instrument panel, she turned up the heater. Images of Francesca's kiva fireplace roaring with piñon and cedar logs and emitting intoxicating scents brought a smile to her face, and a flush of warmth swept up her body to the very tips of her fingers and toes.

But unease quickly returned when she heard a pop, then a hammering sound under her car. At first it sounded as though the tires were bouncing through potholes in the road, but when the steering wheel pulled hard to the right, she realized that her fifteen-year-old Subaru had a flat tire. *It could've been worse*, she thought.

As she braked and pulled off the two-lane road, the rain turned to sleet, then to pebble-sized hail that chattered on her rooftop. Slowing to a stop on the muddy shoulder of the road, she wondered if she could remember how to change a tire, something she hadn't done for years.

After finding the owner's manual, she stepped out of the car, hail now beating against her cheeks. Hurrying to the trunk, nearly slipping on the slick pavement, she stared at the spare tire and the crowbar, hoping Francesca wouldn't be worried. Just as she stepped back on the road to change the tire, a long black Mercedes sped by and sprayed her with muddy water. A number of choice words flew through her mind.

When the Mercedes sedan skidded to a stop, then backed up, Claire tightened her grip on the crowbar. As the car slowed to a stop, through the darkened glass she could see two men inside: a driver and, behind him in the rear seat, a passenger. Looking closer, Claire noticed the words *Ecclesia Dei* printed on the license plate's aluminum frame.

The driver's door opened and a tall, lean Caucasian man with sharp features, wearing a black raincoat, got out. He cut a rather ominous figure, his bearing intimidating due to both his tall frame and severe look.

Claire fingered the crowbar anxiously, despite trying to calm herself.

The driver opened the back door of the passenger compartment and the other man, wearing an identical raincoat and bearing almost a brotherly resemblance to the first, stepped out and glanced toward the setting sun. Then he walked toward Claire, looked directly in her eyes, and said, "I'm so sorry. I asked my driver to stop and offer to help."

He eyed the crowbar. "You needn't worry. We won't hurt you," he added. Without waiting for a reply, he instructed his driver to change the flat.

Claire, caught in the spell of the fellow's commanding presence and piercing blue eyes, handed the crowbar to the driver and stepped aside. As the driver knelt to pop off the hubcap and loosen the nuts, the other man stepped closer. Claire looked into his eyes, which were cold. Her legs and arms began tingling as if she were caught in a nerve-deadening web of subterfuge and malice. She felt helpless while his gaze traveled over her body, an eerie and irresistible force holding her in place.

She forced a tight smile, trying not to show concern, although she wanted to flee, to never see this man again, fearing he would harm her.

"Are you all right?" the man asked patronizingly, as his companion pulled the spare out of the trunk. A smirk traveled across his thin lips. He knew what he was doing, how to do it, and that he was good at doing it.

Irritation snapped Claire out of a seconds-long trance. "Yes," she said sharply, regaining her composure, the authority in her voice evidence that she was coming back to herself and could handle this situation.

She had no doubt that this tall, black-clad, ostensibly helpful man had set her on edge. His light complexion, slim build, neatly trimmed blond hair, and fine clothing all suggested a kind, older gentleman, yet beneath this facade was, she sensed, a person who lurked and then took.

His cold, roving eyes, overly precise speech, and silky tone made Claire feel that he was well practiced in his art. Never had she stood in the presence of anyone so brutally calm, so skilled at projecting a veneer of utmost sincerity. She couldn't deny that his charisma had a certain appeal that drew her but then turned her stomach, like the refreshing waters of the Rio Grande on a hot summer day transforming to swirling white water moving in the direction of sharply hewn boulders.

She recalled where she had encountered such people before—individuals who were outwardly cool but were really predatory, fearsome beyond the normal range of troubling human encounters—the psychopaths at the Turquoise County Mental Health Center, where she had also helped to care for manic-depressives, the severely mentally retarded, and paranoid schizophrenics. In most patients, she had sensed a flicker of life that kindled her compassion, but the psychopaths did nothing to stir her empathy. They were the most fearsome patients because their conscience and capacity for empathy had been destroyed. Their crimes had been both cunning and enjoyed, remorse being as alien to them as water to desert sandstone.

Kept in locked units in a corridor away from the rest of the patient population, the psychopaths had ogled her in a way that curdled her blood, hissing like snakes as they tried to lure her toward them. She'd felt as if she needed to scrub herself clean, which was exactly how she presently felt.

Claire fixed her eyes on the driver as his manicured hands expertly turned each nut in place. He, too, made her recoil. She was glad that her body spoke to her about troublesome events and people. Seeing others in an overly positive light had been a weakness, one spotted by supervisors during her training.

As the driver tightened the last nut, she noticed her breathing returning to normal, her heart settling into its natural rhythm. He placed the flat in the trunk and got back into the Mercedes without saying a word. His manner was like that of a servant; yet he had an officious way about him, not as striking as the one in command but nearly so.

Before turning to leave, the older man visually caressed her from head to toe, then reached out his right hand, which seemed to slither toward Claire like a snake emerging from its hole—mesmerizing but loathsome. On its ring finger was what looked like the world's largest diamond, set in the center of a thick, exquisitely polished gold band, the rays of the setting sun striking it so it radiated a light that was bright yet somehow dark and repulsive. Remembering the religious custom of her schoolmates to bow and kiss the ring of the priest, she stepped back.

Bypassing her insult, the older man inched forward, grazed

his hand over her right shoulder, and said, "Bless you, my child." The hand lay on her as cold and heavy as stone. There was nothing about this man that she liked.

The next thing she knew, the vehicle was speeding away to the north, so that soon it was nothing more than a black dot fading in the distance. The farther it went, the more the atmosphere seemed to clear, slowly pulling her back to her senses. High mountain air was good for reviving a disoriented soul, its freshness better than smelling salts.

The odd meeting with the officious man and his mute chauffeur had briefly cast a hypnotic spell on her, leaving her stunned and feeling vulnerable. Claire noticed that her head and neck ached, and she felt an invisible layer of slime all over her body. The sounds of snakes hissing and men coming forward out of dark places filled her mind. Desperately, she tried to rid her mind of the rush of images—the terrible encounter with the two black-garbed men, Elizabeth's shrieking, her own haunting nightmares, the black car disappearing into the horizon. They whipped in and out of her consciousness with the ferocity of the north wind on a cold winter day, sending shivers up her spine and down through the tips of her fingers and toes. Finally, she hurriedly got into her car, relieved to be in the familiar, enclosed space, and started feeling solace in being once again on the road to her childhood home. She was surprised by the lasting effect the two men had had on her, especially the older one, who had left her most shaken.

The joy of living in northern Aztlan once again stirred in her soul as undulations of mountainous land and wide stretches of mesa, with striations of green, yellow, and turquoise set into play a harmonious inner rhythm. The sun had nearly set by the time she pulled into Francesca's drive, bringing to mind thoughts of her childhood—Francesca walking her to the school bus; teaching her to cook, clean, and read; snuggling with her by the fireplace on cold winter nights. This was the one place in the world that provided a constant, soothing embrace. Francesca, with her warm arms and tender heart, had taken the place of the mother Claire had lost. Francesca had been a lifeline for her during her childhood, and even now she was the only one in the world who knew Claire better than she knew herself. Without her, Claire would have fallen into an emotional abyss; the violence of her mother's death and the resulting memories that incessantly streamed through her consciousness day and night would have ruined all chances for living anything but the most tenuous sort of life.

Stepping out of her car, Claire was overtaken by the aroma of hot red chile and beans, triggering memories of delicious food Francesca had often prepared in the past with loving hands—steaming dinners of enchiladas, rice, and refried beans, garnished with thin strips of shredded lettuce, diced red tomatoes, olives, and grated cheese. But tonight, restlessness curbed her appetite. Not even memories of the comfort of days past could completely dispel the hovering presence of the black-garbed man, which wrapped itself around Claire like the wings of a horrible bat.

The timeworn, oak front door of the hundred-year-old brown adobe creaked as Francesca opened it and stepped out on the red brick porch. She looked as she always had, earthen and strong, her presence one of fortitude and understanding.

Claire hurried to greet Francesca, pulling her into an embrace. Francesca's hearty greeting, the feel of her sturdy body, and the smell of her rosy brown skin was as refreshing as fall breezes sweeping through the aspen-filled canyons of the Sagrado Mountains and as steadying as the solid earth along hiking trails bordering the Turquoise Trail.

"I'm so glad you were able to come, Claire," Francesca said with a warm smile, taking her by the shoulder to pull her inside. Moving into Francesca's home was like making passage from one world to the next as the crisp outside air and twilight sky gave way to the warmth and cozy dim lighting of the adobe living room.

Once in the house, Francesca took the few steps down into the slightly lowered living area, her hand firmly clasping Claire's, then turned and looked at Claire, her gaze steady but inquiring. Her eyes had many times seen through Claire's darkest hidden places with compassion, and now they did so once again.

"Why didn't you come to me earlier?" asked Francesca.

"What do you mean?" replied Claire, suddenly feeling exposed.

Francesca continued, "I felt myself drained the moment I touched you. You are not well."

Claire stayed quiet, her eyes riveted on Francesca's, then she moved to the wooden rocker near the white-plastered fireplace and sat down, the roaring cedar and piñon fire taking away the early evening chill.

She had much to share, but first it helped to calm her mind by enjoying the surroundings in which she had been raised—the comfort of the living room with its rugs from the village of Chimayo scattered across the red Mexican tiles; the warmth of the ceiling's *vigas*, pine logs that offered structural support to the white stucco ceiling; the two-foot-thick adobe walls plastered white and decorated with *ristras*, three-foot-long strings of red chile, and surrealistic Native American paintings of planets swirling through the cosmos, depicting primal forces of earth, air, fire, and water. It was these primal elements that inspired the mysticism and natural magic in the lives of the women of northern Aztlan who were known for their enigmatic ways and dark healing arts. Francesca's own wall weavings made from wool produced in Los Ojos were a particular delight, made with the attention to detail that characterized Francesca's approach to all things.

Francesca went to the kitchen and returned with two bottles of Aztlan micro-brewed pale ale. Unlike self-proclaimed healers and mystics—transplanted East or West Coast pilgrims and psychics searching for the latest spiritual kick under the turquoise blue skies of Aztlan—Francesca enjoyed all facets of life, including good beer, and had taught Claire to do the same.

At least three hundred years old, the tradition of the northern Aztlan medicine women in which Francesca, Lucia, Elizabeth, and scores of other *mestizas* before them had participated was known for its down-to-earth ways.

These women, who natives spoke of in hushed tones, were regarded as seers and healers. They kept to themselves, meeting only infrequently, even with one another. Their solitude nourished a depth, Francesca often said, that could be sustained in no other way. They shunned contrived rituals, incantations, and lifestyles. The medicine women of northern Aztlan were women of Lozen, named after a sister to Apache chief Victorio, a skilled prophet and warrior who was said to have asserted, "Lozen is my right hand... strong as a man, braver than most, and cunning in strategy. Lozen is a shield to her people." She had inspired women, frozen with fear, to cross the surging waters of the Rio Grande as they fled from their oppressors. Apaches proclaimed that she'd had supernatural abilities on the battlefield and such heightened intuitions that she could discern where the enemy was and how

many they numbered. Like her, the women of northern Aztlan had sufficient spiritual powers, strong personalities, and
force of the human spirit to effect healing.

Setting the beers on artistic glass coasters atop a rustic oak
table, Francesca opened them, the flames of the crackling fire
dancing across the bottles' brown glass. Pausing to think
through what she was about to say, Francesca cleared her
throat, handed Claire a beer, then said, "You're twenty-five.
Your mother died at that age."

Claire stiffened and asked, "What's that supposed to
mean?" She immediately wished the question hadn't sounded
so harsh.

Taking a sip of her beer, Francesca continued firmly, but
obviously hurt by Claire's tone, "It means I'm glad you're
here so we can talk."

Claire hesitated before taking a drink, then realizing she
owed Francesca an apology, said, "I'm sorry. I didn't mean to
be blunt, but you sounded so serious."

Francesca set her bottle on the coffee table and said, "You
have a choice to make."

"To be a medicine woman or not," Claire remarked.
They'd had this conversation before, and it always left Claire
feeling cornered. She shifted nervously in the rocker, suddenly flooded with remembrances from her youth of running
fearfully behind Francesca in the grocery store, along a country lane, or in the plaza, times when they encountered a tall
man dressed in black, one of the many priests in northern Aztlan.

Up until her twelfth birthday, Claire had been afflicted by
a daily dread of meeting up with the evil man who had killed
her mother, fearing he would come for her in the dead of a
full-moon night. Then, once Claire had passed her twelfth

birthday, the recurring nightmare started. At first, it occurred occasionally, then nightly, and with it came night sweats and screams when Francesca would come to her room and sit quietly waiting for the terror to pass.

Claire's stomach had tightened so much that she was nauseous, her breaths quick and short. She remained with her arms clutching her stomach and slightly bent over in her chair.

Francesca's eyes moistened, seeing Claire's childhood affliction raising its ugly head. "I love you. I want you to be well, not ill. Alive, not dead. I've cautioned you before that you could become ill if you keep running from who you are," she said.

Francesca had seen through her, and Claire knew she could trust her guidance. Claire sat back up, took a few deep breaths to clear her mind, and felt the childhood ghosts of dread fade to the background of her consciousness. She answered, "I've had a rough day and got a lot on my mind. But the trouble I feel has to do with more than the day's happenings."

Francesca, never known to waste words, asked, "So what happened?"

"One of my patients was finally beginning to open up when a horrible wind tore through the building. Out of nowhere, a huge crow appeared on the window ledge. It stared at us as if it had been listening to our conversation. My patient panicked. I tried to calm her down, but she started screaming at me, said I needed to get away from the hospital while I still had the chance. She left my office in hysterics." Claire's hands tightly gripped the arms of the chair, her knuckles white from strain. She looked at her beer bottle and noticed she had only taken a sip, then she added, "She also told me to remember who I was."

"And what do you make of that?" asked Francesca, folding her arms, her demeanor more serious.

Claire didn't answer.

"So quiet? Come on, Claire. I want to help. This is no time to hesitate," Francesca urged.

"I know what you're getting at," Claire replied. "The patient I'm talking about is Elizabeth."

Francesca became silent, her thoughts drifting. After a short time, she affirmed, "She knows what she's talking about, Claire. She knows your heritage."

"What happened to her, Francesca?" asked Claire.

"That is hers to know, Claire," Francesca answered, a tinge of sadness in her voice. "Destiny is both healer and slayer."

Francesca went on, "You say a crow came?"

"Yes. It scared the shit out of me. It seemed almost human, like it had heard every word and was staring right through us."

Francesca paused thoughtfully before replying, "Black magic works that way. It tries to get you to back off by scaring the hell out of you."

"You think it was black magic?" Claire asked.

"Of course. The black bird comes when death is near. Someone who wanted to scare you sent it."

Claire paled and asked, "Someone wants me dead?"

Looking worried, Francesca rose from her recliner and placed another log in the fire. "What else occurred today? Maybe there's another clue to what's happening."

When Claire told her about the two men, Francesca's frown deepened, and she asked, "What did the passenger look like?" Something Claire said had struck a familiar chord.

"Six-foot or so. Late fifties or early sixties. Sandy blond hair. Dressed completely in black… a priest, I'm sure," replied Claire.

Francesca nudged the cedar logs with a poker. "Ah," she said as if confirming a suspicion.

"Do you know who he is?" asked Claire.

"Just keep your eyes open," replied Francesca. Then before Claire could ask any more questions Francesca added, "Let's eat dinner before everything gets cold."

As they walked to the kitchen, Claire reminded herself that Francesca always waited for the right time to tell her what she needed to know. She sat at the table and waited for Francesca to serve herself. After laying two enchiladas on her plate, Francesca passed the covered dish. Francesca's food was well seasoned with salt, pepper, and garlic, the juicy tomatoes tempering the heat of the northern Aztlan chile.

They ate slowly, Claire trying to let the tension fade while Francesca chatted about mundane things—the tasty red chile, how this year's chile crop had been hotter due to the lack of rain, and the early snows predicted for October. Claire inquired about the well-being of her gardener friend and others she had known throughout her life, good women who were true to themselves and to their friendship with Francesca.

When they finished their meal, Claire went to the kitchen and poured them each a mug of freshly brewed coffee, as was their custom. They enjoyed coffee after the evening meal, neither of them ever complaining of difficulty sleeping. They slept well, unless there were troubles afoot.

As Claire brought the mugs to the table, Francesca said, "Claire, there's something I have to tell you." To calm her agitation, Claire took a long sip of her coffee and pulled over her shoulders a dark blue and ochre patterned Navajo blanket that she had used since childhood to ward off the autumn and winter chill.

Francesca continued, "I've heard that your boss has been asking around about you."

Claire was surprised then asked, "Karl Himmel?"

Francesca raised her right eyebrow and hardened the set of her eyes. "No... not Himmel. It's Archbishop William Anarch who asks about you. I was having dinner at Gordo's one night last week, and the scuttlebutt was flying hard and fast. Church people turned about and stared at me when I walked in, then they went back to their conversations and started speaking in hushed tones that were not all that hushed, like they wanted me to hear what they were whispering. Anarch wants to know about the therapist who's treating a particular church member. I dismissed it at the time until my dreams began acting up. I've been having nightmares about gossipers and back stabbers... the same people who were in the restaurant. There's wickedness in the air."

"Why would he be interested in me? I've never even met the man," Claire said, her insides twisting.

Francesca paused then continued, "Well, hardly anyone outside the church has ever seen him, much less met him. He's rumored to be a recluse."

Claire's hands felt cold and clammy. "So why would he be asking about me?" she asked.

Francesca frowned and answered, "I wish I knew."

3

T he lush grounds of the hacienda of the Aztlan archbishop of the Ecclesia Dei brought a smile to Archbishop William Anarch's face as he surveyed the estate from his second-story office window—horizon-to-horizon vistas showed the miles of ponderosa pine, piñon, and
clusters of aspens; the bubbling brook and footbridge; the
Olympic-size pool and two clay tennis courts. It was from this
vantage point that he best experienced the vast realm over
which he exercised supreme authority on all matters concerning heaven, hell, and eternal salvation.

He also marveled at the many types of rejuvenating rec-
reation that occurred here, activities surrounded by secrecy
because the archbishop had given an ecclesiastical dictum
stating that even one tidbit of information about anything
seen or heard on the premises was concomitant to the act Judas had committed against the Savior.

In total, the Ecclesia Dei in Aztlan owned two thousand
acres of pristine property seven miles north of the plaza, with
numerous brown adobe administrative buildings, including
the archbishop's hacienda, recently appraised at over $100

million, a sum that was significant but expected within the culture of the Ecclesia Dei. "Nothing but the best for the Almighty" was the motto of the black and red–cloaked lords of the Church.

As he continued to survey the estate, Archbishop Anarch thought about how the elderly patriarch of all the Ecclesia Dei throughout the Southwest, His Exalted Holiness Peter Kulten, had praised him recently at the annual clerical banquet in Aztlan for his fund-raising abilities, implying that Anarch might well be the next patriarch. Such a thought brought a smile to Anarch, for the office of patriarch was the most prestigious and powerful on earth. Archbishop Anarch felt that it was his destiny to be patriarch, that he knew the heart of the Almighty as intimately as his own. Thus without fail, he poured money into the patriarch's coffers to solder his relationship with the old man, who it was rumored among his aides, the devoted but talkative Sisters of the Most Precious Word, was nearing his death due to a fatal condition exerting a tortuous plight on a tiny organ not permitted use, at least not ostensibly or regularly.

Archbishop Anarch also mused about how the vicar general and closest adviser to the patriarch, Father Genesis Lukar, visited Aztlan monthly to collect Anarch's tithe of over $100,000 in cash. Lukar's beady eyes would light up when Anarch would open his red leather briefcase to show him the tidy bundles of crisp bills for inspection. Then, with a bit of a tremor to his hands, Lukar would grab the bills and stuff them into a large, soiled canvas bag, saying, "I thank you on behalf of the entire Ecclesia Dei," before expertly pulling the drawstring tight, then sniffing the air and saying, "Ah, the smell of money."

During such visits, Archbishop Anarch would play to the

vicar's weakness for fine wines and gourmet cooking, on the last evening serving him such delicacies as imported Spanish escargot, braised Norwegian pheasant with fresh organic vegetables, mashed purple potatoes, locally baked sourdough bread, thirty-year-old pinot noir from prize-winning vineyards in Aztlan, and truffles made for the evening's celebration by the world-renowned Aztlan chocolatier Father Humongo Dulcelito.

At evening's end, Father Lukar would often luxuriantly sip a twenty-five-year-old port, stretch out on the red velvet divan, and proclaim William Anarch next in line to become head of the half-million-member Ecclesia Dei. Anarch would light Lukar's Cuban cigar and thank him for his support, certain that his future was secure.

A knock at the door interrupted Anarch's reveries. His priest-secretary entered and announced dryly, "Archbishop, Mr. and Mrs. Montoya are here." The man stood motionless with eyes cast down and head bowed.

"Ah, yes. The Montoyas. Please show them in," the archbishop said.

The stoic cleric nodded and closed the door.

Anarch looked around his expansive office, which many high-ranking clergymen had compared to a football field. The tufted leather furniture, luxurious Navajo rugs strewn over polished wood floors, and a gold-brocade sofa all conveyed an air of authority and wealth. Everything was perfectly suited for his meeting with donors to the church. Anarch clasped his hands behind his back, glanced at himself in the full-length mirror next to his desk, adjusted his black cassock adorned with scarlet buttons, and waited.

⚡⚡⚡

Mr. and Mrs. Montoya, a wealthy couple in their late sixties, sat quietly in the reception area of the Chancery Office of the Aztlan Ecclesia Dei. The receiving area was the size of a banquet hall, thickly carpeted in finely woven wool the color of desert sand. Long magenta curtains draped the cathedral-like ceiling-to-floor windows, slightly obscuring the view below of rolling hills covered in piñon and juniper that butted up against the Sagrado Mountains. On the walls were hung oil portraits of previous archbishops, gazing in a way that made everyone entering the room feel like their souls were being penetrated. For many years now, the Montoyas had been privileged with access to the quarters of Archbishop Anarch, whom they considered a veritable Christ on earth. To be granted a private audience was a privilege afforded few, and those so privileged showed their gratitude and from then on never ceased behaving in the expected manner lest they lose favor and have to endure the consequences. For instance, the Vigils, a family of fine repute, politically well-connected and above reproach in matters of social standing and financial stature, had dared question the need for their annual gifts to the Ecclesia Dei, some saying an amount typically exceeding six figures. Mr. Vigil had raised an eyebrow when the archbishop, behind the very doors the Montoyas were soon to enter, had gently, in his godlike manner, stated that the amount of years past was no longer sufficient and had to be increased to a flat 10 percent of the family corporation's annual profit. It was well known throughout Aztlan that the Vigils were one of the wealthiest families in the area, scuttlebutt having it that their worth exceeded that of the entire Ecclesia Dei of the Southwest, perhaps nearing $1 billion. After Mr. Vigil's casual reaction betrayed resistance to the archbishop's demand, a succession of bad things happened to the Vigils, beginning with the unfortunate death of their first grandchild before the infant could be baptized. It continued with the death of Mr. Vigil's mother without a priest arriving in sufficient time to provide the last sacraments to ensure that she avoid eternal hell fire, as well as numerous other spiritual tragedies. It was only with restitution to the Almighty that the terrible occurrences ceased.

The Montoyas knew why they had initially been summoned over seven years ago. It was because of their love of the Almighty and the Ecclesia Dei and their devotion to each other. The archbishop noticed such things and rewarded those of extraordinary virtue with a special apostolic blessing. The rest, the financial proceedings, were just a routine matter.

Benito Montoya lightly stroked the back of his wife Isabel's hand and smiled tenderly. He felt badly about his behavior the previous night. It rarely ever happened anymore, in spite of what she said. Once or twice a month was not bad. Only a year ago it had been more frequent. Besides, the bruises on her arms and back didn't last that long and usually nobody noticed. Any Sunday parishioners who raised an eyebrow were quick to look away for fear of displeasing two of the highest-ranking lay leaders in the Ecclesia Dei.

Isabel returned Benito's smile, expressing a silent knowing that their sufferings, no matter what or how bad, were to be patiently endured for the sake of the Kingdom of the Almighty and the Ecclesia Dei. After all, it was in bad taste to even intimate what happened behind closed doors, especially since every family in the Ecclesia Dei knew that what occurred in the privacy of the home was no measure of church loyalty, faithfulness, or devotion. All that truly mattered was that their archbishop loved them and that they annually made the pilgrimage to the office of the archbishop of the Ecclesia Dei to maintain favor among church officials.

Ten minutes earlier, Father Gall, the archbishop's assistant, asked them to be seated on two Italian oxblood leather chairs. He then sat behind a large mahogany desk with corners carved as heads of lions and legs that ended with claws and balls. After reviewing a copy of their last federal tax return, a required annual submission by all members in good standing, Gall asked the Montoyas about the amount of their annual tithe, which he felt seemed insufficient. They both shifted anxiously.

Abruptly, Father Gall stood, looked at Mr. Montoya, searing him with his arctic blue eyes, then walked to the end of a long, spacious hallway toward fifteen-foot-high mahogany double doors, knocked, and entered. Returning after a brief time, Father Gall showed the Montoyas down the hall, officiously instructing, "His Excellency, the archbishop, is to be shown utmost reverence. To your knees once you are before him. Then kiss his ring. Listen, and do not speak unless spoken to."

The Montoyas glanced at each other nervously as they made their way down the hall to the sanctum sanctorum of His Holiness William Anarch.

The door opened. "Your Excellency, the Montoyas," the officious secretary said, motioning the couple into the archbishop's private chamber.

"Benito and Isabel, wonderful to see you," said Archbishop Anarch, his words flowing like honey as he walked toward them extending his left hand, on which, nestled securely on the ring finger, was the symbol of his office. Benito then

Isabel knelt and kissed the three-carat diamond ring that gleamed with the Latin crucifix carved into each side.

Archbishop Anarch motioned them to their feet and toward the sofa, while telling them how taken he was by their piety and faithfulness. Then for the next hour he explained the Ecclesia Dei's financial needs, emphasizing that the funds provided by generous souls such as themselves were what allowed the Kingdom of the Almighty to grow, pausing briefly now and then to pour sherry from a crystal decanter. After all, he, the Archbishop of the Aztlan Ecclesia Dei, was their humble servant.

"Our Church has plans to expand its missions to the poor of the archdiocese and the three smaller dioceses that I oversee, one, as you both know, in the south of the state and the others in the east and west. We intend to feed the hungry, clothe the naked, and embrace all those seeking salvation. We need—I need—your continued help," he said.

He stepped in front of them and reached out his hands. Hurriedly they both placed their glasses on the coasters that were properly arranged atop the cherry-wood coffee table. The archbishop then pressed their hands in his and finished his eloquent pitch, moving even closer to his prey to make the final strike: "I'm sad to say that without your assistance we may have to close Santa Cecilia's Mission for the Deaf. Nearly a hundred natives will be denied training in sign language and vocational skills." As the words left his lips, he struggled to suppress a smirk. Santa Cecilia's was heavily endowed, but it was the most potent ploy he could think of to break past Benito's businesslike attitude.

Isabel teared up at his words then shook her head when Benito wrapped his arms around her and whispered something. Solemn, Benito then informed Archbishop Anarch that by day's end a check for $100,000 would be delivered to his office. Isabel flung her arms around her husband, his face suddenly alight with the glow of a man whose soul had been forgiven.

Tracing the sign of the cross in the air between them, Archbishop Anarch imparted the apostolic blessing and concluded the meeting by saying, "I am sure St. Peter has added another jewel to your crowns in heaven today."

As the Montoyas left in tears, Anarch retreated behind his ebony desk to bask in his victory. His mother would be elated by his charitable works. It was due to her that he was who he was. He reached for his gold-plated telephone.

His heart leapt the instant he heard her voice. "Mother," he said, "I have great news. Just as we prayed, the Montoyas came through with their gift." Anticipating his mother's approval over his financial prowess always excited him.

"My son, I am happy for you," she answered in a formal voice. "You have attained your ten-million-dollar goal. The Almighty smiles on you, as does the patriarch." The heavens opened.

The voice of the Almighty echoed through Anarch's being. He felt drugged, the room appearing to spin before his eyes, the inebriation terrifying. He massaged the fine, smooth wooden surface of his desk with the tips of his fingers. It was time to change the subject. "Enough about me. How's your health, Mother?" he asked, the ever-dutiful son.

"Ah, my sweet boy. My arthritis and constipation are heavy crosses. None of my doctors understands how much pain I'm in. No one understands but you," his mother said.

"I will offer Sunday Mass for your intention, Mother," he promised. He had to do this every time they spoke or pay hell for it later. Rarely did he forget, but when he did, there would be the howling in the dreams that came in the dark of the night.

"Thank you, my dear. I suffer so much that sometimes I'm sure the Almighty is preparing to call me to heaven," his mother continued.

"Oh, Mother, you still have a lot of years left in you," he reassured her. "Not at eighty-three, I don't," she quipped. Her severe tone made Anarch realize he'd said the wrong thing. She had become obsessed over the past five years with the image of a long-suffering mother on her deathbed.

A few seconds passed before she said, "Don't forget, William, that my lawyer is holding my last will and testament in his strongbox, the will that names you as my sole heir, providing you remain dutiful and loving. Though I must confess that at times I wonder about you, William. About what you're really made of."

He hated the fact that she held money over his head like a well-honed guillotine. Her words seared through him like a cold blade. Tiny shooting pains darted up from his spine and across his forehead, and he felt rage. The chain binding him to his mother was made of gold, and he needed the link snapped. He knew how.

He spoke by the force that enabled him to tolerate, manipulate all circumstances to further his ends. "Mother," he said, "it was you who made me who I am. All those bitter cold mornings when you woke me up to pray with you before serving as an altar boy at mass. All the times you reminded me not to be distracted by the hunger pangs of fasting or the pain of kneeling on the marble steps. You taught me how to suffer as only you know how to suffer." He heard her sniffling, just loud enough to let him know that the tongue magic had worked. His shoulders relaxed, the last of the sensations of pain, tiny pricks up his spine, flittered off, and he smirked, saying, "I love you, Mother. Thank you for everything you've done for me and the church."

He loathed her.

"I do love you, William," she hissed. "You're a good boy. Always pray for me."

"I will, Mother," he promised insincerely, hanging up and swiveling around in the chair.

As he caught his reflection in the mirror, the memory of his mother faded and he imagined himself in the gold-embroidered stole of the patriarch, William restored and established, manhood defined, resplendent. A jolt of white-hot energy shot through him at the thought that the patriarch, now a very ill man, would no doubt die in a few short months. He recalled his mother's words to him decades before as they drove through a snowstorm in southeastern Aztlan on their way to Sunday morning mass. "You're special, chosen by the Almighty. He's told me during my prayers. You'll do great things for him one day." Archbishop Anarch's chest swelled with pride at the memory. It was the one thing that had been true out of all that his mother had said through the years.

But the other things she had said and demanded…

He gritted his teeth.

Palms hitting the sides of his head, he willed the other things back into the black spaces of his mind. He did not want them out. He tightened his snug black collar, fingers pressing the inner white band into the crisp fold of black cotton. He grew cold, only a tiny dripping stayed warm between his ears in a place so deep down only he knew about it, and the headache came.

He couldn't do anything about it. Not right now.

Later.

William smiled at his reflection, then moved closer to the mirror, the headache intensifying. Seeing his own image brought the same thrill he had felt the day he had been installed as archbishop at the cathedral. Two thousand people had clapped as he had walked down the main aisle sprinkling them with holy water. Many had reached out to touch him, weeping as he passed by. He stared into his own eyes, fingers trembling as sparks of light scattered across the periphery of his vision. His followers later remarked that they felt hypnotized by his eyes as he stood in the pulpit during his sermons.

His pupils contracted as he continued staring at himself, the hypnotic quality of his eyes unmistakable, and the dripping burned like minuscule white-hot embers crisscrossing in his brain as his body appeared to change shape. His head twitched uncontrollably, and the image of a man-beast emerged, snout-faced, skin covered with boils. Sneering, revealing rotting gums and sharp, long teeth, a slashed and bloodied serpent for a tongue, the creature hissed Anarch's name, *William*. The stench of its breath was like a blast of sewage. He tried to turn away but couldn't. His legs and feet were mired in sludge. The beast spoke his name again, *William*—louder, jarring him out of the trance. The image was gone, the headache vanquished. He brushed his hand against his face, testing to see if the mirror reflected the same movement, and feeling relieved when it did.

Surely the beast had come to remind him of what he must do before the day's end. Mother words that made his brain hurt and mind bleed, called the creature up from its inferno. During nightmares, William heard its howl from deep inside a black cave, magnetically drawing him into its bowels. William would scramble and claw trying to avoid the hideous roar and the monstrous, fleshy mouth with double rows of spiked teeth that awaited him in the beast's secret lair. Then, as William frantically kicked away from the mouth of the cave, a woman would appear. William would scream, "Her for me." Everything would become silent, go black. Then William would awaken in a cold sweat, sheets drenched, the evening planned out for him. Always, it happened soon after being cut by his mother's razor-sharp tongue.

He reached for his black cashmere coat hanging from the brass butler next to his desk, remembering that he needed to leave for a luncheon appointment. Tonight, he promised himself, he would appease the beast, send it back to its unconscious inferno. At 7:00 pm, a private confession was scheduled. Then and there, the beast would receive its offering. The mind bleed would not return, the headaches would not roar, and even the fiery drips would stop.

⚡⚡⚡

After breakfast at the French pastry shop a few blocks from where she lived, Claire spent the early morning doing laundry and cleaning her one-bedroom apartment on the second floor of one of the many old adobe buildings encircling Aztlan Plaza. The autumn air in the city was crisp, the smell of cedar and piñon fireplaces filtering through the canyon breezes that made their way through the narrow streets encircling the plaza. Sunshine spread its startlingly bright rays across the low brown adobe buildings that nestled shoulder to shoulder throughout the centuries-old hub of life in northern Aztlan.

Dusting, vacuuming, and ironing clothes always left Claire with the sense of having got the cricks out, the jammed-up details of life that had been stored in the corners of her head during the week—whether she should get the oil in her car changed this week or next, whether she should go to Denver for continuing education, or how she should ask her closest friend and lover Anthony if he had purchased the newly developed sculptor's face mask that filtered out particles of stone dust—important things, but obsessing over them was merely a way of discharging anxiety and distracting herself from the real task at hand.

Claire knew what it was that troubled her mind and ate at the recesses of her soul. There was a haunting taking place both within and without. There was no escaping the memories. She knew what she had witnessed as a child, and the memory of it never left her morning, noon, or night, plaguing her like bats flying through corridors of abandoned buildings left to the ravages of weather and time. She recalled Francesca's childhood admonition—*It's best to listen to the whispers so they don't turn to shouts.*

She decided to drive to a nearby forest to hike in a location that medicine women referred to as the Place of the Granite Boulder. It was a spot that called to her when she needed clarity, a sacred site of numinous powers beyond the rational mind. The scenery helped to make the miles speed by, the mind-piercing vastness of hundred-mile unobstructed vistas and cloudless skies that opened up like a cosmic canopy offering shelter to earthen innocents. Parking in an off-road clearing hidden by dense stands of ponderosas, she began the mile-long trek up the mountain.

During the walk, she felt the presence of unseen deities presiding over this place. The land breathed a mystery that came from the gentle stirring of northerly winds as leaves danced in circular motions about her, first to one side, then another. Tears welled up as she continued along the path feeling gratitude for this place and for the life that was still hers.

Soon she was at the Place of the Granite Boulder. To Claire, this was home, a realm enveloped by mystery. Her breathing slowed; her mind hushed. There were no sounds, not even her steps coming closer to the thousand-year-old stone. Looking down, she saw the way cleared of leaves, damp soil and soft yellow grasses beneath her feet.

The granite megalith stood thirty feet high and fifteen feet wide. Squared-off and oriented to the four directions, sunlight radiated different hues on its various sides, of white on the east, black on the north, blue on the south, and yellow-red on the west. According to legend, the natural boulder, extending through the underworld and up into the space-time dimension, was at the core of the medicine woman's universe. Quiet so enveloped the ages-old setting that the mere sound of a distant bird chirping or the creaking of an old tree seemed immediately silenced by an invisible order, restoring the sacred space.

For the past three hundred years, medicine women had gathered around the boulder to celebrate the birthing of healing spirits that transformed human illness to well-being. It was here, Claire remembered her mother saying, and Francesca confirming, that she had been brought shortly after her birth to a gathering of medicine women for a naming ceremony. On that June morning, she had been told, a single shaft of light had illuminated Claire's face, while she had been named Claire by her mother, then by the others. "When you give a name, it is because the name comes from the person as the light comes from the stone," the old ones said.

Nearby was the cave that had sheltered Claire as a child, beyond it the mesa where her mother's blood had been spilled. She looked in the direction of the mesa and quickly averted her eyes. A pressure welled within her chest, and as it did gusts of wind stirred from the four directions and an eagle circled overhead.

Claire knew she had been called here, and she came only when called, drawn by spirits of nature and healing, ancestral energies of Lozen—the mightiest of Apache women warrior-healers whom Warm Springs Apache chief Victorio had claimed as his right hand, *strong as a man, braver than most, and cunning… a shield to her people.* Of Dahteste—the wife of Chiricahua Apache warrior Anandia with whom she fought as she also fought for Geronimo with Lozen and died a valuable woman warrior. Of Ishton and Gouyen and Tzego-juni and many more, all medicine women who had seen that everything in their lives came from the supernatural energies that allowed them to interpret omens and dreams, heal the sick, predict the future, and intuit through visions the presence and location of enemies.

Sitting cross-legged in front of the boulder, Claire breathed scents of pine, high mountain air, pure psychic currents, into nostrils, lungs, marrow, and soul. Time stood still, and the voices of Native American and *mestiza* healer-warriors echoed through meadows and canyons, sounding of ages past and blood spilled on hallowed land, wrongs that had to be righted.

As Claire was driving back to Aztlan for dinner with Anthony, sheets of rain beat mercilessly when she approached the outskirts of the city. Thirty miles seemed like sixty after she decreased her speed, the slick highway and flooded arroyos making the drive treacherous. A mile outside the city the downpour stopped.

She glanced at the digital clock on the dash as she pulled into Aztlan Plaza: 6:30 pm. The tiny park in the middle of the plaza was filled with people, music pouring out of the packed taverns, sidewalks crowded with window shoppers strolling past art galleries, and the sensuous aroma of chile, oregano, and garlic drifting in the air from the scores of neighboring restaurants.

Claire felt a burning sensation between her eyes as she turned into her apartment's underground parking garage. She dismissed it as tension, but it grew stronger, making her realize that this was no passing phenomenon. Her second-sight, as Francesca called it, was opening. "Never be afraid," Francesca had once told her. "Close your eyes and you will see past the world of appearances."

She parked, turned off the ignition, then relaxed against the headrest. A white background emerged behind her eyelids like a blank screen in a theater, and on it flashed an image of Francesca sitting in her rocking chair in front of the fire, holding a small leather book with the gold-embossed title on its spine reading, "Ecclesia Dei." Francesca slowly closed the book as though caring for something precious then rose and walked away, the vision fading like a dream. Claire opened her eyes, feeling as if she'd just awakened from a deep sleep. A block away, the bells of the cathedral of the Ecclesia Dei began tolling, beckoning the faithful to Saturday evening liturgy. For some, it stood as a bastion of faith, while for others it was merely a fulcrum of subterfuge.

Claire recalled a recent conversation she'd had with Francesca about the Ecclesia Dei. Francesca had said it did not have the power it once had, yet it was still a force to be reckoned with among the superstitious and guilt-prone. She also noted that religion exploited the human propensity toward insecurity and fear and that the Ecclesia Dei recruited seekers from the time of their birth into its fold, compelling the vulnerable to yield to its premise of salvation in return for absolute loyalty. From her vision and from Francesca's manner of expression, Claire had surmised that Francesca had discovered something secret about the Ecclesia Dei, perhaps relating to Archbishop Anarch. Claire hoped Francesca would reveal any such secrets in due course to give her a broader perspective on the Ecclesia Dei from the viewpoint of a healer-warrior.

4

As the sun set over the dusty mesa west of the city, Aztlan Plaza glowed with shades of deep purple and crimson. Scores of tourists were whooping with laughter while downing one margarita after another from bottomless pitchers. Teenagers, young couples with children in tow, aging barefoot hippies, and fat-cat politicos talking a mile a minute seemed festive in the Saturday night revelry.

In less than an hour Claire had showered, dressed in a sage green, long-sleeved linen dress with turquoise beads, and fixed her hair so it was pulled up and held in place by a tortoiseshell comb. Then she had dashed down the two flights of stairs from her apartment onto San Gabriél Street, eagerly anticipating spending the evening with Anthony, whom she hadn't seen for over a week. He had called the day before to say he'd be down from the northern mountains to deliver some Italian marble sculptures to the Contemporary Art Gallery of Aztlan and asked to take her to dinner. The more time they spent together, the harder it was to be away from each other. Claire had never had a relationship with a man that was so heartfelt and meaningful in a way that endured and grew with the passing days.

She ran her fingers over the delicate string of Sleeping Beauty turquoise around her neck—a birthday present from Anthony. The two of them had often said that they felt each other even at a distance, and now Claire felt as though he stood by her side, his hand placed, as it often was, on the small of her back. She signed deeply, knowing that the evening would bring happiness. Walking, she let the rarefied air of "*la encantadora*," as every radio talk show host this side of the Rio Grande called Aztlan, soak into her work-weary brain, smiling at the spontaneous mental image she had of Kokopellis-streaking across the park, tossing their invisible magic dust everywhere and bequeathing to people a sudden urge to dance to ancient rhythms.

Stirred by the gaiety and romance around her, she realized how much she had missed Anthony. She thought of the warm, low tone of his voice, his sharply chiseled *mestizo* features, black olive eyes, shoulder-length black hair gathered in a ponytail with a beaded Navajo tie, and his strong hands, the hands of a sculptor.

Francesca had introduced them at her home one spring night two years ago. The *chamisa* had been in bloom, spreading its passionate yellow throughout the desert, while crickets sang a twilight chant in the background. He had come to deliver an alabaster sculpture of a woman giving birth, commissioned by one of Francesca's patients as payment for her services. During dinner, he had spoken about his parents, both of whom had been artists—his mother a painter and his father a sculptor. When Anthony was twelve, they had died in a car accident during a snowstorm on the Raton Pass as they were returning from a Denver art show and a sixteen-wheeler slammed into the side of their car, sending them plummeting over a steep cliff.

Anthony had also explained that his mother's sister, Victoria, herself a sculptor of some renown in northern Aztlan, had finished raising him and had encouraged him to pursue a fine arts degree from the University of Aztlan. From there, he'd gone on to study sculpture in Pietra Santa, Italy, then Tinos, Greece. His eyes gleamed as he had related his accomplishments. Claire had felt an immediate spark between them.

Over the next months, they had discovered that they shared a passion for outdoor activities—hiking, exploring ancient ruins, cross-country skiing—as well as for folk music and native art. Their time together always seemed to end as quickly as it had begun. Each time they parted, Claire felt a desperate desire to see him again, and she knew she had fallen in love.

They had been seeing each other ever since, and Claire felt that their conversation tonight would turn to marriage, as it always had lately—a subject that made her mouth turn dry as desert dirt. It wasn't that she wanted it to be so. Rather there was an uncontrollable compulsion that made her withdraw from that which she knew she wanted, a tendency that left Anthony confused and hurt. The loss of her mother still had a stranglehold on her, making her fear that anyone she loved would be torn away. In her mind, to love meant to lose. She could find no way out of this cornered feeling and was grateful that Anthony seemed to continue to care for her despite her trepidation. Always sensitive, never rushing or imposing, Anthony felt and understood her pain more than she could ever expect from another man.

Claire stopped for a moment and leaned against the adobe wall of La Fonda Hotel, taking in the mountain air, a curious mix of pine, sage, and damp earth. Anxiety concerning the past and the present gradually passed as she listened to a trio singing *boleros* on the street corner, the music calming her until she again became fully present and eagerly anticipating the evening. Up the block, the shadow of the gothic cathedral of the Ecclesia Dei began to loom over the sidewalk, and she picked up her pace. Suddenly, a blackbird fluttered out from an alleyway between two adobe buildings, startling her. As it swooped toward her, Claire jumped back, then turned to see the tips of its wings disappearing into the open doors of the cathedral, soon vanishing into the shadowy abyss.

"Claire, are you all right?" Anthony's called over the noise of the crowd. "Anthony!" Claire shouted as she spotted him crossing the congested, narrow street, darting between cars. He always said Aztlan's streets reminded him of the narrow roads in romantic, high mountain European villages and that the bustle of traffic was part of the charm.

"What's wrong?" he asked, taking her hands in his. "You look like you've seen a ghost."

"Not a ghost, a blackbird," she said, pointing its way; but all thoughts of it started to leave as she looked into Anthony's eyes. She threw her arms over his shoulders and kissed him. Instantly, she completely let go, with gratitude for this relationship she had come to count on despite her misgivings.

"I've missed you," he said then kissed her again.

"I've missed you, too," she whispered.

They walked arm in arm down the sidewalk to their favorite restaurant, Geronimo. Inside the lobby, lit by sconces emitting muted hues of tan and sandy white, was the hum of individuals speaking French, Italian, Spanish, and Navajo—people from all over the world waiting in line to eat at Aztlan's reigning culinary hot spot.

After confirming their reservations, the maître d' escorted

them through a long hallway of Navajo rugs and cedar *santos* placed in well-lit *nichos*, the carved wooden saints glowing mysteriously beneath the track light aimed directly at the hollowed wall space. In the dining room, mariachis were moving from table to table singing songs. Claire and Anthony were led to a choice table next to a fireplace. As they sat down, nestling closely in the linen-cushioned *banco*, Claire reached for Anthony's hands, noticing the calluses as she stroked them.

"What do you make of the blackbird?" Anthony asked, concern in his voice.

She didn't answer; instead, she kept stroking his hands lovingly, her eyes glancing off in the distance thoughtfully.

"You're the one who's always saying that the things we lock up on the inside come to us on the outside. That bird came out of the blue, as if it had a message for you," he said, looking into her eyes, waiting for a response. Then when she remained silent, he asked more directly, "What's bothering you?"

Claire took a deep breath, and answered, "Francesca says I'm soul-sick. My dreams have been saying the same thing. I have the nightmare almost every night now."

"Is it making you ill?" he asked, worried.

"According to the way of the medicine women, illness comes from living out of harmony with nature and destiny. Destiny is both healer and slayer, Francesca says," Claire replied.

Anthony squeezed her hand and said, "Claire, we've talked about this before, and you always come to the same conclusion. You don't want to be a medicine woman."

"I just know that I don't feel well. I'm tired and unhappy," Claire confessed.

"Maybe you're sick for some other reason. Maybe you

should check with your doctor," said Anthony.

Grimacing, Claire replied, "You've got to be kidding. See him and get a prescription for drugs so I can feel good about living bad? No thanks. I need to get through something, and nothing but doing it is going to set me right." Even as the words came out of her mouth, she was gripped by fear that she would not be able to deal with what felt like a horrendous challenge never before faced and not foreseen.

The waiter arrived, and Anthony asked for two glasses of private reserve red from the Dark Forest Winery. They ordered their meals. A few minutes of silence passed between them.

Anthony finally said, "So, what are you going to do?"

"I have to figure some things out," answered Claire.

"Like what?" asked Anthony.

"Things about my past—my mother's death. She was extremely wise for her age, said to have been the most powerful of medicine women. I'd like to understand what it was that left her prey to this man, a killer cloaked in black like some medieval sorcerer," Claire explained.

"I don't mean any disrespect, Claire, but the police never confirmed that she was murdered. She was simply reported missing and finally assumed dead," replied Anthony.

"I was there. I saw it," Claire insisted, her face reddening.

"I know you were," Anthony said, his tone softening.

"Anthony, that man is real," Claire whispered.

"Who is he, then?" asked Anthony, a hint of exasperation in his voice. He felt frustrated about what was outside of his power to influence or resolve.

"I wish I knew," Claire said, sighing. "My nightmare is about him. I hear screams. A rabid coyote in the forest changes into a man dressed in a black robe, carrying a metal staff. He looks right into my eyes."

"You think this man who killed your mother is after you?" asked Anthony, growing more concerned.

"I'm the same age she was then. Maybe this guy is hungry, ready for another kill," Claire answered.

"But why you?" Anthony asked, his eyes widening.

"I don't know. But the nightmare is a warning. Think about it, for the past twenty years women, the majority of them twenty-five years old, have been found in the desert, mutilated—almost like a human sacrifice. The corpses are always found near the Devil's Throne in Cerrillos, which would be a logical place in the mind of a psychopath with occult interests—perhaps the meaning of the black hood and metal staff in my nightmare, like the rod of some sort of evil magician," Claire speculated.

Turning pale, Anthony responded, "I don't like the sound of this. You honestly think you're in danger?" He practically stumbled through his words, something he did only when caught by an unexpected and negative turn of events.

"I've felt that way since my adolescence, when I was to have been initiated. It was when the big dream and then the nightmare first came," Claire explained, gazing out the window overlooking the red brick patio, remembering the dream she'd had on her twelfth birthday that Francesca had called "the big dream," in which medicine men and women had appeared to her as animals—wolves, snakes, mountain lions, eagles, or bears—and a long golden snake had hissed at her and bit her left ankle. She had thought it meant she was going to die, but the next morning Francesca had explained that the bite of the snake wasn't necessarily poisonous. It was a healing bite, unless Claire forsook her calling, and then the energy would become psychic poison—unshakeable sadness, dread, sickness, and death. Francesca had also told her that such dreams were violent because healers often fought their destiny, yielding only after much resistance, sometimes taking themselves to the point of illness and death. Claire felt as if she were caught in a web of memories, like a lost child trying to find her way through a dark forest.

"You're not with me anymore, Claire," Anthony said, his voice barely trickling through.

"I'm sorry, I didn't mean to drift," she replied, turning to him.

Anthony looked at her, worried, and asked, "What else do you know about these killings?"

Claire cleared her voice and answered, "I found out through old newspapers that each victim had contact with a medicine woman just before her death. It's like once the guy connects any twenty-five-year-old female with the legacy of medicine women she's dead. I'm twenty-five, I come from a long line of medicine women, and my dreams tell me that something evil is after me."

"What can we do?" Anthony asked, worried.

Claire tenderly reached for Anthony's hands, looked at him, and remained silent as he drew her close.

A musty smell of old linen, sounds of creaking boards and chirping crickets, and the lingering heat of the ninety-degree night lulled Archbishop Anarch into drowsiness as he sat in the confessor's box. The accusing voice of his mother in his head broke into his peaceful doze just as he heard the penitent's door click open. Its scratching and screeching reminded him of the sound of his mother's voice when she would reprimand him during their unsettling interactions.

He opened his eyes slowly. The young woman behind the sheer veil, Rosita Candelaria, blessed herself, her shadow clear as the passing moon, and said, "Bless me, Father, for I have sinned. It has been one week since my last confession."

Upon hearing her vulnerable voice, Anarch's flesh throbbed. Less than two years ago, at approximately the same time of year, he had heard Rosita's confession then invited her to his private chapel. Few came to where the archbishop himself worshiped. It was an honor he gave only to deserving women. There he did things that exorcised the devils from his body and left the honored person grateful for the privilege of having allowed herself to be used as an instrument of the Almighty. He always told himself that there were private matters and public matters, public theology and private theology. As with all the others, Archbishop Anarch had made Rosita believe that pure intention—ridding himself of evil so as to be a better archbishop—made such action pure, and then to forget about it.

"I have sinned grievously, Father," Rosita continued.

Archbishop Anarch waited in silence. He'd had her and now could see right through her. An image of the wantonness she had expressed months earlier pressed itself into his mind. It was so utterly heavenly that he could scarcely believe the fortuitous nature of it all. The handiwork of the Almighty was marvelous to behold. The sinners positioned so as to be expediently maneuvered. "I am two months pregnant," Rosita confessed, in the voice of a shamed child.

Archbishop Anarch grinned, thinking how delicious it was to have such power over such a woman.

"A most grievous sin, child—compounded by repeated lying to the Almighty himself," he said.

She was twenty-five, unmarried, and had lied during previous confessions. Withholding of impure actions rendered
previous absolutions null and void. Church members had
been indoctrinated since childhood that hell's fires awaited
those who deceived their confessors.

"Father, forgive me," Rosita sobbed loudly.

"You must make severe penance or risk eternal damnation," he said with divine authority. Knowing from years of
having heard her confession that she suffered from disabling
religious guilt, he wanted to make sure to break her will. At
her weakest, rushing through an act of contrition, forgetfully
taking a sip of water before Holy Mass, or entertaining the
slightest impure thought would drive her to confession. These
were the actions of a soul on the path to brokenness. The
breaking was so incredibly and joyously simple.

For months Rosita had managed to hide one of the most
damning of sins—fornication. It was pressed into the minds
of wide-eyed catechumens that above all it was important to
control their passions, especially love, which led to control of
the mind, for the guillotine of guilt inevitably gave a most ex-
peditious cut.

"Father, I will do anything," Rosita pleaded, her tone desperate.

It was so tantalizingly clear to Archbishop Anarch what
the penitent had to do. Inspiration came from on high on behalf of the faithful. Such transmission of divine impulse could
not be doubted since it was both just, the punishment befitting
the crime, and final. "You must expel this evil," the archbishop insisted with the conviction of one who was the earthly
representative of the Almighty. He pressed the images of ripping, tearing, bloodshed, the extinguishing of life's light into
Rosita's conquerable mind. His rage was now stronger than it

had been twenty years ago, when a similar demand had been scorned.

Rosita groaned.

Blessing her, Archbishop Anarch slid the wooden window shut, his imagination hot, anticipating with delight the night's tragedy. A few seconds later he stood outside the mahogany confessional, waiting for the penitent to finish weeping and step out of the rectangular box that always reminded him of an upended coffin.

The pregnant Hispanic beauty came out, red-eyed, trying to tug the black *mantilla* across her face to hide her flushed cheeks and runny nose. She stood before her confessor lifelessly, head down.

"Look at me, child," Archbishop Anarch commanded. He wanted to enter her with his eyes. In actuality, it was unnecessary, the force of feeling already having accomplished its task; but to Archbishop Anarch, the delicacy of the moment could not be missed.

Her cheeks flushed and wet with tears, Rosita sighed and meekly raised her head, gazing directly at him.

Archbishop Anarch locked his eyes to hers and said, "Even one of the Almighty Lord's twelve apostles betrayed him. Then he, Iscariot, made penance. Now, my daughter, go and do the same."

He kept staring, further burning his command into Rosita's mind, his intense thoughts conjuring an image of execution.

As though on cue, her tears instantly dried, and Rosita reverently, mechanically walked out of the archbishop's private chapel.

Back in the sacristy, Archbishop Anarch slipped the confessor's stole over his head, kissed the gold-embroidered cross in the center, and neatly folded it in quarters before placing it in the middle open drawer. Preparing to leave the sacristy, he dipped the tips of the fingers of his right hand into the holy water font near the door, crossed himself, and uttered a prayer of thanksgiving, "Praise be to Thee, Lord Almighty, for having delivered another wretched soul from her wanton ways." Then he looked at himself in a nearby mirror and smiled as a glow of satisfaction at having exercised the will of the Almighty rose up from the pit of his stomach to the top of his head. In no other calling could he have gained such unconditional influence.

Before retiring to his quarters, Archbishop Anarch couldn't help but linger to again gaze at his reflection in the mirror, noting the light that appeared to surround his head just as the saints of old were said to emanate a glow. He flashed a wide, toothy smile, thinking he was handsome, generous, and above reproach. No beast in the mirror tonight.

Then he flicked off the light, anticipating a good night's sleep, undisturbed by roars from the underworld. The bloodthirsty creature dwelt content in his inferno, awaiting the arrival of a tender, young morsel.

Rosita had lain naked in the bathtub full of water for the past twenty minutes. It was cold yet not, for it seemed as though she was no longer present, while eddies of red spun concentrically across her field of vision.

After the first flush of agony, a sense of intoxication had overcome her. The pills were good. The ugly thing floated… looked at her. The room was getting darker, and Rosita's soul was bright white again. The angel came. It was black-robed.

Rosita thrashed, then went limp. She was carried into the night, and things faded to black.

≀≀≀

After dinner, Claire and Anthony returned to Claire's apartment and nestled on the sofa by the roaring fireplace. But an ominous feeling lingered in the night air as though darkness had draped itself over the city like the cloak of some nefarious god. Anthony tried to soothe Claire's restlessness, to no avail. She wanted to relax, but the instant she permitted herself to move closer to Anthony her muscles tightened. She looked at Anthony apologetically.

He understood and lightly stroked her hair. Then he took her by the hand and they made their way to the bedroom, Anthony's touch loving and quieting. Claire drifted toward sleep. In the distance, she heard people talking below her second-story apartment, the north wind tugging at the windows. Dreams rippled in and out of her consciousness. She heard drums beating and voices chanting in a primitive language, then fell into a vortex of shouting and screaming. Tumbling down a black tunnel, she emerged in the realm of the Granite Boulder, its sharp edges scraping her shoulder. The ground shook as the great rock rose to the night sky. Everything turned quiet.

Then there appeared women warrior-healers with colorful streaks painted vertically on their bodies who taunted her and lunged threateningly. Their chants and bare feet on red-hot coals of bonfires terrified Claire. Never had she witnessed such contained yet directed rage. The strangely painted women poked her back with hot staffs and knives. Her mother's people, Apaches, were burrowing into the marrow of her being with their dark eyes as they leapt through flames and cried out with such force that the flames grew higher and higher. Claire tried to shield her eyes from the white-hot blaze as the fire became taller than the piñons rising out of the forest floor, their girth and height five times beyond normal. Claire screamed. Howls echoed in the canyon like wolves wailing at the moon. Dozens of warrior women with the imprint of the healer—a coiled snake branded on the outside of their right biceps—surrounded her. Red welts on her right bicep morphed into a coiled snake.

The warrior-healer women screamed furiously as they formed a tunnel, their teeth bared menacingly, and whipped her legs with willow branches. Tiny beads of her blood dripped to the ground. She tried to break away, but they locked themselves in formation. The oldest of them, a woman with leathery skin, shoved her toward the passage then spun her around so that she was facing their rage-filled eyes. The old woman forced Claire's head down then shoved her through the tunnel of muscled legs and interlocked arms. She now recognized the eerie, low sounds they were making as the incantation of a medicine woman's initiation, which her mother had described to her many times. As she crawled through the passageway, hands and arms beat her with clubs and thorny branches. Claire squeezed her eyes closed with the pain.

When she opened her eyes again, the scene had shifted. The warrior women had vanished, and she was lying in a sun-lit meadow, the sun's rays healing her wounds. The wounds on her arms and legs no longer bled but burned like beestings. Hearing a rustling from a nearby stand of lilacs, Claire turned her head. As she did, something nipped her left calf, causing a blistering pain to shoot up her leg. She saw a rabid black coyote run past her, then turn back, poised for another attack. It growled, its snout and teeth blood red. Claire tried to run, but a mysterious force kept her from moving as she peered into the creature's eyes. In her mind, she saw the face of Elizabeth screaming, "*El diablo, el diablo!*" The coyote stood its ground, white foam mixing with the blood dripping from its distended tongue. Then its hairy body began morphing limb by limb into a human shape until a man with a hooded cloak stood before Claire, lifting a staff with a bronze crook threateningly. The air was still, and the sky was dark with ominous clouds from which lightning flashed. He turned the tip of the crook toward Claire as if to incinerate her with its evil magic, the sight of it taking her back to when she had been a girl hiding in a forest to stay alive while a black-cloaked figure killed her mother with a similar staff.

The next instant Claire awoke, heart pounding. Looking at the digital clock on her nightstand, she saw it was 5:30 am, Sunday. She was due at the hospital by 6:00.

Getting up, she noticed reddish streaks on the skin along her right shoulder and on her legs, which faded after she had showered and toweled herself. Then, in the steamed-filled bathroom, she thought she saw the image of Elizabeth behind her in the mirror. Feeling dizzy, she leaned against the sink. When she looked in the mirror again, the image was gone.

She dressed quickly and hurried out to her car without waking Anthony. Adjusting her rearview mirror, she thought she saw Elizabeth hunched over limply in the backseat. She turned around, but no one was there.

With her heart racing, Claire gripped the steering wheel tightly, backed out of her parking space, and sped away to the hospital.

5

The votive candles flickering on the back chapel wall, the smell of incense, and the crisp fall air reminded Archbishop Anarch of a night more than twenty years ago, the only time when his standing as a priest, which he loved, had been seriously threatened.

After many months of passionate secret rendezvous with a woman, one midnight with the stars spread across the black sky of the high mountain desert, the woman, whose hands were softer than rose petals and whose cheeks shone with the luster of moonlight, mentioned marriage. That night he had hesitated for an instant, nearly overcome by the woman, before angrily declaring, "I am a priest, and I cannot." From then on, he had steeled himself against the wiles of women, growing to hate them all.

One evening after he had resisted the temptation of the woman, he rededicated himself to his priesthood by kneeling down beside his bed and praying for power from the Almighty to recommit himself to leading lost souls to eternal life, to restore the Ecclesia Dei to its former glory, and to grant him the title of Archbishop of the Ecclesia Dei. That night in a dream, the wind began howling and a ghastly being appeared before him, with a pale luminescent face, red eyes lacking irises, pupils twice the normal size, and fire raging at its feet.

"William," the being said.

"Yes, Lord," he answered.

"Your will be mine," it hissed.

For so long he'd prayed to hear those words, the Almighty's acceptance of his ambition to lead the Ecclesia Dei, to ensure its glory, to proclaim hell an ever-present reality and that the way to heaven depended on blind faith and unquestioning obedience to the shepherd — the Archbishop of the Aztlan Ecclesia Dei.

"As you wish, my Lord," William had answered, a cold wind touching his soul with its arctic fingers.

"I will send you a helper to enact my will at the altar of sacrifice," said the old god.

William's heart beat frantically.

"Restore my church," the old god continued, blood pouring out of his mouth as he tilted his head back and howled with holy fury.

William permitted himself only a glance, remembering the Old Testament curse of death for gazing into the face of the god of wrath and judgment. But his soul absorbed the god's fury, becoming a weapon to wield against unbelievers and others who would threaten his divine calling. His wish had been granted. One year later he was installed as the Aztlan Archbishop of the Ecclesia Dei, commissioned to spread the good news of the gospel, rout out all infidels, and restore the Ecclesia Dei to its former glory.

Now Archbishop Anarch looked at his watch and realized he still had three hours before the chosen remnant would gather for Sunday mass at the mission church twenty miles away. He finished his prayers and walked out of his private chapel into the sacristy, where a floor-length mirror was fastened to the wall just below a small, ancient crucifix. Admiring himself, he reached toward the reflection of his hand bearing the coveted ring and grinned. Then gathering his vestments and chalice, he walked to his private dining room.

"Excellency, your morning papers," his priest-secretary, Father Gall, said, placing the *Aztlan Crier* and the *New York Times* on the white linen tablecloth of the twelve-foot dining room table. Father Gall knew that the Archbishop liked to read the papers before being driven to the mission for the early Sunday morning mass to get inspiration for his homilies from real-life examples of corruption, despair, and tragedy.

Archbishop Anarch smiled at the local front-page headline that read, "Pregnant Heiress Commits Suicide" The three-page article, illustrated with pictures of the philanthropic socialite, brought back memories of his own private encounter with the woman. The article confirmed that a maid had discovered Rosita Candelaria dead in her bathroom at 10:30 Saturday night. According to the police report, a hot bath had been drawn for Ms. Candelaria at 9:00 pm. The maid told reporters that Ms. Candelaria seemed preoccupied that evening. For nearly an hour the employee did not hear her stir, and, troubled by the unusual quiet, she finally knocked then entered the bathroom to find Ms. Candelaria dead in the bathtub, drowned in a pool of her own blood. An emergency autopsy had revealed she had taken an overdose of opiates, slit her wrists in the form of a cross, and wedged a hanger in her uterus to cause an abortion—the suicidal end of one of Aztlan's and the Ecclesia Dei's wealthiest benefactors.

One year earlier, Archbishop Anarch had graciously accepted her promise to will her sizable estate to him and the

Ecclesia Dei, with the stipulation that $10 million would be deposited directly into his personal Swiss bank account upon her death. He had humbly thanked her that day, knowing the beast would soon find its way to her bank account.

Elated, Archbishop Anarch commanded, "Father Gall, get my personal attorney on the phone. We'll wait till tomorrow to call the church's corporate attorney." For the next ten minutes, Archbishop Anarch related to his high-priced attorney the details of Rosita Candelaria's death and stressed the importance of the immediate transfer of her funds to his personal account. Archbishop Anarch told the attorney that the pathetic girl had always suffered from an irrational fear of dying young, meanwhile thinking to himself that of course he never hesitated to exploit this obsession during her confessions, inspiring her to see death as a new beginning, like a butterfly breaking out of its cocoon.

Chuckling to himself as he thought of Rosita's gullibility, Anarch hung up the phone and signaled to Gall to prepare the black Mercedes. He wanted to go to the psychiatric hospital on a matter of mercy, before celebrating mass.

Another matter had to be settled.

Claire stopped outside the door to her office, fumbling for her keys. She felt pressured after a restless night's sleep, anxious about what the day might bring.

No sooner had she turned the key in the lock than a frantic voice echoed down the hall, calling, "Claire! Claire!"

She turned to see Raphael, a young mental health worker, running breathlessly toward her. "I'm glad you're here. Elizabeth needs you," he gasped. Raphael was one of the few staff people Claire trusted. They had often worked side by side in group therapy, trying to calm patients who were out of control. When Raphael came to her about hospital or patient matters, Claire listened.

She quickly set her briefcase on the desk and followed him, locking the door behind her. Neither said a word as they left the administrative building and hurried to the locked ward on the other side of the twelve-acre lawn. Unnerving images flitted through her mind—the nightmare about Elizabeth, the evil man cloaked in black, and the illusion of Elizabeth slumped over in the backseat of her car. There was an electrical charge in the air, indicating a storm was brewing. The wind kicked up, scattering litter across the lawn and into the nearby arroyo. Claire felt her skin begin to crawl.

They reached the inpatient ward and ran up the dozen steps to the front door. Raphael unlocked it, and as they walked down the corridor Claire's dread grew. She felt as if she were moving in slow motion. Each second that passed seemed like a minute, every sound ringing irritatingly in her ears.

Instead of going to Elizabeth's ward, as Claire had expected, Raphael turned down the hallway leading to the isolation unit for the dangerously psychotic.

"She's in there?" Claire asked, frowning.

"Yeah. She's really in bad shape," replied Raphael.

The electronic triple-locked doors suddenly crashed open as three nurses and a couple of psych-techs rushed out. "I don't know what's going on. Everyone's falling apart," one of the nurses exclaimed.

A psych-tech chimed in, "Maybe there's gonna be a full moon tonight." The group laughed nervously.

No sooner had Claire and Raphael stepped inside when

the charge nurse, Wardene Black, a red-faced stocky woman, marched toward them, stopping inches short of Claire's face.

"It's about time you showed up. Your patient Elizabeth Gonzales is about to rocket to the moon. You're the only one she's likely to listen to, if she listens to anybody! You'd better settle her down or we'll put a truckload of dope into her," Black said, grinning.

"So where is she?" Claire asked, glaring.

The nurse hesitated and then said, "Follow me."

Walking down the dim corridor of gray cement covered with hairline cracks, Claire looked up at the bare bulbs hanging from the ceiling. She hated this part of the hospital, one of the few remaining pre-World War II structures. *Hell's alleyway*, she thought.

Raphael stopped to peer inside one of the units. "I'd better check on this patient," he said. "See you later."

Claire nodded. "Thanks, Raphael."

Wardene Black had bolted ahead, stopping at the last door at the end of the hallway. She turned toward Claire with a sneer, slammed the palm of her hand just below the door's steel-mesh window, and said, "She's all yours."

Claire clicked the deadbolt open and saw Elizabeth huddled in the far corner, looking like a discarded human carcass. The grunting and snorting sound she was making reminded her of a pig at feeding time. Shocked to see Elizabeth in such a state, Claire resisted the impulse to run, unable to abandon Elizabeth to a megadose of antipsychotic drugs.

Stepping inside the small cell-like room, she called softly, "Elizabeth." Now a catlike cry sounded from the corner.

Claire inched closer, the smell of the urine and feces on the floor turning her stomach.

Then Elizabeth purred, and Claire felt the blood draining

from her face. As she moved closer, Elizabeth let loose a bloodcurdling scream.

Claire froze, wondering if this woman she thought she knew so well might hurt her. Claire wanted to touch Elizabeth's shoulder, whisper that everything would be all right. Since they had worked together for nearly a year, Claire believed that in some deep recess of Elizabeth's mind, the place where memories of feeling safe and loved are inscribed, Elizabeth knew who she was and wouldn't feel threatened. Still, in this condition Claire couldn't fully trust her.

Suddenly, Elizabeth lunged, and Claire's head hit the concrete. With Elizabeth's large, filthy body splayed on top of her, Claire struggled to breathe under the weight and felt pain radiating across her eyes and down her neck and spine, making her wonder if her ribs were broken.

Elizabeth's tongue curled into Claire's left ear, shocking Claire as a glob of saliva rolled down her neck.

Mustering all her strength, she shoved her arms and legs into Elizabeth, who arched up and laughed, staring into Claire's eyes. Claire pushed again, this time managing to knee Elizabeth in the stomach, knocking the wind out of her.

Elizabeth's eyes rolled up in her head as she slumped to one side, then collapsed to the floor in a semiconscious stupor.

Claire's first impulse was to scream for an orderly, but she knew he'd only call in a team to strap Elizabeth down in leather cuffs on a hospital bed while Wardene Black doped her. Days or weeks would pass before the dosage would be decreased enough for Elizabeth to speak coherently again.

Elizabeth whimpered, curling into a fetal position. Claire noticed bruises on her wrists and ankles, telltale signs of an orderly's roughness. Claire reached out a hand, still hopeful that she could handle the situation herself, but the split second the tips of her fingers touched the nape of Elizabeth's neck Elizabeth sat up on her haunches and glared at Claire with a fiendish grin. Her mind was gone, and her body began to convulse as if her soul were trying to break free of its psychotic prison.

Then just as suddenly as it had begun, the convulsing stopped. Elizabeth's expression softened, and she looked at Claire as if recognizing a long-forgotten friend. Her old smile returned, but there was a hollowness in her eyes that made Claire's heart race. Afraid to trust the change, she waited for her patient to make the next move.

Elizabeth's eyes sparkled with the innocence of a child. She rocked her head from one side to the other, giggling as if Claire were making funny faces. Then she drew closer and touched Claire's face with wet, smelly fingers, after which Claire felt a warm trickle of urine spraying down her leg.

"Orderly, help!" Claire called out, hoping her voice would carry down the corridor. Claire finally had to admit that Elizabeth's personality had fractured into tiny pieces like a shattered porcelain plate and that there was nothing more she could do.

Within seconds, a young Navajo man opened the door as he hollered for more help.

Elizabeth stood up and sneered at him, then grabbed him by the jacket, pulled him inside, and dropped him on the floor like a sack of potatoes.

Two more orderlies appeared and, when they saw her sitting on the man's chest, covering his mouth and nose with the palms of her hand, bolted for her. The instant they touched her, her forearms flew straight back, slamming them both in the nose. Blood trickled down their faces as they lunged at her again, this time managing to throw her to the floor and pin down her arms and legs.

Elizabeth struggled a few seconds more before she finally went limp, groaning like a dying wolf. She lay quiet for a moment and then stopped breathing.

"What the fuck!" one chief orderly shouted, his face paling. Pushing the other two away, he flipped her over, lowering his head to her heart. "Can't hear a heartbeat. Let's get her out of here."

The young Navajo man ran for a stretcher, and in less than a minute, Elizabeth was being wheeled to the intensive care unit.

Claire watched from the doorway, hesitant to step over the threshold, as if doing so would close the door on Elizabeth forever. She glanced back inside the dark chamber and, for a second, a mist, a form of a woman, Elizabeth, seemed to be huddled in the center of the room. As she rubbed her eyes and looked again, the bluish gray vapor drifted past her, vanishing outside the door.

She heard the orderlies barking out orders to the floor nurses, telling them to call the pharmacist and the attending physician. A moment later, Claire felt clammy, light-headed, a bitter metallic taste creeping over her tongue. She crouched against the wall and pressed her head between her knees, fighting the urge to vomit.

"Claire!" yelled Wardene Black, her voice like nails on a chalkboard, jarring her back to reality.

"What is it?" Claire sighed.

Snarling, Black came toward her and said, "Elizabeth has escaped."

⚡⚡⚡

The Mercedes had just started down the hospital's long gravel drive when Father Gall stopped the car and exclaimed, "Archbishop, look. Isn't that Elizabeth Gonzales, the patient we're here to see?" A barefooted woman in a hospital gown was trying to hide behind one of the piñons that lined the path to the administration building.

Archbishop Anarch rolled down his window. It had been at least fifteen years, but he recognized her. "Let's stay right here and see what she's going to do," he directed, enjoying the little game of cat and mouse.

Within seconds, she came out of hiding, walking proud as a peacock straight for the car. He felt nothing but contempt as he watched her limp toward him, noticing her badly soiled clothing.

A few weeks before, Elizabeth had requested a private appointment. She was told that the archbishop's demanding schedule didn't allow him to visit the hospital more than once a year, at Christmas, and then only to deliver a special homily during mass. Elizabeth persisted, threatening that someone who knew about his past would tell all if he refused to see her, whereupon Archbishop Anarch quickly agreed to the meeting.

Elizabeth stopped about ten feet from the car, close enough for him to realize that her gown was smeared with excrement. She bent over, exposing her ample bust, muttering lewd things that so-called sacred celibates were really participants in nighttime trysts in alleyways off Aztlan Plaza and peep show frolics in parks along Central Avenue, that there were more clergy freaks of kid flesh in the Ecclesia Dei than angels dancing on the tip of Aquinas's pen. Then Elizabeth gawked at them, lifted her gown, and peed.

Anarch was revolted, although he, too, had read the editorials in which the Ecclesia Dei had been accused of closing its eyes to rampant promiscuity and pedophilia among clergy. The location of the Ecclesia Dei's corporate headquarters was repudiated by journalists as a place where "every parish was a hothouse and altar boys had best beware of what pops out from under pretty robes."

Anarch and his secretary both knew of Elizabeth's propensity to engage in shocking acts and say blasphemous things. He'd had Father Gall investigate everything about her, prior to and during hospitalization. The attending physician, psychiatrist, and Wardene Black—all devoted members of the Ecclesia Dei—had agreed that Elizabeth, despite periodic outbursts, was usually a good patient.

Archbishop Anarch had also scrutinized Claire, one of the few staff members who didn't belong to the Ecclesia Dei, after learning that Claire had been orphaned and raised by a medicine woman. Elizabeth had been a medicine woman, a friend of someone he had tried to forget. Also, he decided it was best not to ignore Elizabeth, who might, he thought, get a little carried away with revealing memories during her therapy sessions. And medicine women were trouble, as he knew only too well.

"Archbishop, shall I put a stop to this?" Father Gall asked.

"Not yet," the archbishop answered, watching Elizabeth with a cold smile and wondering how it was that so many years ago he had ever had such a ludicrous oaf, even for a night.

Elizabeth glared back defiantly, knowing that since she was a member of the Ecclesia Dei, talking badly about priests and then exposing herself was very bad. Archbishop Anarch had preached about the Ecclesia Dei's stance on sexual morality frequently in his sermons, reminding his followers that celibacy was the highest of callings. Priests were to be regarded as Christ himself. Sex and the body's private parts, unless used for the procreation of true believers, were instruments of Satan.

As he matched her stare, Archbishop Anarch's blood boiled at her behavior.

Noticing, Elizabeth ran toward a nearby arroyo.

Archbishop Anarch leaned back in his seat with assurance that the Almighty had ways of dealing with such wayward members of his flock. He ordered Father Gall to follow her, saying, "Make sure this matter is completely taken care of."

As Father Gall got out of the car, Archbishop Anarch whispered a prayer to St. Augustine, praising his wisdom regarding the foul nature of women. The cleric returned a few minutes later, nodding at archbishop before getting into the car and driving away.

≀≀≀

Claire surmised that evidently for a brief time Elizabeth had been left unattended in the intensive care unit, regained consciousness, and escaped out the back door that had been left ajar by a careless employee.

As the stern face of Wardene Black peered at her, Claire asked, "Did you find her?"

"We need your help. Maybe she'll show herself to you. She trusts you," Wardene Black answered.

"I'm on my way," Claire replied, moving to the door.

"By the way," Wardene Black added, "if you find her, you will bring her back, right?" Claire smiled, letting the door slam behind her.

Once outside, she decided that the mesas and dense trees

on the edge of the desert would be her best bet. Jogging past a clump of sprawling sagebrush, she spotted a rattlesnake winding its way down a lone arroyo. As she reached a stand of piñons, a strong feeling of Elizabeth's presence overwhelmed her as well as lingering energy of rage and terror. Gray hues seemed to lace through the atmosphere, warning that Elizabeth's energy was fading. Francesca had taught Claire to be sensitive to the energy that people in highly charged states of rage or fright left behind, which, she had instructed, was as powerful as electrical currents in a thunderstorm. Sensitive souls, she had stressed, could intuit not only the nature of a place but the type of people who had been there—good or bad, frightened, lonely, or desperate. Claire had learned how to interpret such energy and now knew she urgently needed to find Elizabeth, whom she felt was in danger or worse from designs by outsiders, staff, or from her own scattered mind.

For one thing, over the past three months the medical staff had been threatening electroshock therapy for Elizabeth, and her escape would give them all the excuse they needed. "Touch the brain, never the same," Claire recalled a senior neurology instructor saying. She didn't want that for Elizabeth, no matter how dangerous her behavior had been. Claire knew that if she could talk to Elizabeth, she, if anyone, had the best chance of getting through to her, eventually learning the rest of her story and helping her to keep healing.

The morning sun was shining brilliantly against the Sagrado Mountains, and it was getting hotter by the minute. Claire knew that given her weight and overall poor health, Elizabeth would soon fall victim to injury, exhaustion, heart attack, or stroke.

Claire walked on, careful to watch for broken branches,

footprints, or pieces of torn clothing caught in the limbs as clues to Elizabeth's location.

Suddenly, she heard someone call, "Claire." It was Elizabeth's voice, coarse and weary, but there was nothing nearby for anyone to hide behind.

"Claire, where are you?" the voice spoke again, now with greater desperation.

Claire realized that the voice was coming from her intuition and that somewhere out in this ecclesiastical nowhere land Elizabeth struggled for life and was thinking of Claire. In the culture of medicine women, listening to intuition was crucial to a life devoted to healing. Claire knew that if she wanted to get to her patient, who might be dying, it was essential to let her intuition do the work. She closed her eyes, letting her mind drift to that still place deep inside where she could pick up the feelings of others and see things from a distance.

Immediately a faint image of Elizabeth lying face down in the dirt came to her, but the surroundings resembled any of a dozen sites along the arroyo. Focusing more intensely, Claire willed the image to become clearer. She heard a rumbling, the sound of cars passing on the highway, and thought Elizabeth must be at the outside perimeter of the hospital compound.

Claire headed for the arroyo about a hundred yards away, following it toward the two-lane highway, then started up the hospital's main road. Arriving at the exact place she'd seen in her mind, Claire spotted her patient lying motionless in the sand near the edge of the arroyo.

She breathed a sigh of relief and ran toward her, certain that Elizabeth's sheer exhaustion had finally subdued her demons, allowing her to rest.

"Elizabeth," Claire called softly. But there was no response.

Moving closer, Claire noticed a small turquoise crucifix

on the ground a few feet away and a pool of blood surrounding Elizabeth's head. Her eyes were wide open, lifeless.

6

Claire fought back tears as Himmel coldly informed the hospital staff of Elizabeth's death in the employee cafeteria, which resembled an army mess hall with shining, stainless-steel countertops, metal folding chairs, and grimy tables.

"I called this meeting both to announce that we now have the money we need to expand the locked ward beyond its present hundred-bed capacity and to say that the hospital and Ecclesia Dei have ruled Elizabeth's death accidental, and she will be privately interred tomorrow," said Himmel. Despite the fact that it had been less than six hours since Claire had discovered Elizabeth's corpse, the hospital administration already had the body taken to the morgue—without pause for an autopsy—then embalmed and prepared for burial.

Upset with Himmel's nonchalant demeanor, Claire asked Wardene Black, "Where's the burial going to be?"

The sour-faced woman stopped fidgeting long enough to reply, "Like Himmel said, it's private."

Claire turned away, choked by grief at the image of Elizabeth dying alone and now being buried without friends in attendance.

As Himmel tossed Elizabeth's file into his open briefcase and talked about the plans to build the ten-thousand-square-foot addition, Claire envisioned herself demanding that something this important shouldn't be so easily dismissed, that there had to be more to it. Elizabeth's psychotic break, the way she had bolted out of the locked ward, all on the day she was to have met with the archbishop, left too many questions unanswered.

Himmel droned on, describing the up-to-date facilities that would provide ample space for isolation units, hydrotherapy, and shock treatments, saying that the additional wing would enable the hospital to be more efficient in caring for the increasing number of Ecclesia Dei members.

Claire recalled one of her last patients who had received shock treatment.

Emily Sandoval, a thirty-year-old woman from Puerta de Luna, had been to see her for only a few sessions before the wizards of the ward—the staff psychiatrists—strapped the electrical conduits onto her head and fried her gray matter. She and Emily had laughed at their last session when Emily shared that the people in her village were convinced she was a witch.

"Yes, and you did your part to make them believe it," Claire had said. "Like the time you drew a circle around yourself in the dirt and told the kids chasing you that you had cursed them, so if they stepped inside the circle, the earth would swallow them up and they'd drop down to hell."

Emily had laughed, her eyes twinkling, and said, "Yeah, and it worked. They ran off screaming and never bothered me again."

Claire had thought it tragic that Emily's psychiatrists had

diagnosed her as chronically violent with a poor prognosis, meaning that the hospital had become her permanent home.

Himmel's gruff voice detailing building plans brought Claire out of her reverie. During the past year, she had grown to dislike the man—his cold nature, superior attitude, and gray weasel-eyes.

Claire listened as he said, "This fine psychiatric institution is looked on as a model for mental health care, emulated by other hospitals throughout the country. We have a lot to be proud of and a lot to thank the good Lord for, as well as Archbishop Anarch, of course. Ladies and gentlemen, this work provides our daily bread. Let none of us ever forget that."

Business. That's what it always boiled down to, Claire realized with horror. Elizabeth's death was being hushed up because it was bad for business. Trying to suppress her anger and grief, she remembered how Emily had looked the day after electroshock therapy—an automaton who barely knew who she was. Like Elizabeth, she'd had enough gumption left, though, to escape the hospital, even if, in Emily's case, it involved suicide. One night a nurse who noticed Emily wasn't in her bed, checked the bathroom, and found her hanging by a belt from an exposed pipe in the ceiling. The administration had brushed her death away like dust off shoes, just as Elisabeth's death was being quickly dismissed. For Claire, the cover-up of tragedy after tragedy was sounding an alarm that persuaded her to investigate motivations.

Summoning courage, Claire stood up and said, "Elizabeth was alive one day and dead the next, out of the blue. We can't gloss over it as if nothing's happened."

A hush swept through the room. Himmel raised his eyebrows and replied, "Ms. Sanchez, we are all saddened by Elizabeth's death, but we must get on with caring for the living."

Everyone shifted nervously in their seats, whispering among themselves, then abruptly stopped as though directed to do so by an intimidating glance from Himmel.

The outside light coming through the cafeteria windows dimmed as dark clouds formed a canopy over the grounds. The afternoon winds suddenly died down, creating a strange silence. Himmel glared at Claire, then sighed in disgust and began discussing a portfolio of slides, "These architectural renditions of the new wing will enable you to see the magnificence of the project we're undertaking," he said, making a point of ignoring her.

But just as he inserted the first slide into the projector, Claire spoke up again, saying, "Mr. Himmel, may the staff attend Elizabeth's funeral?"

Seconds passed like hours before he answered, "As I said, Ms. Sanchez, her burial is a private matter."

"Elizabeth and I went through a lot in the past year," Claire replied, her voice gaining strength, "and I'd like to go to her funeral."

"You'll have to grieve privately. Now, please sit down," Himmel insisted. Claire ignored the order and repeated, "But we're treating her death so casually."

His eyes flaring with anger, Himmel said, "Ms. Sanchez, I have a hospital to run. If a patient chooses to disregard the hospital rules meant to ensure their well-being and safety, the results may be tragic. But we must go on."

Several heads nodded in agreement, but then, to Claire's surprise, a usually timid nurse came to her defense, saying, "Claire's right. Otherwise, we're more like a death camp than a hospital."

Then Raphael, who was sitting toward the back, said, "People come in here, die tragic deaths, and no one pays any attention."

"Yeah, like it's expected, even hoped for," a new psych-tech added.

"Don't forget who butters your bread," Himmel said, threateningly. "This is a private institution. If you don't want to play by the rules, get out."

Claire noticed that only employees who were not members of the Ecclesia Dei had dared to speak up.

Himmel continued, "I hope everyone feels better after having had their say, especially you, Ms. Sanchez. Let me reiterate, we're here to serve the Church. If that's not your intent, I'll expect to find your letter of resignation on my desk."

"Are you firing me, Mr. Himmel?" Claire asked.

Grinning, Himmel answered, "We'd love you to continue working here, Ms. Sanchez, but since you seem to be so dissatisfied with the way things are run, I have to wonder if you might be happier working for someone else."

"Mr. Himmel, I work for my patients. This hospital pays me to do my best for them. That's what I've been doing, and I intend to continue," Claire declared.

"I'm glad to hear that, Ms. Sanchez. You do such fine work with your patients, and we'd hate to lose you," Himmel said in an artificially sweet tone. Then glancing at his watch, he placed the portfolio of slides in his briefcase and announced, "Time seems to have gotten away from us, so we'll postpone hearing more about the building project. Let's all get back to work now."

Claire sat down, satisfied that she had voiced her concerns and resolving to look deeper into Elizabeth's death regardless of Himmel's lack of cooperation.

❧❧❧

By five, the sun had nearly set. Crisp, cold air warned of the possibility of snow. A chill crawled over Claire's neck and arms. The day had been stressful, to say the least. After Himmel's shocking and ruthless treatment of Elizabeth's death, Claire had found it nearly impossible to concentrate on her work. She felt despair at the thought that there might be nothing she could do about what she now saw as a tragedy, hidden by subterfuge and administrative double talk. If only she had been able to get through to Himmel there might have been hope within the institutional corridors of the Hospital of the Ecclesia Dei—but there had been no human feeling from the man, his words cold as a corpse. Worse, there would be a price to pay, Claire knew, for having spoken up so boldly.

Throughout the day, every time she walked through the hallway or entered the lounge to ice her tea or relax for a while, Claire overheard the opinions of others who had been at the meeting. "Bad idea. She shouldn't have said a thing," a middle-aged, frail doctor known to do as he was told mumbled.

A young nurse added, "She's going to be sorry."

Nearly all the twenty or twenty-five persons present agreed that Claire had been right, but she shouldn't have voiced her opinion publicly, especially since the Ecclesia Dei was cutting her check.

As she unlocked her car door to leave for home, a hand touched her shoulder, startling her. "A professional recommendation, Ms. Sanchez? Mind your own business," Wardene Black advised, smirking at Claire.

"Good night, Wardene," Claire said and got into her car.

But Wardene Black kept her from closing the door and added, "Sanchez, one day you're going to learn that it isn't smart to mess with people in high places."

"People in high places? Please go on," Claire said, remembering the turquoise crucifix on the ground near Elizabeth's body.

Sounding uneasy, Wardene Black continued, "You were hired to do a job. Just do it, then go to your *casita* at night and we'll get along just fine."

Anger rose in Claire like a fierce desert wind. She held Wardene Black's gaze.

A snide smile flashed across Wardene Black's face as she turned and walked away, then glanced back, adding hatefully, "Your mother died around your age, didn't she?"

Stunned by what appeared to be a threat, Claire started up her car and laid her head on the headrest, trying to calm herself. Wardene Black's viciousness, Claire thought, was just another sign that the administration desperately wanted to keep Elizabeth's death under wraps.

Claire was eager to get to Francesca's to tell her in person about Elizabeth's death, since the two women had been friends, once sharing the spiritual kinship of the medicine women. Considering again the details surrounding both Elizabeth's and Emily's deaths, Claire felt increasingly certain of her gnawing suspicion that they just might be two in a long line of tragic deaths the Ecclesia Dei had written off as accidental or self-inflicted. She knew she wouldn't rest until she'd discovered the truth.

As Claire pulled into Francesca's driveway past the first stand of piñon trees, she felt relieved, like the feeling that comes from a comforting embrace. Claire parked her car where she always did, behind three ponderosa pines that stood less than fifty feet from Francesca's front door. But as she turned off her engine, she had a sense that it wasn't safe to get out of the car and walk in the dark to the front door. Being overly tired made the mind play tricks, she realized, especially after a tragedy. Light-headed and stomach queasy, she laid her forehead against the steering wheel, closed her eyes, and tried to fight off the dizziness. Then she sat up quickly, experiencing a sense of the earth opening up and an evil, medieval sorcerer, his cape fluttering in the wind, carrying her into its bowels. As she clutched the steering wheel tightly, a headache started up the back of her neck and sent shooting pain right between her eyes.

Francesca always said, "When you're exhausted and dark images knock at the door of your mind, don't answer. Let them pass. If entertained, they'll cause havoc, needless worry, anxiety, and despair." Claire knew how to do this. In a few minutes, she had reassured herself that the fear would fade.

She was relieved when she saw Francesca looking into the car with a concerned expression on her face, saying, "What's wrong? I saw you drive up, but you never got out of the car." Without waiting for an answer, Francesca opened the car door, took Claire by the arm, and hurried her into the house. Claire waited in the living room, taking a chair by the fire, while Francesca went to the kitchen to pour them each a cup of hot coffee.

Returning, Francesca set a cup down in front of Claire and asked, "What in the world has gotten into you?"

Claire walked to the blazing fireplace, warming herself, before answering, "When I drove up, I thought something evil was out there. I suppose the day finally caught up with me." She went back to her chair, sat down, and reached for her coffee mug, cradling it thoughtfully. Then she told Francesca about Elizabeth's death and described her psychotic episode, searching for her after she'd run off, then finding her body in the sand with the turquoise crucifix beside it. Francesca lowered her head and cried over the loss of an old friend. Then she stared into the fire, lost in thought.

"What are you thinking?" Claire asked after a while.

"The turquoise crucifix troubles me," answered Francesca.

"It troubles me, too," Claire replied. "I was one of the last people to see Elizabeth, and she wasn't wearing a crucifix. The hospital doesn't allow patients to have any jewelry."

Francesca nodded, then clasped her hands together and asked, "But why so fearful, Claire?"

"Himmel basically told me to 'bug off' at the staff meeting this afternoon when I voiced my concerns about Elizabeth's death. Then, when I was leaving this evening, Wardene Black threatened me. She met me at my car and told me to mind my own business, reminding me that my mother had died at my age."

Francesca raised her eyebrows and said, "They're talking about you. Claire, Wardene Black works for the Ecclesia Dei, which knows how to use fear. She made you doubt yourself. Self-doubt is a curse. It's sent to stop you in your tracks."

Claire nodded.

"What did you say when she told you to watch out?" asked Francesca.

"Nothing. I tried to brush it off," replied Claire.

"That would've been the time to have sent her little curse back to her," Francesca remarked.

"How?" asked Claire.

"With a big broad smile," Francesca answered.

Claire chuckled then said, "Self-doubt is deadly. Wardene

Black won't get me again."

Francesca continued, "She is only a small desert rat with a tiny bite. It's your deeper fear of ending up like your mother that concerns me. It's what's making you vulnerable. You have your own choices to make, as did she. People live or die by their own decisions, not those of their parents."

"My fear is about more than ending up dead. I've been afraid of what I'm capable of," Claire confessed.

Francesca held Claire's gaze, then said, "I have something else to tell you. Through the years, I've had in safekeeping some things that were entrusted to me by an old friend. One of those things is a diary containing recollections about the Ecclesia Dei and Father William Anarch. Lately, I've felt drawn to read through it, and I've discovered something troubling."

Remembering her vision in the underground parking lot, Claire listened intently.

"Evidently, William Anarch's mother, an oil heiress and noted benefactor of the Ecclesia Dei, promised her fortune to her son provided he remain faithful to the priesthood. As a young priest, he had an eye for native beauties. One of them was the writer of this diary," continued Francesca.

Claire's interest piqued since this was at odds with rumors that Archbishop Anarch was a woman hater.

"When faced with the choice of giving everything up for the woman he professed to love," Francesca went on, "he left her cold."

"Who was she?" Claire asked.

"In due time, Claire," Francesca said, standing to tend the fire. "I also found a letter inside, written to the author by someone we both knew—Elizabeth." Claire had a strange feeling of knowing who had written the letter a millisecond before Francesca had spoken the name, Elizabeth's presence slipping into the living room as quietly as the wisps of snow falling outside.

Francesca moved to the window, smiled as she watched the flakes dancing in the darkness, then sat back down beside Claire and said, "The quiet brings a friend." After a few moments she continued, saying: "One night many years ago, the old medicine women spoke of a profound disturbance that disrupted their sleep. Someone of great influence had entered into a pact with evil—a foul alliance that would last years and harm many lives. Elizabeth knew about this and had suspicions about who that person was. Her letter was a warning to the diary's author. She wrote, 'William Anarch has left behind all human feeling, prayed to become archbishop of the Aztlan Ecclesia Dei, and the devil has answered his prayers.'"

Claire shuddered.

7

Claire stood on the balcony feeling discouraged as a cold evening wind slapped fine particles of sand against her cheeks. The week's troubles ran through her mind—Elizabeth's death, Himmel in the staff meeting on Sunday, and Wardene Black's threat and vicious barbs. Her subsequent investigation into Elizabeth's death over the last few days had also gone poorly. Encountering closed door after closed door had frustrated her determination to get to the bottom of what she was convinced was a cover-up by the Ecclesia Dei. The usually talkative executive secretary, who had scheduled Elizabeth's appointment with Archbishop Anarch, had suddenly become tight-lipped, brushing Claire off when she asked about the reason for the meeting. Therapists, doctors, and nurses had also been abrupt and cold. No one had been willing to talk to her about anything except clinical matters, which they had discussed with robotic detachment. Claire hoped that dinner in her apartment this evening with Anthony and a good night's sleep would refresh her. Closing the French doors behind her, she stepped back inside her living room then went to the kitchen to stir the hearty broth she'd prepared for dinner. Rich aromas of fresh garlic, onions, and vegetables mixed in a base of tomatoes and bouillon made her mouth water. Taos Pueblo flutists played on her stereo.

In the distance, winds kicked up and then began howling furiously. The apartment lights flickered then went out, so she couldn't see beyond the tip of her nose. Gradually, her eyes adjusted to the darkness, aided by the embers of the dying fire in the fireplace. Looking out her window, Claire saw the lights of the plaza and realized that the power outage was only in her apartment complex. Lighting the candles on the dining room table, she hoped it wouldn't last long.

A knock at the door startled her, then she realized it was probably Anthony. "I'll be right there," she called.

A cold draft swept through the room. She wrapped her arms around herself as she walked toward the front door. Everything grew strangely quiet.

She reached to open the door, but the knob wouldn't turn.

"Anthony?" she called out.

There was no reply.

She dead-bolted the door then asked, "Who's there?" There was still no answer.

A gust of wind flung the balcony door open. She ran to slam it shut, her heartbeat echoing in her ears. Then the electricity surged back on as footsteps creaked down the stairway in the corridor.

She went back to try the door, hesitated, listened, and then tried again to open it. This time it clicked open to an empty hallway and the barren foyer of the first-floor apartment. Suddenly her breath caught in her throat as the front entrance door swung open. Anthony walked in and smiled at her, arms outstretched, carrying a bottle of wine and a bouquet of flowers.

"*Querida*," he said, hurrying up the steps to take her in his arms.

"It's so good to see you," Claire breathed, comforted by his presence. They lingered in a kiss.

"Why were you coming out?" he asked as they stepped inside her apartment.

"I think someone was trying to break into my place," Claire explained.

"And you opened the door?" Anthony asked, worry lines creasing his face.

"I thought it was you who had knocked. When I tried to open the door, the knob wouldn't turn, as if somebody was holding it from the other side. Then the wind blew the balcony door open, and after I went to shut it, I again tried the front door and it opened. I walked out to check things—that's when you came in," said Claire.

Anthony handed her the flowers and set the bottle of wine on the dining room table. "Maybe we should call the police, Claire, and tell them there was an intruder in the building," he suggested.

"I don't want to deal with the police. Every once in a while, something like this happens in the building. Nothing comes of it. I'll just make doubly sure the doors are locked," Claire insisted.

"I don't know, Claire. I saw a van whip around the corner just before I came in. I thought it was a service person of some sort, in a hurry. But it could've been the person at your door," Anthony replied.

"Maybe," Claire conceded. "I want to let it pass, for now. We're together. That's all that matters."

Anthony put his arms around her, still concerned, then

kissed her cheek. He picked up the wine and went into the kitchen. "I brought a great cabernet sauvignon from the Dark Forest Winery in Embudo," he said proudly.

Claire smiled. She stayed in the living room stoking the dying embers in the fireplace until the cedar and piñon kindling blazed and crackled. The earthy scent would help soothe the unspoken feelings between her and Anthony.

Soon Anthony returned with two glasses of wine and handed her one.

"*Salud,*" he said, tapping his against hers.

"*Salud,*" she echoed, taking a sip of the wine.

Anthony tasted the wine, then smiled and said, "Definitely a winner. Like us. You look lovely this evening." He put his arm around her waist, kissing her again, then adding a big cedar log that would burn a few hours.

Anthony's warm voice dispelled Claire's shadowy thoughts. She enjoyed watching his every move, his skin glowing a rich bronze as the flames curled over the logs. She felt a familiar longing to spend every day and night with him for the rest of her life; but then she again experienced the anxiety that surfaced whenever she thought about marriage. Distance meant safety, that the evil of the night was unable to steal Anthony away.

"I love you," she whispered.

"*Querida,* I love you, too. But I'm worried about you," he replied.

Claire was also worried about what she was facing, as reflected by her increasing inner visions about evil entities as well as the rituals of medicine women of the past. Francesca had taught her that the boundary between inner and outer worlds could disappear during times of turmoil and that spells of bad luck and weird happenings sometimes came from disturbed emotions, like an underwater earthquake generating a mammoth tidal wave. But Claire didn't want to worry Anthony even more by describing her inner visions now. Gazing at the fire, she confessed, "I've been exhausted. I've let discouragement get the best of me."

"You've been too stressed from your job and everything else," said Anthony, trying to reassure her.

"I know, but I felt something with Francesca. And I'm frustrated because I not only have unfinished business because of Elizabeth but also my own unfinished business."

Anthony rubbed her back understandingly then said, "How'd your investigation of Elizabeth's death go this week?"

"Didn't get anywhere. One dead end after another. No one will talk," Claire told him.

"But you're going to go on?" Anthony asked.

"If I don't, I'll be running from a ghost the rest of my life," explained Claire.

"So, what's your next step?" asked Anthony.

Claire hesitated then answered, "Right now, I'm going to do what I've been most afraid of."

"What?" Anthony asked, turning to face her.

"I'm going to Sunday mass to see the archbishop for myself. Nothing happens without his okay. So, it's time I check him out."

"But you can't do that, can you? You don't belong to the Ecclesia Dei," Anthony replied.

"It's not necessary. They don't have armed guards at the entrance checking IDs. There's nothing to stop a person from going to a mass. And I've decided to go to where the real action is, to Archbishop Anarch's first Sunday morning mass in the tiny village of Oro, the area of rich *rancheros*. The Sunday

9:00 am mass draws about two hundred wealthy parishioners. Archbishop Anarch's supposed to be at his fiery best there. Doctors talk about it in the lounge. His sermon and pageantry at the noon mass at the downtown cathedral doesn't compare. It's only a quarter full, while Oro is packed," replied Claire.

"I don't know about this, Claire. It gives me the creeps to think about you out in the middle of nowhere with a bunch of religious fanatics," Anthony replied.

"That is where I need to go. The mission in Oro is only a couple of miles from the Devil's Throne. It's a psychic hot spot," Claire explained.

"Then I'm going with you," Anthony asserted.

"No, I want to go alone. That way, I can slip in and out of the mass as inconspicuously as possible," Claire replied.

"I don't like it," Anthony said, as he walked to the balcony windows and stared out at the tiny garden area, which was perfectly lit by the plaza lights. Abruptly, he said, "You told me that the wind had blown the balcony door open. Are you sure there wasn't someone out here?"

"Why?" Claire asked, walking over to him. "Look at what has happened to the concrete statue we found last summer near Las Golandrinas." Anthony pointed to a section of the balcony near the fire escape stairs. Claire's eyes shot first to the iron balcony gate that led to the fire escape, which she never used and was always latched. It was now open, and the statue of two lovers embracing, set in the middle of a grouping of redwood planters, was now on the ground—broken to pieces.

༑༑༑

Drifting off to sleep that night, Claire wondered if she'd done the right thing by not having Anthony stay until morning, but she needed to be alone, to think, to dream. Anthony's warning as he'd left her home that evening floated in and out of her consciousness: "Be careful, Claire. You're going into dangerous territory."

As Claire slept, she slipped into a realm where the night sky was glistening with stars over a forbidding desert. A black-robed figure stood a great distance away, beneath an imposing jagged sandstone edifice that looked like the surreal throne of some ungodly king. Desert rats screeched and scampered beneath an ancient granite altar the size of a human body and a nearby cave that was partially hidden by low-lying scrub brush, the air perfectly still as though all life had been sucked out of the atmosphere.

Drawing closer, she saw that a naked body lay on top of the granite slab, obscured by the figure's black robe in such a way that she at first couldn't tell if it was a man or a woman. Then telescopically homing in, she got a better view that revealed the legs of an overweight woman and long tresses hanging over the sharp edges of the altar. The black-robed figure stood in the shape of a cross with his arms outstretched, holding a long knife in his right hand, which he lifted heavenward, saying, "All praise be to the wisdom of the Almighty." Then, in a pontifical voice, he continued, "As a jewel of gold in a swine's snout, so is a fair woman which is without discretion." His hand trembled with an unearthly energy that made Claire want to turn away, but she forced herself to gaze back as he proclaimed, "As you have promised, so you have done. As I have promised, now I do."

The rats grew quiet as a strong wind came up, swirling around the horrid throne and altar, spiraling upward, born from ancient depths.

Claire was both horrified and fascinated. She recognized but couldn't place the voice. She wanted to move closer to see more details, but invisible forces kept her legs and feet frozen in place. The victim's face was turned away, exposing her neck—a dead white dove beside it.

Then the black-robed figure lowered his knife and cut into the flesh of his victim. His robe billowed open like the wings of a bat. Blood spilled onto the desert floor, pooling around his feet as he performed the ritual with the cold precision of a surgeon. After cutting the body from head to toe, he laid the knife down beside it and cradled a strip of raw flesh in his right hand, muttering, *"Et verbum caro factum est."* Opening his mouth, he swallowed the bloody sacrifice. A voice whispered in Claire's ear, "The word becomes flesh." An unseen hand caressed her from head to toe, causing her to cringe. Then it stopped.

The black-robed figure picked up a sparkling gold chalice and placed it under the ledge of the altar to catch some of the overflowing blood. Then he lifted it upward, crying out another incantation. But his words were lost in the escalating screeches of feasting rats. Draining the chalice dry, he set the empty goblet on the altar and staggered from inebriation. The rats grew silent again as the blood-red moon emerged from behind dark clouds. Its beams descended to earth, surrounding the altar, and slithered toward Claire like the claws of a ravenous beast.

Claire bolted awake, her sheets twisted and damp.

Archbishop Anarch reeled, the black night swirling about him like a hurricane. The taste of human blood intoxicated him, its velvety richness a perfect complement to the sacrificial victim's sweetbreads. He would store the corpse deep in the frigid bowels of the cave to cure for a week before savoring the flesh.

He steadied himself against the granite altar and looked at the corpse. This insolent female had dared expose herself to God's chosen and for that had paid the price—eternal damnation—one less wanton woman in the world.

With the back of his hand, he wiped his bloodied mouth and watched as the nighttime clouds parted to reveal a constellation of stars in the image of the Almighty—with razor-sharp teeth and vicious eyes that always watched him. Pointed funnel clouds scooped downward like blood from the mouth of this divinity of wrath, who loathed the most carnal and corrupt of creatures—woman.

Anarch lifted his arms heavenward and cried out, "Into your hands, O Lord, I deliver the woman."

Anthony sat on the sofa in his living room with a sketch pad and charcoal pencil, making a drawing for a mother and child sculpture he planned as a birthday gift for Claire, symbolizing her work nurturing patients and reflecting his hope for their future. Sketching the contour of the mother's breast, he thought of Claire's beauty, her soft yet firm manner, the love in her eyes when she spoke of how much he meant to her, the fear that she expressed when they talked of marriage. Twice now they had agreed to set a date, but each time she had said that they shouldn't rush into it. After much painful talk, she'd finally admitted that she desperately wanted to marry him but was too haunted by her past, too terrified that someone evil would steal him away. No amount of reassurance could assuage her anxiety. Anthony had promised patience but secretly feared she would be forever captive to childhood ghosts.

Glancing outside, he noticed that the odd light he'd awakened to at 6:00 am was still lingering. Its unnatural grayish hue gave the impression of a sun eclipsed by soot. He could sense when something foul was afoot, especially when the lighting of a place or surrounding dimmed. His sixth sense, a protective and aggressive instinct to which he had grown sensitive since meeting Francesca and Claire, was being activated.

Intent on going to his studio situated at the entrance to his property for further work, he picked up his sketch pad and went to the door, then hesitated, reluctant to step into the strange atmosphere. Never had he felt such uneasiness that it made him shy away from stepping outside, onto his land. Finally, after bolstering himself with a deep breath, he stepped outside. The gray hue seemed to intensify, making him fear that his premonition had been right.

As he walked the thirty paces to his studio, a sudden urgency, not for himself but for Claire, overtook him. He stopped, looked around, and listened. A car engine turned over in the distance. Tires spit gravel behind the steep embankment of an arroyo and thick sagebrush adjacent to his studio. He realized he'd had an unexpected visitor. Tension gripped his neck and jaws as he remembered a conversation he'd had the day before with the yard supervisor at Aztlan Rock and Stone. The man had told him that a black Mercedes sedan had driven up on Friday and that the chauffeur had gotten out to ask if he knew a young sculptor who specialized in Italian alabaster and marble. He'd told the driver where

Anthony lived, happy to refer business. Now, Anthony wondered if he'd just missed their visit, but his instincts said otherwise. He hurried to his studio to make sure nothing was amiss.

From a few yards away, he saw something near the door-jamb and words painted on the weather-beaten door. As he drew closer, he saw that a dead dove was nailed to the door through its heart, its blood used to scrawl the message below it:

A love nest built for two.
One will be taken, her or you?

The two-lane highway leading to the isolated adobe Oro mission of the Ecclesia Dei was free of traffic save for a few cars carrying families on their way to the 9:00 am mass. Halfway there, Claire decided to pull off to the side of the road for a few minutes to think before driving the last ten miles. She got out of her car, walked a short distance, and sat on the top rail of a wooden fence. She was troubled by the previous night's dream, instinctively feeling that such an occult place and such a wicked being could exist behind the everyday scenes of her native Aztlan.

As the morning sun highlighted the bright yellow cotton-woods nearby, she realized just how reluctant she was to spend the morning in a setting that medicine women referred to as a "haunted place clouded by incense." Soon she would be witnessing a ceremony she'd heard about since her youth but always thought had undue influence over unquestioning minds. Having been raised in the way of medicine women, Claire had been taught that the human spirit could never be constrained without severe consequences. It followed the natural flow of life—a path of instincts and inspirations in which visions and dreams helped guide the course of daily living.

A black Mercedes whizzed by, the passenger in back turning to look at her as they passed. Claire recognized him immediately as the man whose chauffeur had changed her tire two weeks earlier. She grew angry at the thought of his roving eyes as the car disappeared over the horizon.

Walking back to her car, she stopped in surprise to see a large crow perched on the roof of her car, its black eyes staring right through her. It stood so utterly still that a feeling of desolation and death emanated from it. She wondered if it was real. Francesca had told her the legends of witches and warlocks who lived along the Turquoise Trail, some of whom had the magical power to shape change into large blackbirds that could hypnotize the unwary or ward off intruders with their unearthly caws.

On edge, Claire got into her car and started the engine. A dark voice spoke in her mind, telling her that she had no business entering this cultic site. Wardene Black's words—"Your mother died at your age"—rang in her ears. The admonition had been forceful, as though dictated by someone outside of herself. Claire's resolve, however, was like an eagle soaring through a turbulent sky.

She quickly drove the remaining distance and found the two-hundred-year-old adobe church standing atop a desolate plateau. It had been abandoned as a missionary outpost for nearly thirty years. Once William Anarch had been installed as archbishop, he had cultivated connections with the church-going ranchers in the area, offering to restore and expand the site as a functioning mission for the Ecclesia Dei in exchange for tithes.

Driving up the steep incline to the parking lot, Claire noticed that nothing was growing within a hundred-yard radius of the mission save some hundred-year-old cottonwood trees that softened the austere setting. The surrounding land was desolate, fit only for lost souls and bad spirits. Claire turned into the parking lot but hesitated getting out of her car. She watched as a Cadillac parked in a reserved space near the church and an elderly Hispanic couple got out and hurried up the wide flight of whitewashed steps to the church.

When Claire finally opened her door, a rank odor like rotting meat assaulted her senses, and a mental picture of decaying corpses hidden in the church's cellar filled her with disgust. She hurried up the crumbling adobe steps to the mission's ten-foot-high double doors.

An usher dressed in a gray wool suit smiled at her wryly as he held the doors open. Straining to see in the darkness of the church, her eyes moved to the neatly arranged, red votive candles flickering on either side of the two rows of pews. The nauseating smell of incense, the drone of worshipers mumbling their prayers, and the darkness made her feel claustrophobic. Small bells rang at the front of the church as an entourage of six altar boys, a priest, and the archbishop, who was holding a golden staff in his right hand, emerged from behind an ornate altar.

She sat down at the far end of the last pew, where she could hide in the shadows and watch the enactment of the five-hundred-year-old ritual of the Ecclesia Dei liturgy. The archbishop and assisting priest, whose features were obscured by cowl and robe, but who looked vaguely familiar, intoned incantations in Latin, while three hundred parishioners chanted the responses. Twenty minutes later the archbishop ascended the steep marble steps to the pulpit looming above the congregation. He blessed himself then silently surveyed the crowd. His soul-piercing gaze moved slowly from one individual to another. For a moment it seemed to stop at Claire then move on. The assembly remained quiet, awaiting judgment from on high.

Archbishop Anarch's voice broke the silence like a rock shattering glass. With fist-pounding and shouting, he began a spellbinding fiery sermon on the corruption of the true faith, his eyes wide with the righteous conviction that damnation awaited those who refused to accept the one true faith, his medieval raiment of luxuriously woven red and gold vestments adding a touch of divinity to his already thunderous stature: "The chair of truth, the seat of the representative of the Almighty, set up as a light of salvation for all nations, is being threatened more and more each day by a network of unbelievers that influences the hearts and minds of unsuspecting people everywhere, seeking to place doubts in their minds regarding the Ecclesia Dei—the very institution that ensures the salvation of their souls. People you least suspect can be instruments of this unholy alliance established by none other than the Prince of Darkness. People are taught that our religion is not needed, that human beings are sufficient unto themselves. Little do they know that the Almighty is not the Lord of benevolence and mercy to those who do not believe. These faithless ones will, in the end, meet not only our maker but theirs. And for them there will be no mercy. They are an abomination of wickedness. We, members of the Ecclesia Dei, must stand firm in our beliefs and rout out all impurity of thought, word, and deed from our lives, lest we, too, be corrupted and spend eternity suffering the flames of hell."

The people stared up at Archbishop Anarch, their unwavering devotion to the man stronger than the pungent incense clouding the air.

"Should the Antichrist himself appear on the face of the earth, he could not match the wickedness of the unbelievers in our midst," Archbishop Anarch continued, his eyes sweeping toward Claire.

Exaggerated images of the consequences of her beliefs crowded her mind. She saw herself being dragged before the pulpit, exposed as the daughter of a medicine woman, and punished in the manner of the Inquisition, when more than 2 million unbelievers had been drowned, burned at the stake, or had limbs torn from their sockets.

Claire felt herself growing even more uncomfortable as he continued, saying: "They are emissaries from the kingdom of sin, death, and hell. Even as I speak, these Antichrists are positioned in our community to destroy the Kingdom of Our Lord. We members of the Ecclesia Dei are the Almighty's true mystical body on earth. As such, we must resist all unholy forces that oppose our sacred mission, for mankind's salvation depends on us. We have been chosen by him. Let no one lead us astray or stand in our way."

Anarch suddenly stopped speaking and seemed to look straight at Claire again. She held her breath for a second, then wondered if the darkness, his towering position, and the relatively cramped space just made it *seem* as if he were looking directly at her.

But then the usher who had let her in tapped her on the back and whispered, "Father wants to see you."

She glanced at the altar and noticed that the priest who had been standing beside Archbishop Anarch was no longer there. She looked back at the usher, confused.

He took her by the arm, saying, "Please come with me."

Any hope of exiting was out of the question. There were another six ushers in the back of the church, and they would certainly stop her if she tried to leave. So she followed the thin, mustached man to the back of the church and down a dark hallway.

As they passed the restrooms, Claire said, "You'll have to excuse me for a moment. I haven't been feeling well." She turned into the ladies' room without waiting for a reply, where she closed her eyes and tried to catch her breath. She pictured the archbishop's assistant pulling her in front of the congregation as a dramatic conclusion to Archbishop Anarch's sermon, exposing an unbeliever who had desecrated their sacred place.

A moment later the usher knocked on the door impatiently and asked, "Everything all right in there? Please hurry. Father has only a moment."

"I'll be there in a moment," she called out. Realizing she had no choice but to let things play out, Claire ran some cold water over her hands and pressed her palms over her eyes, which were bloodshot from the incense. Her brown irises and dark pupils seemed to emanate a strange light. Then drawing a deep breath, she stepped back into the hallway just as the usher was reaching out to open the bathroom door.

Claire walked beside him, pulling her arm away when he tried to take hold of it and guide her down the dank, narrow hallway, which reminded her of a condemned mining shaft in Cerrillos. They stopped in front of the last door at the end of the corridor, which was slightly ajar.

The usher gently knocked, then pushed it open, motioning her in. The large room was lined with old pews set flush against three of the walls. Against the fourth, directly in front of the door, stood a floor-to-ceiling, ornately carved confessional.

No one else was in the room. Claire glanced back at the usher. He motioned her to the confessional door on the right, pressing his hand against the small of her back to urge her forward.

"It's all right," he said softly, "he just wants to talk to you."

"Why can't he talk to me out here?" she whispered. The usher put a finger to his lips, shaking his head, then opened the confessional's door. As Claire moved forward into the booth, she touched the wooden pew within it and felt a prick on her finger, as if a splinter or sharp pin had punctured it. The usher closed the door. Immediately, she was overwhelmed by a musty, putrid smell emanating from the priest's side of the confessional. Her finger began throbbing as she stared at the kneeler and the latticed screen, the silhouette of a man behind it.

"Welcome to the Ecclesia Dei, Ms. Sanchez. Kneel, please," a deep, authoritative voice said.

Claire remained standing, silent. The confined space, the lack of circulation, and the stench made her light-headed. Her finger was on fire, sending waves of sharp pains through her hand. She leaned against the door, fumbling for the lock but couldn't find it.

Things started spinning, and she felt herself blacking out.

When she awoke, she was lying on the cold floor outside the confessional, the back of her head hurting. Two beady-eyed ushers were peering down at her. The thin one, who had showed her in, grinned and said, "You passed out. A little air and smelling salts work wonders, though. You'll be all right in a few minutes."

The other man who had the build of a bodyguard, also smiled and said, "Father had to leave on an emergency. He asked me to assure you that the Ecclesia Dei welcomes you with open arms and that you're also welcome to stay for the rest of the liturgy."

Claire felt an immediate loathing for them and their feigned concern. As she struggled to get up, the two men helping her to her feet, she noticed that the pain in her finger had subsided. "I'm really not feeling well," she said, as she lightly massaged the back of her head. "I'd better be on my way."

"As you wish. We'll help you to your car," the ushers said.

"Just outside, please. I need a little fresh air before driving," Claire replied.

They escorted her out a back door. Once outside, she took a deep breath, then turned to thank them, hoping they'd leave immediately, but they lingered ominously before finally turning away. Before stepping inside, the stocky one looked back and said in a menacing tone, "Come and see us again."

⚡⚡⚡

Claire turned her car onto the highway. She was still feeling disoriented but knew she had to get away from the church. The memory of the words, the warning—*A haunted place clouded by incense*—paled in comparison to what she had witnessed firsthand.

She decided a soak in the hot lithium springs near the Place of the Granite Boulder would help wash away the psychic grime she felt after having been in one of the foulest places she had ever experienced. Driving helped free her mind from her horrid, oppressive experience at the church. The air sparkled as if the spirits of the night had swept over the terrain with cleansing winds.

Still, she remained frightened about what might have happened during the time she had passed out at the church. Standing in the small coffin-like confessional chamber had felt like struggling to get out of quicksand. She hated the feeling of not being able to control the situation, which had left her feeling vulnerable.

She realized that fainting after the finger prick had likely not been an act of cowardice, a fear-induced withdrawal, but had been deliberately caused by the prick to her hand from a door handle that had been dabbed with a central nervous system depressant potent enough to knock her out. Angered, her thoughts shifted to Archbishop Anarch's sermon, his hypnotic voice and eyes. There was no doubting the power of the man who towered above the congregants as he pontificated his gospel of hellfire and damnation. His religious fervor seemed to have deadened him to human realities, the vulnerability of less-educated minds, the susceptibility of mesmerized spiritual seekers to whatever spiritual spin would hasten their deliverance from the misery of their daily lives. It seemed evident that he'd stop at nothing to achieve his ends. The fact that she'd been singled out during the service told her that she was going in the right direction with her investigation. No doubt Elizabeth's death was part of a covert operation within the Ecclesia Dei, and they were trying to fend her off by pretending to welcome her with open arms.

The walk from the parking lot to the bathing area of the hot springs was less than two or three hundred yards. She shed her cotton dress and leather sandals and slipped into the pool, her muscles immediately loosening. From horizon to horizon, her eyes traversed the otherworldly landscape, hills and valleys of red clay with sandstone striations, towering pines, and clouds floating majestically across turquoise skies, as she absorbed the peaceful energy.

Sinking more and more into her relaxed reverie, Claire closed her eyes and became more conscious of the water's gentle caress, allowing its warm fingers to realign her with the oneness that breathed through the mountains, a mestiza's surrender of mind and body to invisible forces that replenish and renew. Minutes later, Claire felt herself slowly drawn back to the day world. She opened her eyes as a roadrunner whisked by, a mountain breeze came up, and the Gah'e, protective mountain spirits, cast the scent of piñons her way—signals that it was time to drive back home and continue her investigation.

Driving across the expanse of sagebrush and sandstone desert, she pondered what step to take next. Elizabeth's death, she was sure, had been orchestrated by Archbishop Anarch or his underlings. He was cunning and manipulative enough to have orders executed while he remained calm and collected behind the scenes of pontifical splendor. Going to the police was out of the question since there was no concrete evidence linking Elizabeth's death to the Ecclesia Dei. And it would be difficult, she realized, to get past the Ecclesia Dei's veneer of goodness and piety to find proof of its unholy alliances. At the moment, she had to have faith that the next step would present itself, as Francesca always said, as long as she remained sincere in her quest.

As she pulled into her garage, Claire realized it was nearly time for dinner and looked forward to preparing her evening meal, hoping that cooking would comfort her. She walked up the stairs and down the hallway to her apartment, suddenly feeling as though it were a long way, her limbs becoming heavier with each step. The relaxation of the afternoon was overtaken by dread as she saw that her apartment door was partly ajar. She inched the door open, afraid that the intruder might still be inside.

Everything in the living room was just as she'd left it—the television, the DVD player, her stereo—but she felt like she was being watched. She carefully made her way to the kitchen. Everything was in order there, too. The sense of being followed, watched from a ways off, stayed with her and could not be attributed to nervous edginess.

After making sure no one was lurking behind the sofa or the drawn drapes at the balcony door, she headed for the bedroom. From the threshold she saw that the light on her nightstand was on, just as she'd left it that morning, something she routinely did in case she didn't make it home before dark. Cautiously, she walked in, visually scanning the medium-sized room.

The walk-in closet door was closed. She picked up the tennis racket propped against the chair near the side table, drew a deep breath, and flung the door open. No one was hiding in the closet.

A moment later she heard sounds coming from the bathroom. Tennis racket firmly in hand, she walked toward it, peered in, and saw that the window was cranked open. She didn't remember having left it that way. A shadow passed. Something fluttered, and she saw a black wing, then a huge blackbird cawed, its silhouette now fully visible behind the crinkled glass before it flew away.

As she turned around and faced the medicine cabinet, she saw that the word *Querida* had been scratched into the cracked mirror, and in the porcelain sink lay a dove with its throat slashed.

8

Blood of doves, blood of virgins. Blood of doves, blood of virgins," Archbishop Anarch whispered over and over, entranced by the violent images it conjured. Darkness veiled the room. Shadowy images of himself in the full-length mirror gave him secret pleasure, wrapping him in a certain tranquility. He glanced around his sacred study, in which few were permitted during such moments of intensive contemplation.

Father Gall, seated in a lone wingback chair positioned under a floor lamp that remained off, barely breathed. His hands were steepled beneath his nose. He, too, was caught in the spell of the chamber's dark magic like a trout following a worm. In a hushed tone, Father Gall said, "We must hurry. She doesn't frighten off. Her will is strong, and the forces of the old medicine people seek to empower her."

"Then it's time to exterminate her," announced Archbishop Anarch, as the corners of his mouth turned upward, delighted at the prospect of ending a life that for so long had plagued him.

"And if *her* powers fend *us* off?" Father Gall asked.

"Then we will get to her through him. We will abduct him, then draw her down to the dungeons. From there, we will go to the holy site," declared Archbishop Anarch, growing more excited. "The Almighty's sacrifice must be made. Her blood must be spilled in the desert. We'll leave him as a feast for the buzzards."

In a stronger tone, Father Gall affirmed, "Yes. She must be stopped or the kingdom of righteousness will be threatened."

"Never again," Archbishop Anarch said, clenching his fists and gritting his teeth. "With her death, the lineage of the medicine women will finally end."

Father Gall walked to Archbishop Anarch, placed a hand on his shoulder, and whispered, "She is so much like her mother. She's learning to use the deeper powers."

Anarch pounded his fist on his desk and confessed, "At each sacrifice, it's Lucia's face I see. Once her daughter is dead, her memory will surely fade. Then, and only then, will I find rest and will the kingdom of the Almighty go forward as it should."

Father Gall moved in front of Anarch and bowed his head, saying, "Lord Archbishop, I take my leave."

Anarch lifted his hand, allowing Gall to kiss his ring, and added, "I want the artist dead, too. Michelangelo blasphemed His Holiness Paul III, painted him as a lost soul falling to hell. Artists are profane."

"As you wish, my archbishop," said Father Gall.

"We must act before the next full moon. Her powers grow stronger when the moon is at its peak. We can afford no risks," stated Archbishop Anarch.

"Yes. We will give her no opportunity to learn what must be kept secret.

"The Ecclesia Dei cannot afford scandal," Father Gall agreed.

After the terrifying discovery of the word scratched onto the cracked bathroom mirror and the sight of the dead dove in the sink, Claire had called Francesca, who had told her to come immediately and plan on spending the night.

She wasn't sure who had broken into her apartment but felt certain it was related to her visit to the mission. No images entered her mind, as if whoever had broken in had no presence, no soul.

As she drove up the twisting mountain road, headlights appeared behind her. The driver flashed his brights twice, speeding up as if to pass, then dropping back. Claire inched closer to the shoulder and slowed down, giving the car room to pass on the narrow highway, but it stayed behind her. When she moved onto the road again and sped up, it pulled up beside her. Someone rolled down the passenger side window, and she heard several drunken teenagers laughing wildly. Then the roar of a huge vehicle barreling around a curve in the oncoming lane pulled her attention away from the kids.

Claire slammed her hand on the horn. The kids screamed as their driver dropped his speed. Claire sped forward. The kids managed to slip back in behind her an instant before the truck whizzed by. Its driver shouted something and flipped off the kids as he passed.

Glancing in her rearview mirror, Claire saw the teenagers skid to a stop, spin into a U-turn, and tear after the man, leaning out the windows, shaking their fists and swearing.

She had a sudden psychic vision of the man in the other vehicle. He was a heavyset, backwoods type who looked as if he had just returned from a hunting trip in the northern wilderness of Aztlan. His gun was mounted on the truck's back panel, and Claire sensed that he wouldn't hesitate to use it to scare off a carload of obnoxious teenagers. She winced as the vision shifted to one of the kids lying on the side of the road, blood soaking his shirt and crying out for his friends who were driving away.

She pulled over, stopped, and focused. Francesca often said that prayer was really a way of sending strong feelings to others. It was a force that came not from some faraway god but from our own protective powers. A sensitive soul could pick up such energy. Hopefully, there was one in this ornery group of unsuspecting teens.

After some seconds, Claire looked in her rearview mirror again but saw only miles of dark, empty pavement. Leaning over to the passenger side, she looked down the gorge to her right, and finally spotted the teenagers' sedan about a hundred yards behind the other vehicle.

Now an image flashed in her mind of the teenage driver, who said to the fellow in the passenger seat, "I think we better turn off. I just got a creepy vibe that that guy up there could pull out a shotgun and blow our heads off."

As Claire watched their car, the driver slowed down and turned into a campground area. Claire breathed a sigh of relief. She recalled a morning two years earlier when Francesca had told her it was time she learned to use her mental powers, both for the benefit of others and herself. Now that hell's hounds were snapping at her heels, she realized the importance of Francesca's instruction, and this incident had helped her gain confidence in those powers. She reflected on the teaching of the medicine women that there was no reason for anyone to suffer if suffering could be prevented.

About ten miles from Francesca's house, Claire saw a flare going off ahead, and a van pulled over on the shoulder of the road. When she slowed down, a man slid out from under the van, waving his hands, his face streaked with black grime.

Straining to see past the glare of the flare, Claire had a sudden urge to drive on but told herself that checking on the man now would save an evening's worth of concern and that he was probably a family man on his way home, with a wife and children worried about him.

As Claire stopped, the man walked to the side of his vehicle and pointed. Maybe someone had sideswiped him, she thought.

She got out of her car, pocketing her keys as she walked toward the tall, lanky man. "What happened?" she asked.

"My damn van broke down. Look here," he said, crouching down beside the van.

But when Claire stepped closer, he suddenly twisted her arm behind her back and shoved her against the side of the van. "Claire Sanchez, isn't it?" Up close, his face looked purposefully blackened by soot or charcoal. Stunned, Claire didn't resist as she knew he could easily break her neck.

"Aren't you going to try to get away, bitch?" he hissed, shoving her harder against the van. "Won't talk, huh? Doesn't matter. What I have in mind doesn't call for conversation." His voice was familiar, but he seemed to be feigning an accent of a lower class.

The heat from her solar plexus became white hot, and she heard the sound of barking in the distance. The man turned to see three gray wolves coming toward them from out of the dark foothills, poised to attack. The wolves drew closer. One glanced at Claire then shifted its penetrating gaze to the assailant, leaping at him.

"What the hell?" the man screamed, flinging Claire around, trying to shield himself with her body. The wolf tore a sleeve off his overcoat, its eyes intent. The two others crept closer, growling viciously. Nearly crushing her throat with his forearm, the man reached into his back pocket. Something clinked on the pavement beside Claire's feet. She looked down and saw a hypodermic needle roll under the van.

The man grabbed her by the shoulders and yelled, "You want meat, puppies, you got it." He flung Claire into the pack, but the wolves moved away.

She tumbled down a steep embankment. Midway down, she grabbed a sandstone boulder, stopping her fall. She tried to figure out how she was going to fend off three angry wolves when a mental image of wolves as protective spirits formed in her mind as she saw through her childhood eyes. After lying motionless for a few seconds, she became aware that the wolves had retreated and were now howling in the distance.

She crawled up the hill, stealing a glance past a clump of sagebrush as she heard the van speed off.

"Tell me again why you stopped," Francesca asked, as they sat on the bed in Claire's old bedroom.

"He looked desperate," Claire replied, now fully realizing how she had put herself in danger.

"Evil can mask itself as neediness," Francesca answered, emphatically.

"I have a sense that he wanted to scare me as part of a plan to make me stop my investigation," explained Claire.

"Be careful, Claire. I think they mean to stop you even if

they have to kill you to do it." Francesca warned. A pensive look crossed her face, then she continued, saying, "I also think, as you do, that the prick from the confessional door was intentional. There are drugs used by people skilled in the black arts to render their victims unconscious. A little applied to a dart, the head of a pin, or a splinter is all it takes."

Suddenly very tired, as though her mental and biological battery had just run out, Claire said, "I feel like I am still experiencing the aftereffects of that drug."

"You need a good night's sleep. If he'd injected you a second time, it could've been fatal," Francesca replied.

"Maybe, but why kill me when they think they can just frighten me away?" Claire asked.

Francesca insisted, "They've already figured out that you can't be scared off. That cargo van was meant for your corpse."

"Why the charcoal, then?" asked Claire.

"So, you couldn't identify him if something went wrong. Like it did," replied Francesca.

"But I think I can. It was Father Gall," Claire said.

Surprised, Francesca asked, "Father Gall, not Archbishop Anarch?"

"Yeah. Father Gall probably has access to hospital drugs, and I've heard he's an expert on untraceable toxins. According to the hospital's grapevine, he's a weird sort," Claire explained.

Claire remembered a hospital groundbreaking party for a new administrative wing when people had gossiped about their strange experiences on missions in the Orient, Europe, and Africa and with Father Gall, who had then been the director of missions for the Ecclesia Dei. "The nurses who've been to the missions when he was there say that everyone from African voodoo priests to East Indian magicians feared him," Claire stated.

Someone knocked at the front door, and Francesca went to verify that it was the police she had called an hour earlier. Claire heard Francesca inviting two officers into the living room, then ask "Ready?"

Claire nodded.

"Officers Ortega and Yellowhorse, this is my stepdaughter Claire," Francesca said.

Claire shook their hands and noticed that Yellowhorse, a paunchy Native American, was wearing a silver ring with a turquoise cross. "Your ring is striking, officer," she commented.

He looked down at it proudly and replied, "Thank you. It's a symbol of my faith. The Ecclesia Dei means everything to me and my family. The archbishop put in a good word and got me into the Aztlan Police Academy." Claire glanced at Francesca, heart sinking. "Life seemed hopeless before we joined the Ecclesia Dei," he went on. "Now doors seem to be opening for us everywhere. My wife got a job as a maid in a big hacienda, and she's making good money." Then he added, "I'm sorry for going on and on. Ms. Mirabal said that someone attacked you out on the highway?"

Claire carefully explained, "It all started earlier this evening when I got home. I discovered that someone had broken into my apartment, scratched the word *Querida* on my bathroom mirror and put a dead dove, its throat slit, in the sink. Nothing was stolen."

"Did you report it?" asked Officer Yellowhorse.

"No. I called Francesca, and we decided I should come straight over and spend the night here," Claire explained.

"You should've reported it," Officer Yellowhorse scolded.

Claire nodded, but she knew her call would have taken the police the better part of an hour to answer and would not have produced anything but a report.

"And then you met up with some kind of trouble on the highway?" Officer Yellowhorse asked.

"A stranded motorist." Claire went on to describe the entire episode. "You say his face was grimy, maybe camouflaged, but can you give us any description of him?"

"His voice was familiar," said Claire, pausing, stomach fluttering, then adding, "I think it was Father Gall, the priest who's always with the archbishop."

Silence descended on the room.

Officer Yellowhorse scratched his head then huffed, "The archbishop's secretary, Ms. Sanchez?"

Claire said nothing, looking him directly in the eyes. He shifted his gaze away and reached for his notepad.

"What else, besides his voice, makes you think it was Father Gall?" asked Officer Yellowhorse.

"His height and build," answered Claire.

"A lot of people have a similar height and build, Ms. Sanchez," challenged Officer Yellowhorse.

"And the same voice, too?" she questioned.

"Ms. Sanchez, Father Gall was sent by the patriarch to serve as assistant to the archbishop the day after his installation. Some call Father Gall the archbishop's guardian angel. He's been here twenty years, and he's helped many people. You're saying he's some kind of night marauder? Why would he do such a thing?" asked Officer Yellowhorse. His demeanor had changed radically, from a soft-spoken professional to a religious zealot.

"I'm not sure, but I know what my impressions are," she stated.

Closing his notebook, Officer Yellowhorse looked up at her and said, "I've documented everything you told me. Without something concrete to go on, though, there's nothing we can do but file a report."

"I understand. That's all I expect. At least there'll be a paper trail if anything else happens," Claire replied.

"You anticipate more problems?" he asked, as though suddenly suspicious that she knew more than she was letting on.

"I don't know. I just want to make sure my bases are covered," Claire said. Officer Yellowhorse turned to Officer Ortega, and the two men exchanged a quick but knowing glance.

When Claire caught Officer Ortega's eye, he shuffled his feet nervously, shifting his gaze downward. "Something wrong, officer?" she asked.

Officer Ortega hesitated, then mumbled, "That patient who died..." He stopped abruptly as Officer Yellowhorse's eyes widened.

"What patient?" Claire asked, her heart beating faster.

Officer Ortega didn't answer; Officer Yellowhorse held his gaze.

"Officers?" she pressed.

Officer Yellowhorse turned away from Officer Ortega and said, "Officer Ortega is new on the force, and sometimes he says more than he should."

"I'd like to hear what he has to say," replied Claire, trying to control her anger.

Officer Ortega took a step back then said, "My grandmother used to say that if you talked bad about a priest, it would bring you bad luck. I don't want no bad luck."

Claire asked, "You mentioned a patient who died. What's that have to do with a priest?"

Officer Ortega looked panicky, his expression begging Officer Yellowhorse for help.

"That's a confidential police matter, Ms. Sanchez," Officer Yellowhorse responded. "I'm sure you understand. Some of the old church members still have silly superstitions. That's what this is about, isn't it, Tom?"

"Yes, sir," Officer Ortega answered with obvious relief.

Officer Yellowhorse gave Claire a cold look, saying, "Superstitions, no matter how silly, keep people silent." Then he paused and added, "You'll be spending the night here, is that right?"

"Yes," Claire confirmed.

"Good. This is probably the safest place for you. At least for now," he said in a threatening tone. "But call me if there's any more trouble."

He walked toward the front door, leaving behind a rank odor that reminded Claire of what she had smelled on the grounds outside the mission of Ecclesia Dei and made her think of spilled blood and rotting meat.

Francesca looked her way and nodded, then rubbed her nose with an index finger, letting Claire know that she smelled it, too.

Officer Yellowhorse turned to face them and added, "As I said, Ms. Sanchez, all I can do is file a report."

Just after Officer Yellowhorse crossed the threshold, Claire heard a metallic clink on the outside tiles.

"My ring!" yelled Officer Yellowhorse.

"What's wrong?" Francesca asked, as she and Claire stepped out to find Officer Yellowhorse searching the walkway.

"My ring just slid off my finger," he explained.

"I'll get a flashlight," Francesca offered, barely concealing a grin.

"Thanks, but I have one on me," he replied. He unhooked it from his belt, flicked it on, and shone the light around but didn't see anything. After a few minutes, he seemed shaken as he said, "Well, there's no use looking any longer tonight. I'd appreciate it if you'd keep an eye out for it. Strange magic in your home."

Francesca smiled, shutting the door behind them. "Ortega almost spilled the beans," she said.

"It's clear that the police and the Ecclesia Dei are in cahoots," Claire stated. Just as she had suspected, there would be no help from the police. They had their own agenda and weren't about to let her get in the way. She wondered how Officer Yellowhorse would make good on his threat, and how Officer Ortega, an easily intimidated buffoon with a loose tongue, could manage to keep their secret under wraps.

"Everyone's scratching everyone else's back, and no one's the wiser," Francesca agreed, sighing in disgust. "Keep your courage, Claire. No self-doubt. They'll smell it."

"I'm not interested in dying young," Claire replied resolutely.

Francesca walked toward the kitchen and asked, "How about some tea and a little something to eat?"

"That would be good," Claire said, her stomach churning from the experience with two of Aztlan's finest. Francesca soon returned with some tea and *bizcochitos*, sugar and anise cookies that had always been Claire's favorite treat in winter. They ate quietly.

Then Francesca pulled out an old leather book and turned the conversation to her further discoveries in the old diary. It was a slim volume of yellowed pages filled with a woman's graceful handwriting. She held it protectively in her hands, turning each page tenderly.

Claire sat beside her and read aloud the page Francesca pointed to:

I no longer know this man… from what I hear, he's a real conquistador with the ladies now. It's been so long since I've seen him. It's rumored that he knows I'm living in the mountains and about the tragic things that have happened in my life. I should never have trusted him. He always said that his soul belonged to the Almighty, and he would go into a rage whenever I countered that it belonged to his mother. I'm sure he'd stop at nothing to protect "The Kingdom of the Almighty" — the kingdom of William and his mother. My dreams have been warning me never to see him again.

Francesca closed her eyes and touched Claire's hand, her face flushed with pain. She nodded after a few moments, signaling Claire to continue.

Claire hesitated then turned the page.

My soul is still trying to heal from his betrayal. I should never have left the sisterhood for the short time I did. Joining the Ecclesia Dei to be closer to him was a terrible mistake. The night before my baptism I mentioned my condition. He flew into a rage, demanding that I leave the state and spare him any disgrace. He pushed me away and disappeared into the dark night.

"Look at what she writes a few years later — one month before her death," Francesca urged, quickly turning to the last pages.

My friends say he's been searching for me. I know he's afraid I'll topple his kingdom by revealing our secret. I'll avoid him for as long as I can, but I pray that if I do encounter him, I'll be strong. The other members of the sisterhood have promised to support me, especially if I fail.

Francesca closed the diary and said: "These entries prompted me to visit the oldest of the medicine women, who lives in Ojo Caliente. She's over a hundred, but her mind is clear. Many years ago, she said that the evil loosed on this land and its people demanded the offering of human flesh and blood. I wanted to talk to her about what she'd said back then."

"When did you visit her?" Claire asked, stunned by the similarity of her dreams and the old medicine woman's insight.

"Just yesterday. She told me what I needed to know before I even asked. 'The sorcerer feeds on flesh, drinks blood, and is more beast than man,' she said."

"More beast than man?" Claire asked.

"He has his religion but no true conscience. Human feeling is dead," explained Francesca.

Claire thought of her first encounter with Archbishop Anarch, his cold eyes, the way he made her skin crawl. Thoughts of the symbolic sacrifice at the mass, Anarch's magnetic presence, and the priest by his side flooded her mind.

"Thinking of Archbishop Anarch?" Francesca asked.

"Yes, and his guardian angel, as Officer Yellowhorse called him," said Claire.

"Priests who offer flesh and blood sacrifices in the land of Aztlan," Francesca said, and shuddered.

Claire nodded, adding, "Evil always collects its due and uses the ones nobody would suspect to do it. But I need to keep my eye on Himmel and Wardene Black, too. I have a feeling they'd stop at nothing to protect Archbishop Anarch and the Ecclesia Dei."

"Evil uses weak minds," Francesca mumbled as though thinking out loud.

"They're strong only as long as they remain hidden," observed Claire.

Claire remembered the priest hidden in the confessional

and the sorcerer in her nightmare who had stood with his back to her.

Francesca concluded, "Truth draws evil out of hiding. Behind every evil lurks a secret. Only when the secret is made known can the forces of light battle the forces of darkness. It is then that fate decides who lives and who dies."

❧❧❧

Claire lay snuggled in the warm bed she'd slept in as a child, thinking about the generations of medicine women. She was the last of the lineage and, secretly, felt proud of her heritage.

She got up, put on the robe and slippers Francesca had left for her, and went into the kitchen thinking a little warm milk might help her relax and sleep. As she waited for it to heat up in the microwave, she became aware of an inner despair that went beyond the events at the hospital and the Ecclesia Dei. It was rumbling from somewhere deep inside her, from a little girl abandoned in a forest, wondering if death would bring freedom from pain. She feared that her world would be destroyed again, that Francesca and Anthony would be brought down by the evil man who had killed her mother, that she, too, would die at his hand.

She was so overcome by despair that she thought of killing herself. Glancing at a butcher knife on the counter, she considered how simple it would be to take it, step out the back door, walk down to the arroyo bordering Francesca's property, and end her life. It would be a sure way out. Francesca and Anthony would no longer be in danger, and her own fears would be permanently put to rest. Francesca would mourn, but she was a strong woman and would go on with her life. Anthony would also eventually find a woman who would be able to give him the love he deserved.

Suddenly shocked by the strength of her impulse, Claire tried to shake it off as she sipped her milk and tried to think about something else. But the morbid pull to pick up the glistening knife grew stronger.

Her being felt empty and her head crowded with ghosts of intimidation and fear—rank odors from the soot-masked attacker, scowls from Wardene Black's twisted face, and Archbishop Anarch screaming that she had no business coming against a force that even her mother could not defeat, that during two decades had grown even more powerful, that stood by their religious icons, inflicting pain and grief and death on anyone who dared oppose them. Then she heard a hostile voice say, *"Alone and abandoned, those you love will die and you will die, Medicine Woman."*

Claire took a step toward the counter and reached for the knife. But then her arm brushed against a book Francesca had left on the counter, knocking it to the floor, the sound jarring her out of the hypnotic spell.

Trembling, she picked it up, and looked at the dog-eared, open page before her.

Speaking of suicides, the lecturer said that self-murder was no escape from the miseries of the present but only a preparation of greater sorrow for the future. Suicides, he declared, cannot shirk their responsibilities so easily. They must return to take up life exactly where they laid it so violently down, but with added pain and punishment for their weakness. Many of them wander the earth in unspeakable misery till they can be reborn in a new body—generally a lunatic or weak-minded person who cannot resist the hideous obsession.

Shocked, Claire looked at the book's cover and recognized the name of Francesca's favorite gothic writer, Algernon Blackwood. With her mind now clearing, she was stunned that she had considered killing herself. Finally, today she was feeling freer of the drug, which, she suspected, had caused her suicidal thoughts. Never had anything so undermined her reason. It was a confirmation that those she was dealing with were skilled in ways potentially fatal.

She was grateful that the book had so powerfully spoken to her in a time of desperate need, and knew Francesca must have intuited her state of mind and intervened in a way that she knew would be effective. Their relationship had time and time again borne out the truth that genuine caring and love were both guardians and seers.

As if to confirm Francesca's extraordinary gift of intuition, now as Claire's mind turned to the crow perched on her car that morning, suddenly

Francesca appeared at the kitchen entrance and said, "Black bird, bad spirit."

Claire's heart nearly stopped at the sound of Francesca's voice. "It's been a frightening night," Claire said.

Francesca glanced at the knife on the counter, the book beside it, and replied, "Yes, but all that has passed now."

"I feel like death is snapping at my heels," stated Claire.

"More than death. Self-doubt—not about the investigation but about you and Anthony," insisted Francesca.

Francesca paused, as if giving her words time to sink in. "Not even your mother's death could make you suicidal. But self-betrayal could," she explained. Claire said nothing, still shaken from moments earlier.

"You love him. Distancing yourself weakens you both. It's a form of self-betrayal," said Francesca.

"I don't want him to get hurt," explained Claire.

"He's already been threatened," revealed Francesca.

"When?" Claire asked, catching her breath.

"He called me this morning to say that he had received a threat that one of you would be killed. You must stand together."

"Why didn't you tell me before?" demanded Claire.

"I was waiting for the right time," explained Francesca.

Just then there was a knock on the front door. Claire could see headlight beams shining across the front porch through the window.

"Who in the world could that be? It's two in the morning," Francesca muttered as she went to the door. "Who's there?" she asked.

"It's Officer Yellowhorse. Are you two all right?"

Francesca unlocked the door and ushered Officer Yellowhorse in. "I was patrolling your area and thought I spotted a prowler. I saw your light on, so I thought I'd better make sure you were both okay," he explained.

"I didn't hear anything," Claire replied, her voice rising in alarm.

"So was there a prowler?" Francesca pressed.

"Well, a van—like the one you described, Ms. Sanchez— was coming off your property and drove a man off the road. The car was forced into that shallow arroyo and got a flat. He had just finished changing it and was getting back into his car when I pulled up," said Officer Yellowhorse.

Claire glanced out the window. "I don't see anyone out there," she replied.

"Oh, I let him go. He was on his way back home after giving someone the last rites when that lunatic sideswiped him. So, it couldn't have been Father Gall you had a run-in with because Father Gall was with a dying church member all evening," claimed Officer Yellowhorse.

Officer Yellowhorse paused, his eyes glazed like a fanatic's, and added, "Oh yeah, Father Gall gave me something for you. Said you might want it." He reached into the breast pocket of his leather jacket and pulled out an object wrapped in tissue, handing it to Claire.

She unwrapped it, her heart quickening as she saw the same weathered turquoise crucifix that she'd found lying next to Elizabeth's body. "Where did he get this?" she asked.

"From Archbishop Anarch, of course," Officer Yellow-horse replied, his tone reverent.

9

Rats scuffled and screeched through sticks and brambles that covered a corpse lying in one of the cave's hollowed-out recesses. The atmosphere, dark and rank, filled Archbishop Anarch with such pleasure that he momentarily experienced a quality of being outside his body, of looking down on the darkened, starlit cosmos from the outer reaches of space, a realm where the Almighty alone abided. Never before had he reached such heights, a sign that the winds of fortune were indeed turning his way, aided by powers and satisfaction akin only to what saints, angels, archangels, and the Almighty must experience. Practically oblivious to the presence of Father Gall and two companions standing in the background of the shadowy grotto, Archbishop Anarch preferred the company of rodents and the fluttering of an occasional bat across the high sandstone ceiling. Utter aloneness, the unadulterated presence of himself, intoxicated him nearly as much as the taste of fresh blood.

A large fire, encircled by hand-sized granite stones, flickered brightly in the center of the cave. Its flames freed his mind to travel to distant realms, other places and times he longed to visit again, having severely missed them since entering this earthly incarnation. The voice that had spoken twenty years ago told him what he had been preordained to do. After the initial visitation, it had returned that night, saying, "You are a high priest of the Order of Melchizedek. Before time began you were."

Archbishop Anarch envisioned universes outside of human perception that he had once inhabited and ruled over as a god—all willingly forgone to undertake a divine mission to save the spiritually lost souls of earth. Visions had told him that from ages past other skilled initiates in the mystic arts had also found solace here. As the Savior had gone to the garden to pray, Archbishop Anarch retreated to his cave when weary of his responsibilities as archbishop. Focusing within cleansed him of the voices that populated his mind when tired. Dealings with underlings, purveyors of religious sanctimony, and financial benefactors taxed him greatly, for interactions with such people required feigned sociability. Secretly, he loathed those who admired him, those who surrendered control over their eternal well-being and ultimate salvation. He knew he was a god. The privacy and quiet of this ages-old cave allowed him to commune intimately with the god whose nature he found most replenishing—himself.

As a cold wind blew through the cave, he tightened his black-hooded cloak around his shoulders and thought about when the Almighty had first offered him the opportunity to exchange his heavenly position next to the Archangel Michael in the courts of heaven for the power he secretly craved. Although he only remembered the blessed voice that had spoken to him as a young priest, he reasoned that one such as himself—more god than man—had been preordained for greatness, having once stood at the right hand of the Lord of Lords and King of Kings. He believed he had been called to tread the earth as another Christ, giving up celestial standing for mere worldly influence and wealth—a small gesture of appreciation from the Almighty for his willingness to gather the scattered sheep. It was his eternal mission, no matter the cost, to draw in the wayward so that those who were blind might understand the necessity of loyalty to shepherd and sheepfold.

This knowledge, which no one could cause him to doubt, was fortification against ever thinking twice about the taking of human life, which was a small price to ensure the salvation of the victim's soul and the souls of countless others. Consumed by a burning desire to cleanse the earth of infidels, he knew that—as quickly and easily as most people swatted a fly—he would kill anyone who stood in the way of his sacred duty.

Each day brought new summits of spiritual potency—people weeping as he sermonized, thousands of dollars pouring into Ecclesia Dei coffers because of his silver tongue, assistants carrying out his every wish from the purchasing of exquisite foods and clothing to the placement of victims on the altar. He pulled out a finely honed German knife from its leather sheath, the nine-inch blade reflecting the yellow and red flames that danced furiously. "We have traveled through many times and worlds together, my friend," he said, stroking the steel blade with his fingertips. He sharpened the edge of the blade on the grinding stone in front of him. He touched the knife to his tongue, withdrew it, then cut the tip of one finger, and sucked. "After disposing of the artist and the old one, we will consummate the vow with the sacrifice of the tender flesh and sweet blood of the daughter of the powerful medicine woman, the last of her line. All memories and evidence will die with her," he said, howling with such force that scores of rodents stopped dead in their tracks. The second the earsplitting echo ceased, a violent wind tore through the mouth of the cave deep into the mountain, into the center of the earth. He smiled with this evidence that his divine powers even controlled the forces of nature.

He had never wavered in any sacrifice, yet now he suddenly wondered if he should risk less and simply abduct the medicine woman and leave her for dead in the desert—food for the coyotes. So far, he had managed to minimize public attention, but Claire Sanchez was a visible person in the community. His stomach churned with an unfamiliar wrenching sensation, but soon apprehension burned away.

A strange smoke curled up from the center of the fire. The gray and white cloud remained perfectly centered between the ring of stones and grew into a ten- to twelve-foot-tall grotesque phantasm with a pointed head, long white beard, and searing red eyes. As it opened its mouth, multiple rows of pointed teeth framed the dark orifice, its tongue a vicious serpent. A familiar, sulfuric smell emanated from it. Its pencil-thin lips began to move with indiscernible mumbling. A black crucifix was emblazoned on the center of its chest, and a horizontal, white-lettered imprint in place of the corpus read, "Vox Ecclesia Vox Dei."

"The voice of the Church is the voice of God," Anarch stated, and the message vanished, replaced by the crucifix of the Ecclesia Dei. "I am honored by your presence, Almighty," he said.

The Almighty spoke, his voice similar to the archbishop's own, "You are the chosen one. Do not disappoint me."

Archbishop Anarch briefly closed his eyes as the words burned into him. Then he affirmed, "Majesty, I am honored to do your will."

"So you have chosen, so you will do, and not cease the doing," said the Almighty.

Anarch's blood turned to ice. His mind conjured up images of the damned—those who refused the Almighty's command suffering unending hellfire. Church fathers had written that a lost soul, one who stepped outside the fold or abjured divine calling, was given a coffin-sized cubicle carved into the side of a stone wall that surrounded a burning pit. Nightmares frequently took Archbishop Anarch to this place of eternal misery, where he was shown his lot if he did not fulfill the task of ridding the world of the irreligious. The sooner Archbishop Anarch ate the flesh and drank the blood of the young medicine woman, the sooner the nightmares would cease and his everlasting redemption be assured. Unlimited power and money would be his earthly reward. And, as archbishops before him, he would be accorded the ultimate designation of holiness at the time of death. He would be buried in the sacred vaults beneath the cathedral of the Ecclesia Dei.

The faithful, the world over, would forever speak of how Archbishop Anarch had served true believers everywhere. There would be legends about how he dwelt in his eternal home—a well-deserved mansion in heaven, even grander than the one in the oil lands left to him by his devout mother.

As the fires died down, he saw two figures standing stiffly on the other side of the circle of dying embers, their faces expressionless. Father Gall stood behind them near the mouth of the cave.

"Ready?" he asked them firmly. They didn't reply.

He realized the effects of the drug hadn't worn off, leaving them in the hypnotized state Father Gall had induced some hours earlier. Their complete cooperation during a sacrifice was assured through a combination of hypnosis and an untraceable, exotic sedative. In this suggestible state, they followed precise instructions about the kidnapping, delivery, and placement of bodies. Archbishop Anarch walked toward them and said, "Remember each and every step we have gone over. First the artist, then the old one, then the young medicine woman. She's not to escape this time. I want to make sure she's terrified. Adrenaline always makes for a bittersweet offering. Just the way I like it."

Then he ordered, "Leave now," and motioned the two entranced persons toward Father Gall. Turning back to the dying embers, he passed his hands over them, reigniting the blazing fire, for him evidence that the Almighty confirmed his presence and blessed his actions. As he walked out, the fire died. At the mouth of the cave, he swept both hands across the entrance to the cave, whereupon blowing sand flung huge tumbleweeds and tree branches over it. He pulled his black cape tightly around his shoulders and walked to the altar a stone's throw away. Touching the granite surface, he mused with conviction, "Before the next full moon she will be dead."

Francesca slept fitfully after Officer Yellowhorse had left. Images of him handing Claire the crucifix, blood oozing from its turquoise stones, and two shadowy figures stalking Claire plagued her dreams. Then she saw a man with his back toward her, gazing in a mirror at an image that distorted into a beast with blood drooling from its mouth. The man knelt and prayed. Next, she dreamt of walking through a maze of dark stone tunnels, the passage seeming to last a lifetime. As a hologram on the shadowy walls, she saw the face of her mother, a sturdy woman with the compassionate eyes of a medicine woman, and her grandmother, also a medicine woman. Reputedly, both had mastered the art of shape-shifting into gray wolves. They called her name, gazing intently at her. Claire's face faded in and out of the background.

Francesca's mother spoke first, saying, "Evil is preparing to strike." Her grandmother, in a gravelly voice, added, "The young one must accept her calling on her own. Only then can she battle the forces of evil. Should she retreat into fear, she will die."

The ground shook, and a loud wind whipped through the passageway. Cracks streaked across the walls, and chunks of stones fell from the ceiling. Francesca covered her head with her arms, sand and pebbles pelting her skin. Finally, the shaking lessened, and she was surrounded by clouds of dust and debris. In its wake, the wind left an odor of decayed flesh and bone-chilling cold—the stench and chill of evil, Francesca knew.

The images of her mother and grandmother flickered and faded, their voices muffled by a background roar. A few moments passed before the roar weakened to a rumble. Then Francesca heard her mother's commanding voice say, "The black dog of death has also been set on you."

Her grandmother reiterated, "Let her go or evil will gain the upper hand, and both of you will die." Then suddenly the dream ended.

Francesca's eyes shot open. Sitting up in bed, the words of warning echoing through her mind, she saw a note on her bed stand that read:

I've taken the day off work. I need to see firsthand the place in my dreams. I'll be hiking through the desert to the Devil's Throne. Claire

≀≀≀

Looking at the sacristy window, Archbishop Anarch observed how his compound glowed with a heavenly light as the early morning sun shone across acres of cottonwoods, clumps of green grasses, and pueblo-style buildings. It was a welcome sight for someone who had slept fitfully through the night after having been engaged in the most psychically depleting of tasks, the taking of life.

The groundskeeper walked toward the ten-foot-wide wrought-iron gate. After mass, it was unlocked precisely at 7 am each weekday for those in residence. No one was permitted outside the ecclesiastical grounds until then. Typically, the archbishop took breakfast in his private dining area after the service. Today he felt a strange prodding to return to the chapel. He turned away from the window, blessed himself, and locked the sacristy door behind him.

It was a short walk down the hallway to the dark chapel. Votive candles cradled in red glassware flickered, reflecting off the stained-glass windows, the highly polished granite floors, and the Italian marble altar. He stood in the shadows, behind a wall next to his private pew.

A back door creaked open and two figures, wearing the black-hooded robes that lay members of the Ecclesia Dei donned during religious ceremonies, slowly entered the chapel from a rear storage area.

"The time draws near," the taller one, a man, said, standing at the bronze altar railing. His voice was authoritative, unfeeling.

"I am confident that the final sacrifice will be made," the shorter one, a woman, remarked tersely.

"All things will then come under his dominion. We will

have our places beside him, lives of ease and wealth," the man said, with a tone of ruthless ambition.

The woman lowered her voice and added, "We cannot tell him about the lies being spread through the archdiocese."

"No, we must not. I fear his rage. *We* would end up as food for the vultures," said the man.

"But rumors about his past are flying behind his back," said the woman.

"His past does not matter. He is a great man," replied the man.

The woman, her voice becoming a little louder, countered, "But those who say his past is littered with sins of the flesh could ruin him. Someone from his past might confirm what they are saying. Then the patriarch would be forced to remove him from office."

"Father Gall says the last of the old medicine women and her stepchild are responsible for the rumors and that all traces of the archbishop's past will be washed away with the final sacrifice," added the man.

The woman nodded and touched his shoulder. They turned to face the gold tabernacle on the front altar, genuflected in the center of the aisle, and left through a side door.

Archbishop Anarch was infuriated at what he had overheard. Seeds of destruction were being planted in the fields he had so meticulously cultivated. He stormed down the hallway to his office sure that Father Gall, not wanting to distract him from his plotting, would sooner or later tell him about the talk. He must finish off the young medicine woman and her friends swiftly. An end to the lineage of the medicine women would mean freedom. Hauntings would be gone. Diseased tongues would wag no more.

Archbishop Anarch slammed his office door shut, secured

the deadbolt, and walked to his desk. A fireproof vault was hidden in the large walk-in closet near his desk. He opened the closet door, stepped inside, and lifted a life-sized picture of the Almighty incarnate off the back wall (a rendering that a local artist of sound repute had made to resemble, although not too closely, the archbishop), then paused to remember the safe's combination. It was a place for hoarding treasures no one suspected he had. And, except for certain items, he didn't like going in because it might stir unwholesome emotional states. Yet, he knew that memory itself served a purpose, one that could add to and not detract from that which was meant to be enhanced.

In the safe were hundreds of thousands of dollars in neatly wrapped bundles, deposit slips from his Swiss bank account, stock certificates, his mother's $30 million life insurance policy naming him as beneficiary, and private papers tucked into an old leather satchel. Taking out the satchel, he withdrew two letters, both dated twenty years earlier. One read:

William,

Now you know. The truth could not remain hidden forever, but I beg you not to harm the child. I fear that in trying to get to me, you will stop at nothing. Her father died in a construction accident a month before her birth. The entire village knows of this tragedy. Spare her the loss of her mother as well. I beg you to leave us in peace, and the secret will die with me.

Lucia

The other, slightly crumpled, letter, written on the letterhead of

the Chancery Office of the Patriarch of the Ecclesia Dei
in Turquoise County and dated a week earlier, read:

Dear Archbishop Anarch,

*As per my previous correspondence, I trust that you are doing
what is necessary to put an end to the vicious rumors of licen-
tiousness circulating about you. The devil is always at work
trying to bring scandal and infamy to God's chosen and the elect
of the Ecclesia Dei. My son, make sure to use whatever means
necessary to stop him in his tracks. Father Gall will help you.
As you know, I have always considered you my crown prince.
Continue to remain faithful to your vows, especially that of celibacy, and I know that the Almighty will one day appoint you
to occupy the seat of the patriarch of the Ecclesia Dei.*

Sincerely,

His Exalted Holiness Peter Kulten
Patriarch of the Ecclesia Dei

Shortly after his arrival twenty years ago, Father Gall had instructed the archbishop to keep all correspondence securely
filed away for future reference, saying that remembrance of
the past provided perspective for present action. He felt how
the advice had indeed kept him sharp and prepared. With this
keenness came the motivation to always strike while the divinely ordained white iron was hot. The shackle of Ms. Claire
Sanchez was clanging loudly and burning white hot.

Laying the papers aside, he clasped his hands, fingers
pointed to his lips, and thought, *I saw the child eaten by wolves.
Yet I trust Gall. He would never deceive me. Twenty years ago, I*

should have done away with the child myself; one stroke of the crook would have cracked its little head. Hatred for Lucia and her child bubbled up in him.

He returned the letters to the vault and removed a brown manila envelope from one of the steel shelves, then reached to the darkest corner of the man-sized safe and pulled out a bronze crook crested with the head of an openmouthed serpent. Propping the crook against a wall, he unsealed the envelope and looked at a photograph of a young woman in her early twenties holding a five-year-old girl in her arms. An enclosed lock of the child's hair had been meant to arouse sympathy for the young mother. He touched the picture, saying, "How sweet the flesh and blood of one who knows not of their beginning nor anticipates their end."

Father Gall had taught Archbishop Anarch about the dark side of spiritual powers, to be used only for the highest purposes, a foul magic ignited when hatred burned from the core of the soul. Then and only then would the sordid wizardry accomplish the nefarious deed required for the most godly purpose. Archbishop Anarch took the lock of the child's hair and curled it around the top of the crook. Stroking the head of the serpent, he repeatedly whispered, "Curl and coil, tease and frighten, strike and bite till her blood begins to boil." The crook became white hot, aglow with his hate. The viper writhed in his hand, its eyes fixated on him. Soon the crook was no longer a crook, and the snake slithered away.

≥≥≥

Claire didn't want to go back through the country that bordered the Oro mission of the Ecclesia Dei, but something drove her to go to the Turquoise Trail and look for the place of sacrifice depicted in her nightmare. The landscape sparkled as the eastern sun slowly crept over the Sagrado Mountains. Rays of sunshine burst through clumps of sage and stands of piñon. Several roadrunners dashed across the road, offering a brief distraction from her uneasiness. Even more than about Archbishop Anarch, the Ecclesia Dei, or Elizabeth's death, Claire was troubled about Anthony. She knew he could take care of himself, but she didn't want anything bad happening to him. The images that flew through her mind were nothing she dared entertain, for to do so might bring the worst to pass in the same way that arguing with a foul soul inflames its rage.

Her mind returning to the archbishop, she pondered the fact that to rock the Ecclesia Dei's most highly revered boat was dangerous business. Religious fanatics would do anything to maintain their security. She and Francesca had often discussed, due to the nature of the suffering of many of their patients who had come from religious backgrounds, that men and women could experience great loss of soul because of money, lust, liquor, and religion. Each of these four powers could either inspire or devour. Their sickest patients had been devoured by religion.

But Claire knew that if Anthony were with her right now, he'd tell her to finish up what she'd started; he could handle whatever came his way. And she needed to complete her investigation, no matter how much fear knocked at the door of her heart and tried to turn her away from her path.

She pulled to the side of the road, got out, and stretched, looking at a long barbed-wire fence edging a limitless expanse of property. The landscape here was unlike anywhere else, the crisp light, the dry air, the turquoise sky so close it made you want to reach up and go into it. The horizon seemed to be both near and far, creating a familiar sensation of being simultaneously close and at a distance. The mystic aspects of the land often altered perceptions, so things were not as they appeared, reminding her of some basic truths—that what was true on the outside could be far different on the inside, and that the greater the outer luster the less the inner substance.

She glanced at a tin sign nailed to a wooden post that supported a crudely made gate, with words scrawled on it by what seemed to be a nervous and angry hand:

NO TRESPASSING.
VIOLATORS WILL BE PROSECUTED TO THE FULL
EXTENT OF THE LAW.

- SISTERS OF PERPETUAL MERCY

Chuckling at the disparity between the message and the name of its authors, she got back into her car and drove on. About two miles up the road, she saw a popular eatery famous for its *huevos rancheros* and decided to stop for breakfast. Pulling into the rather sad-looking hole-in-the-wall restaurant, she parked next to a red Cadillac, wondering if this was a place frequented by members of the Ecclesia Dei after services since it was just a few miles away from the mission church, and people loved to get together after having fulfilled their religious obligation to rant and rave about things they were prohibited from discussing on church property.

Claire locked her car then walked up to the restaurant, traipsing across the sandy parking lot. As she drew closer to the front gate that opened to the inner portico, a dust devil blew up out of nowhere and danced around her, causing her to cough from the dust.

Ahead, the warped screen door to the dining establishment stood partway open. Going up the two wooden steps to the porch, she reached for the screen door, which creaked open only after she had given it several tugs. Peeking through the glass-paned front door, Claire saw what appeared to be the picturesque original family living area of the two-hundred-year-old historical structure. The restaurant bustled with activity. People looked as if they were having breakfast on their way to work. Groups of women with black prayer shawls draped over their shoulders talked noisily.

Chunky, with a coat of badly chipped white paint lapping over its window, the door also resisted opening, as though it too were warped. As she walked inside, her eyes immediately lit on a large framed photograph displayed over the mantel in the center of the room of a Hispanic family smiling happily as they knelt in front of Archbishop Anarch, who extended his arms over them.

"Breakfast, *señora*?" said a husky voice, snapping her out of her reverie. The heavily built man seemed initially friendly but then, after looking at her more closely, appeared to recognize her and grew more distant. Seeing her gaze at the photograph, he said, "It is the archbishop of the Ecclesia Dei. He is very close to our family. Some say our little establishment here is the archbishop's favorite restaurant."

"Oh. How wonderful," Claire said, unsettled by the influence the Ecclesia Dei seemed to have even in small communities of the area.

Before Claire knew it, the owner had found her a table, a tiny wooden plank fixed drop-leaf style to the wall. She walked into the adjoining room where he stood, smiled graciously, and sat down.

Her feelings of being ill at ease intensified as whispers flew from table to table and people looked away when she caught their eye. Claire felt like an intruder in the midst of a malevolent cult.

The owner, his mouth slightly open in a waxy, sardonic grin, handed her a greasy, laminated menu. Despite not wanting to touch it, Claire accepted it and decided to order some coffee first, but before she'd had a chance to, he asked, *"Cafecita, señora?"* The smirk still on his face reminded Claire of one of the life-sized plastic figurines of saints she had seen in the display window of a religious goods store on the plaza.

"Yes, please," she answered, trying to conceal her unease.

After a few moments, he returned but without the coffee. He stood looking at Claire, his finger wagging as though trying to place her. He shook his head slightly and said, "Don't you work at the psychiatric hospital? I have a niece there, and I thought I recognized you from one of my visits."

Claire scooted her chair back and replied, "Yes. I am on staff at the hospital. It's my day off." She looked him straight in the eye, hoping he'd back off.

He got the message and brusquely turned away again, saying, "Your coffee will be right up." Motioning to a waitress near the kitchen to bring coffee, he made his way from table to table, schmoozing with customers, who shot hostile glances at Claire. But she had made up her mind to stay, despite the hostility in the air.

A waitress with thick red lipstick and a black and red fiesta dress, appearing like a life-sized flesh-and-blood replica of a Hispanic Kewpie doll came to her table with a coffee pot, barely watching as she poured. Her eyes were on the owner, who was now talking hurriedly on the telephone, his gaze darting back and forth from Claire to the tablet on which he was furiously scribbling.

Claire glanced at the menu and said to the waitress, "*Huevos rancheros* over easy with green chile, please."

"*Gracias*," the waitress replied in a high-pitched voice switched on automatic pilot as she walked away.

Sipping her coffee, Claire shifted her attention to the booth in front of her, trying to overhear the conversation.

"When our archbishop is consecrated as patriarch, we will have a direct line to the most powerful man in the Ecclesia Dei," said an old woman in a gravelly voice.

"Yes, and as his friends, we will have brass plates put on our own special pews at the cathedral for special feasts and holy days when we go there," a man chimed in.

A young woman asked, "How much do they cost?"

"No more than ten thousand, I'm sure," the old woman quickly replied.

"Very reasonable," the man remarked.

"But you know church politics. In Washington your back is stabbed by a devil, in the church by an angel," the old woman said with authority.

"What's that mean, *abuelita*?" asked a younger woman.

"*Mija*, in the world you expect to be betrayed, in the church you don't. Beneath the halo are the horns," explained the old woman. Everyone at the table groaned in affirmation.

She continued, "We must take care of our archbishop so that no one gets in his way. He is a *real* holy man and deserves to be the next patriarch."

"Who would get in his way?" her granddaughter asked in hushed tones.

The grandmother paused then answered, "Father Gall says someone at the hospital is trying to hurt our archbishop. If the higher-ups in Turquoise County believe the lies, then they, as Judas of old betrayed the Almighty, will turn against the archbishop."

A middle-aged man sitting across from the grandmother looked sternly at Claire, and suddenly Claire realized that she was being allowed to overhear the conversation.

"The Almighty always deals with whoever stands in his way," the grandmother asserted. A moan of understanding drifted across the table. "Father Gall told me privately that any bad things we might hear are from the evil one. We are not to listen to the words the devil tries to plant in our souls. The Almighty will remove the evildoer from our midst."

"Father Gall is the archbishop's guardian angel," the girl said.

The waitress, plate in hand, suddenly appeared at Claire's side and placed the meal on the table. "Anything else, *señora*?"

"More coffee, please," said Claire. The waitress had partially blocked Claire's view of the grandmother's booth, but once the waitress had left Claire could see the grandmother and entourage leaving, the granddaughter looking directly at Claire with a twisted smile.

As the waitress poured Claire some fresh coffee, she hummed a popular tune Claire remembered her mother singing to her as a child.

Claire commented, "*Que sera, sera*," and looked at the waitress, expecting a warm reply of acknowledgment.

"Yes. Whatever will be, will be," the waitress said coldly. The waitress's thinly veiled threat took Claire aback. Hurriedly, she finished her breakfast, realizing she was now alone in the dining area.

The waitress, the owner, and everyone else in the peculiar eatery reminded Claire of those a lecturer at the School for Natural Therapeutics had referred to as the "functionally insane." "We have to consider," the lecturer had stated, "that it's not the ones locked up in psychiatric hospitals who are necessarily the sickest or most dangerous, but those who look okay on the outside and are rotted on the inside."

Claire got up from the table to pay the bill but no one was in sight.

Finally, the owner stepped out from behind two swinging doors that led to the kitchen.

"I'll just pay up and be on my way," said Claire, eager to get on with her desert hike.

"Where are you off to this morning?" he asked as he took her money.

"Here and there," answered Claire, not wanting to reveal any specific location. Dislike for the owner churned through her stomach like gravel in a concrete mixer.

As he gave her change, he remarked, "You better watch your step. Rattlesnakes everywhere, they say."

Claire took this as another threat and left without saying a word. Hurrying to her car, she saw the door wasn't locked. She hesitated before opening it then froze. On the driver's seat was a coiled rattlesnake.

Hiking through the desert, Claire felt adrenaline pumping through her bloodstream from the earlier encounter with the snake. The rattler had lunged at her but had only struck the door before escaping into the shade of a nearby boulder. Obviously, it had been planted to taunt or harm her. The incident was nothing she could have reported to the police since it would have been easy for the snake to have crawled into a car door mistakenly left partway open, although she knew she hadn't done that. Plus, nearly everyone around was on to her and would disregard any explanation having to do with who she knew was behind this. She decided not to draw any more attention to herself but to proceed with the investigation in her own way.

Walking on, she felt a menacing presence in every hill and valley, plateau and mesa, boulder and cave and thought of the assailant who had nearly packed her up in his van as a newly scored corpse. She decided Francesca had been right about him. The reason she hadn't seen through his ruse at first was because she wanted to believe that things were not already at a life-or-death level. Hiking through tumbleweed-strewn mesas and narrow passages between sandstone cliffs, she halfway expected the charcoal- and grease-smeared man to bolt out from behind the next boulder.

As she turned around a bend in a sandy three-foot-wide clearing between limestone and sandstone cliffs, like a bad omen a cow's skull jutted out from a shoulder-height ledge. Claire's heart skipped some beats momentarily as she stopped to look at it then moved on with greater urgency.

Down through a clearing, three or four buzzards feasted on a carcass. They looked her way, hesitated, then flew to a nearby rocky outcrop. Claire climbed down and walked past the half-eaten remains. The hungry birds flew from boulder to boulder, landing near stands of scrub oak, following Claire for a while as she continued her hike.

After walking more than a mile, Claire saw the harsh desert sun shining on something huge and primitive in the distance. Even in the light of day Claire recognized it as the place of her nightmare: two upright stones tightly joined to a stone slab on top. The remembrance made her skin crawl. Approaching slowly, Claire noticed that the atmosphere became increasingly eerie the closer she got to it. Unable to venture any closer than twenty feet, she sensed that an invisible shield guarded the circumference of the weathered stones, the way a person can tell that the mood in a room has shifted from mellow to mean.

She heard a light hum that gradually got louder until it turned into screeching, as a pack of rats appeared, running and scratching across the altar's surface. Covering her ears, Claire watched the rodents as they devoured morsels of food and licked splatters of blood on top and beneath the flat stone surface, hissing, then baring razor-sharp teeth.

The rats suddenly stopped, cocked their whiskered noses in the air, looked her way dismissively, then went on gorging. She thought again of trying to approach, but then the largest and most vicious one looked directly at her, a maleficent being peering through its eyes. Claire squinted to see the hideous rat beast. The rat's eyes took on a reddish hue, and its back arched as its fur bristled. Then all the creatures hissed and looked her way. She felt as though she were reliving her nightmare. She tried to turn and run, but her legs and feet wouldn't budge. Panicked, she pictured the rats circling then leaping and gnawing at her body.

Next there was a loud pop, like boulders crashing onto boulders. She snapped free of the rats' gaze, and the rodents vanished, along with the altar.

Where it had stood, there was now an inviting crystal-clear pond of shimmering water, flanked by cottonwoods.

With her mouth parched, Claire automatically tried to step toward the oasis, but it also disappeared, leaving nothing but barren ground. Francesca had said that magical illusions were cast to hide the obscene deeds of the profane, Claire reminded herself. Then remembering how her visions had enabled her to see through the deeds of members of the Ecclesia

Dei, she realized she was now caught in the magic of those who had orchestrated their powers behind the scenes of what appeared to be religious devotion but was not. Shaking her head, she knew she had peered into *el* diablo's lair.

Once back in her car and driving down the last stretch of highway to Francesca's house, she breathed a sigh of relief. It was nearly dinnertime, and the day's warmth yielded to a descending evening chill.

Suddenly, a bright light flashed from the eastern, treeless slope of the mountain. As she drove closer, she saw that the evening sun was reflecting off a chrome bumper on an old pickup in the gully. Seeing it was Francesca's truck, her mind raced through a million different scenarios. After getting out and slamming the door shut, she ran past skid marks on the highway and in the dirt. The truck's front end was smashed into a granite boulder, stopping a descent that could have flipped the truck end over end. Francesca wasn't inside. Relieved, Claire carefully opened the driver's side door. Everything was neat, in perfect order, as Francesca always kept it.

Next to the truck she saw a woman's footprints. They went down the ravine and seemed to slide as if the woman had been moving quickly. After a few yards they stopped. Several feet away Claire saw another set of prints, appearing as if someone had caught up with the woman and dragged her back to the road. Pieces of ocher-dyed wool—bits of Francesca's shawl—clung to a nearby scrub oak.

A rattler sounded. Claire stopped breathing, unable to tell where it was but imagining its loosely joined horny pieces of tail vibrating and erect, fangs bared. She knew if it was close enough, it could strike her in an instant. With the sun quickly going down over the western slope, in a split second she could slip, fall, and be bitten.

Darkness settled on the land. The rattling stopped, but now she heard a rustling through leaves and pine needles as if something were moving away. A pack of coyotes howled. Claire trudged back up the slope, tears streaming down her cheeks and fearing the worst for Francesca.

As she got in her car, an image of the desert altar flickered then faded away. She was sure that whatever had happened to Francesca had to do with Claire's investigation into the Ecclesia Dei and her discovery of the vanishing altar. At Francesca's she'd call the police. Even Officer Yellowhorse couldn't deny the wrecked truck and Francesca's disappearance. The thought of losing Francesca was unbearable. Next would be Anthony, she feared. But one thing was different— a prim and proper cleric, no matter how violent, would be no match for a stone sculptor used to carrying a hundred pounds of marble in each arm.

Tears ran down her face as her fear about Francesca's fate combined with grief over the fate of her mother twenty years before. She blamed herself for not protecting Francesca somehow, just as she had also blamed herself for her inability to save her mother that day in the forest.

She was the last of the medicine women lineage. For too long she had lived as half a woman, cringing and hiding. But now she could no longer retreat. Too much was currently at stake for her not to assume her rightful role in this seeming battle between good and evil, human liberty and servitude. Trembling, she reached for the ignition, heard the rumble of the engine, and got back on the highway. As she pulled into Francesca's, everything was dark except for a small table lamp shining from a window, the one Francesca left on whenever she'd be home late.

Claire walked to the front door. An owl perched in a nearby

tree hooted, its eyes luminescent. A note tacked to the door, written in Francesca's flowing hand, read:

All is not as it seems. Stay the night.

I'll see you in the morning. Francesca.

A rush of emotion overcame Claire. Then she heard a raspy noise coming from behind an old clay pot on the porch, less than a foot away. The rattler struck, its fangs piercing her leg, and she cried out and fell to the ground, her head slamming against the porch floor, causing everything to go black.

10

My headache's gone," said Francesca, sitting up in bed in the intensive care unit of Aztlan Hospital. "Raphael, thank you for your help." Raphael was a new friend she had met just a few weeks before at a Saturday morning farmer's market in Española. Francesca had been struck by the glow from his eyes and face, and also learned he worked with Claire, a fact he spoke of proudly while buying his monthly supply of freshly ground red chile. Raphael had seen Francesca's crashed truck on his way home from the afternoon shift at the hospital. He had pulled off to the side of the road and slid down the dusty embankment to reach the truck.

"When I saw your head against the steering wheel, I thought you were dead," he said to Francesca.

Francesca rubbed the tips of her fingers together then massaged her temples with firm, warm strokes. "I hit hard, that's for sure. The speeder came out of the blue. I swerved, then went down."

Sitting next to the bed, Raphael leaned closer and said, "By the time I got there, no one else was in sight. Did you see who it was?"

Francesca's anger swelled. "I think so," she answered, pausing as she saw an image of the reckless driver speeding past, his rubbery jowls bouncing as he laughed like a fat imp who figured he'd gotten away with something.

"Who was it, Francesca?" asked Raphael.

"Someone who wanted me out of the way and then Claire," Francesca replied.

"Francesca," Raphael pressed, "who forced you off the road?"

She finally answered, "Officer Yellowhorse."

Raphael's muscles tightened, but he remained silent.

Francesca continued, "I need to leave. Claire's in trouble, I know it."

"Your X-rays and CT scan are all normal. There's nothing keeping you here, but you need rest. She's a grown woman, Francesca. She can take care of herself," admonished Raphael.

"Of course she can, Raphael! But when crisis hits, and it will hit, I must be there!" She nimbly slid out of bed like a woman twenty years younger. Picking up the canvas bag that held her belongings, she walked behind a curtain partition.

Raphael heard the rustling sounds of Francesca dressing.

Then Francesca said, "Please, drive me home."

The two of them hurriedly checked out of the hospital, feeling the urgency to find Claire.

It was 8:00 pm. Stars sparkled against the black sky. Archbishop Anarch still had over an hour before presiding at the hospital's worship service. Scrub oak brushed against the pant legs of the expertly fitting, black nylon suit he wore whenever killing was at hand as it easily zipped off once the deed was done. Tonight, he would taste Claire Sanchez's salty blood and sweet, tender flesh. After surgically slashing her carotid, he would then tilt her head to one side, allowing her blood to drain into a sacred vial before drinking it. His mouth watered at the thought.

Power tingled in his arms and hands, coursed into his fingertips. His senses always became sharpened when he was about to encounter the dividing line between life and death. He had many times snuffed out corrupt women quickly and inconspicuously. In his view, all women reeked of sins of the flesh. To sacrifice them was a divine pleasure that caused a certain excitement, as he privately confessed in his nightly act of absolution.

Archbishop Anarch picked up his pace. He now had less than a hundred yards to go before he would be standing over Claire Sanchez's fallen body. He would put it in a zippered canvas bag, sling it over his shoulder, and pack it in the van quicker than the rod of Moses turned into a serpent.

As the trek got steeper, he stumbled momentarily and cactus bit into his palms. Steadying himself next to a waist-high granite boulder, he picked two cactus needles out from his left palm, flicked them into the dirt, and sucked pleasurably on the wound in anticipation of the human blood from Claire Sanchez's wounds.

He hated women. Even as a child, he had hated them— his mother especially. Young William had heard the fights between his parents late into the nights, observing them while hiding in the pantry and watching through the slightly ajar door. Inevitably hollering would echo through their seven-thousand-square-foot Aztlan adobe house, penetrating the air with more hatred than an entire battalion of bloodthirsty medieval Spanish crusaders.

"You are no kind of father. No kind at all," his mother would chide. A plea to stop always came, with his mother saying, "No more of your nonsense. Keep your friend away."

William's father would clench his teeth and begin slapping and punching, manflesh and knuckles cracking against bony womancheek like the butting of Rocky Mountain longhorn sheep.

Bleeding, his mother would then say, "William is *my* son," smirking before she fainted on the marble floor, blood stained a dark apple butter brown.

Loud enough for the servants in the carriage house to hear, William's father would repeat, "Are you okay? Are you okay?" like a holy ritual.

Eyes glazed, his father would reach down to lift up bloodstained fingers and suck them before walking away. The hatred of his father had grown in William like wildfire moving through Aztlan's parched alfalfa fields. His father had died while surveying oil properties when William was twelve, a twister ripping his plane to shreds. People there said the inky-black funnel cloud flew out of the sky like the finger of the Almighty flicking a bug off his sleeve.

The tragedy left townspeople thunderstruck, but William's mother had smiled. On the night of his father's funeral, his mother had cuddled William, the first time ever, and whispered, "The Almighty removes anything in his way." William had been happy for a while since his parents did not fight anymore.

It was then that the patriarch began to freely visit their estate—the virtuous act of a virtuous man, his mother would say. But the stray cats with gray and white stripes, like his mother's prematurely graying hair, made William angry.

They'd screech and writhe like a woman in pain when he did things to them. He did those things on a little sandstone altar in the middle of nowhere.

Afterward, he always felt better, like he had done them a favor because they had seemed unhappy when they looked at him, and their hissing and clawing meant that they were surely agents of evil.

As Francesca's home came into view behind a stand of piñons, Archbishop Anarch's reverie ended. Sharp and keen as the finely edged carbon blade in his pocket, his mind raced.

His prey was near. His rage was stoked. Gripping the trunk of a piñon tree, he squeezed tight. Madness crawled like maggots into marrow. He saw his father's red fingers and heard his mother's chiding.

His breaths became quicker, shallow, as banging and screaming echoed inside his head. He dropped to his knees and rocked back and forth until everything became quiet.

Draped by darkness, Francesca's home stood still as a corpse.

Walking again, he savored the calm as he stepped out of the brush past the rounded corner of the garage. Claire was sprawled on a little patch of grass, her head cocked to the side.

"Mother?" he whispered as he approached. She didn't stir.

Then his gaze darted to the coiled rattler lying under the faint glow of the porch light. He walked out toward the snake with its fangs protruding.

Gazing intently at it, he ordered, "Be gone."

Following the wave of his hand, it crawled into the darkness.

Popping loose the snaps on his back pocket, he reached for his carbon steel scalpel. Claire moved her head.

"Mother?" he whispered again.

Under the starlight, Claire's flesh glowed succulently. He had dreamt of this moment for so long. He would have some exquisite foreplay and then make the cut. Drinking the blood of someone bitten by a snake would be immensely exhilarating.

Car tires crunched along the driveway gravel. Without looking to see who was coming, he lunged at Claire.

❧❧❧

Something cold and sharp pressed at Claire's throat.

Dark clouds of memory swirled around Claire—Francesca's accident, the note, and the snake biting her. Medicine women howled—the spirits of Lozen, who had single-handedly killed a steer with a knife, Dahteste, who had been skilled in ambush and attack, and Gouyen, who had sunk her teeth into the enemy's neck and cut off his scalp before the victim had even died. Claire saw war, with men plundering and raping and taking what was not theirs. Coming to, Claire kicked the perpetrator's crotch hard then shot to her feet, leaving the dark-clothed man writhing. Claire knew who he was, what he had done, and what she had to do. She envisioned grabbing his knife, and cutting his groin, the cry, ending the life of one not fit to exist.

Instantly, he seized her by the wrist, threw her to the ground, and approached her again with the knife.

Claire again heard the chanting and howling, and bolted to her feet to face him.

He retreated to the edge of the forest, and she followed as he was one moment visible and the next invisible among forest shadows.

Then suddenly Claire felt a hard blow to the back of her head and fell down.

A car door slammed shut.

Winded, breathing heavily, Archbishop Anarch towered above her as she turned toward him, stunned.

A second car door slammed.

Dropping his knee on her back, he pressed the blade against her neck. Claire felt a round metal object in the dirt under the palm of her limp right hand.

Barely audible, Anarch whispered, "A meal rushed is a meal ruined. I'll be back. Be afraid, little Claire." Withdrawing the sharp blade, he jabbed a knee into her kidneys.

Resisting passing out, Claire clutched the hard metal object and flung it at him, hitting him between his eyes. He stumbled backward, hands to his face. "I'll be back, cunt," he muttered from a distance. Claire slumped back to the ground.

Energy drained out of her quickly as Archbishop Anarch looked at her again, smiling. Teasing held its own pleasure. Snapping off a branch of brush, he whisked away his footprints, then stole into the night, hearing a distant voice say, "She's not breathing."

Denim-clad patients entered single file down the green marble aisle of the Chapel of the Precious Blood, located at the center of the psychiatric hospital's campus. It was 8:30 pm, time for Compline, communal evening prayers presided over by the resident chaplain or the highest-ranking visiting clergy. Like automatons, the patients walked past rows of a hundred dark wooden pews, men turning right, women left, filling each pew with twelve somber faced people. It was precisely orchestrated with little chance of anyone failing to fall into line, for their fate for eternity depended on such scrupulousness. At the front of the chapel, surrounded by a three-foot brass altar railing, was the gothic sanctuary of the priests. It gleamed with scores of two-foot-long, tapered, beeswax candles reflecting off the glassy marble walls, brass candelabras, and silver chalices. Seated at the front of the sanctuary, on an elevated bronze chair that resembled a medieval throne, was Archbishop Anarch, surrounded by an entourage of visiting clergy from throughout northern Aztlan and remote regions of the Southwest.

Since it was a holy day, the Feast of the Innocent Souls, the archbishop had sent word to Karl Himmel that he would attend Compline and deliver a brief homily about heaven, hell, and the need to avoid sin, stressing fidelity to the Ecclesia Dei, the patriarch, and the archbishop. The faith and loyalty of both staff and patients had to be stirred now in case Sanchez's influence survived her.

Earlier that day Father Gall had informed him about Officer Yellowhorse's confrontation with Ms. Mirabal and Ms. Sanchez, and Sanchez's accusation of Father Gall. Archbishop Anarch didn't want any gossip about trouble leaking out to the office of the patriarch. The patriarch had continually warned Archbishop Anarch to quell all dissent before the first rumbling. The last of the congregants turned into the pews as the organ began playing "Salve Regina," the archbishop's favorite hymn for Compline, ending the day's toil with a chant to heaven's beloved mother, the only true Virgin Mother, who sincerely loved her divinely conceived son. At the end of the hymn, Archbishop Anarch stood, blessed himself, and intoned Psalm 91, concluding, "You will not fear the terror of the night nor the arrow that flies by day... It will not come near you."

At the end of the psalter and prayers for the living and the dead, Anarch motioned for the assembly to be seated and began, "Inspired with a message for this Feast of the Innocent Souls, I decided to lead this evening's Compline and end with a brief homily."

He paused for effect, closing his eyes to convey the appearance of receiving a message straight from a hotline to heaven, so his homily would more easily reach the minds of the susceptible. Then opening his eyes reverentially, he took a deep breath and continued, "In heaven there is perpetual springtime, succulent fruit hanging from eternally replenishing orchards, crystal clear streams that quench the most parched of throats, and a brotherhood and sisterhood of believers who love one another and never speak ill of each other."

A gasp swept through the audience, for the archbishop's voice seemed accusatory, making everyone in the pews feel guilty by contrast to the described behavior, whether or not they had committed any transgression. The archbishop believed in the power of shame and guilt helping to avert religious misdeeds. To further intimidate them, he gazed at the center of each row, looking into their souls to detect the slightest lies, which was as easy for him as peering into an empty cardboard box and guessing what was there.

He went on, "Satan is a serpent slithering through the tranquil garden of the Ecclesia Dei, whispering thoughts of disbelief and mistrust into the ears of believers. Wickedness sneaks in among us and sows seeds of divisiveness. Listen not to anyone who casts aspersions or concocts scandals. To listen means mortal sin, and those who die in such a state forfeit paradise and tumble into a pit of unending fire and torments comparable to the most pain-ridden day of one's life magnified thousands of times."

The spiritual alarm had been sounded to patients, staff, and visitors. They didn't dare stir or convey nervousness, for to do so, in their minds, would be tantamount to confessing wrongdoing.

Anarch continued, "We are all no more than pitiful creatures hanging by a silk thread, dangling above the wails of hell, saved from falling downward only by the grace of the Almighty. We are loved but not coddled. At the instant of mortal sin, we, as the transgressors, cut our own thread—and are forever lost." With a look of horror and pity, imitating the Almighty, Archbishop Anarch gazed downward as if into hell's abyss and made a scissor-like movement with his right hand, then stretched out both arms. He loved the theatricality of his preaching and was in his element.

The congregation gasped again upon hearing that, under the pain of mortal sin, they dared not so much as entertain any doubts regarding his character or that of his staff.

Archbishop Anarch bowed his head, let a few moments pass, then tearfully looked at the dumbstruck assembly and said, "And there is nothing the Almighty can do for a soul who knows better yet willingly chooses sin." He let his eyes sweep over the crowd, then concluded by lifting his right hand, blessing them, and saying, "*In Nómine Patris, et Fílii, Et Spíritus Sancti. Amen.*"

Piously walking toward the sacristy, followed by his entourage, he congratulated himself. *As always, splendid,* he thought. He could summon up any emotion necessary to get across whatever point he wanted anytime he wanted. He was thrilled at his talent for unadulterated manipulation of souls who did not know their own way without the aid of one who created the twists and turns of spiritual gangways.

Throughout the chapel there echoed the sniffles of elderly ladies in black mantillas, the fire of their faith kindled by the sermon.

Archbishop Anarch grinned as he caught sight of the granddaughter of one of the Ecclesia Dei's wealthiest benefactors, who looked like Lucia had twenty years ago with her slight build, flowing brown hair, sparkling eyes, and bronze skin. Momentarily, he wanted to stay in the place of wonder and pleasure he had known those many years ago with the one woman who had brought to his mind and body a humanity he had never before felt. While awaiting her baptism, Lucia had devoutly sat in a chapel pew and watched as he walked by at the end of Sunday morning mass. The sight of her had transfixed him more than the sight of the consecrated host. This experience with a woman had surpassed everything he had felt with any women, although he'd had since then many encounters. But he could never again experience what he had felt with Lucia because he had killed her.

Taking the last few steps into the sacristy, he gritted his teeth and reminded himself that this was not twenty years ago, that the woman in the pew was not Lucia. Lucia was dead, and there would not be a then for him to return to, for the last spark of it would soon be snuffed out with Claire's death. He entered the private large oak-paneled sacristy—the changing and storage area for the archbishop and altar boys of exemplary virtue and talent. It was replete with finely embroidered vestments, chalices of silver and gold, cherished relics, and a red velvet divan. He handed his silk vestments to one of the fair-haired altar boys, who hung them in a huge cedar closet.

A smile crawled across his face. As had Lucia, Claire had

dared act counter to his purpose, and for that—should she last beyond the night—she would pay a price she would never anticipate.

He knew that he must act soon lest images of the past overtake his mind and usher him into another reality in which the past consumed every minute detail of his present-day existence. Such an occurrence could not be allowed to happen, for the past, with all of its sordid acts and mischievous but understandable deeds of a young cleric, no longer existed, and all he wanted of events associated with the past—all manner of things, acts, persons, accusations, and threats—to permanently stop troubling his divinely consecrated mind.

Despite being the anointed and appointed Archbishop Anarch, for a moment he shook with such violence that there was nothing in his powers that prohibited the advance of total irrationality and utter loss of control. But never would he sanction a loss of control. He was the archbishop. He demanded, ordered, willed, forced, and executed. Finally, after a few seconds he again became his composed self.

Father Gall came to his side, sensing the archbishop's innermost thoughts, and said, "Your troubles will soon cease." Agreeing that sacrificing Lucia's daughter would end his troubles and fulfill his vow to the Almighty with the eradication of the lineage of medicine women, he recalled how this scenario had been anticipated for quite some time. Almost a year ago, one unseasonably cold autumn night at the Devil's Throne in the heart of the Aztlan desert, Father Gall had told him that the year would bring an aggressive, young enemy. Initially he had hoped such an enemy did not exist; but as he learned it did, he had prepared himself. Now due to detailed plotting, he was ready to fulfill the twenty-year-old vow. Then no further sacrifices would be required by the Almighty, and the office of the patriarch would be his within the month. It was only right that a little bonus—the office of the patriarch—had been added to sweeten the deal. Father Gall had assured Archbishop Anarch that the Almighty willed it so.

He laughed, thinking how everything he orchestrated was so delightful. Father Gall touched his shoulder knowingly and said, "The sooner the better. Once we've made sure she's dead, all power will be ours."

"Where are Himmel and Black?" Archbishop Anarch asked as he looked around to make sure no other clergy were in his private chamber.

"Preparing for their morning mission," Father Gall answered, looking out into the sanctuary then shutting the door behind him. "They'll knock when they arrive."

Archbishop Anarch and Father Gall walked into the adjoining meeting room used for visiting with clerical dignitaries. The archbishop sat at the head of the long mahogany dining table, with Father Gall to his left, and motioned for the brandy in a crystal decanter surrounded by six sparkling glasses, all resting on a silver tray. Father Gall poured as Archbishop Anarch continued, "Tomorrow morning we will both be celebrating the sacred liturgy with the monsignor in charge of operations at our mission in Piedras Negras, Mexico, correct?"

"Yes. That way our whereabouts can be attested to by the monsignor, his priests, and the dozens of faithful attending the mass and fund-raising brunch afterward," replied Father Gall.

"What precautions have been taken to prevent the artist from escaping?" asked Archbishop Anarch.

"Himmel and Black will wear dark silk ski masks. He'll be injected with a double dose. It is doubtful that even a person so young and strong will be able to dodge the quick prick of the needle."

"Remember the botched highway incident?" the archbishop reminded him.

Father Gall stared at Anarch, his face flushed with anger, and said, "I did not anticipate that Francesca's powers had grown so strong. As for Ms. Sanchez, my plan is foolproof. If she manages to escape the sting of death tonight and is left with her wits about her, she'll be desperate to save her beloved. Her mind will be distracted and her powers scattered. She'll be on our turf. We'll have the upper hand," Father Gall assured him.

Then Father Gall walked to a wall of glass-encased bookcases packed with mammoth editions of the Tridentine liturgy and music bound in red leather with gilded lettering. He unlocked the middle case and withdrew three volumes in succession, each from a different shelf, then took a step back. The bookcase slid forward, and the spring-loaded door clicked open. He walked inside. After a moment he came out carrying a small wooden box and laid it on the table in front of the archbishop. As he lifted the lid, a sweet scent of cedar rose from its interior. It held yellowed letters, and beneath them a locket containing a picture of a couple embracing.

Archbishop Anarch didn't speak, feeling suddenly drymouthed and tense. "Sanchez will weaken the moment I show it to her. She'll be shocked but convinced," Father Gall said, smiling wickedly.

Archbishop Anarch cleared his throat and took another sip of brandy as he was transported through the years to the time when Lucia had presented him with the locket.

After a few moments, he looked up at Father Gall and said, "Years ago I threw that into Black Lake."

Father Gall smiled from ear to ear, his eyes gleaming with a reddish light, then rolled his tongue over his pencil thin lips.

An electrical energy, stronger than a high desert mountain thunder and lightning storm, flowed through the archbishop's mind, the inspiration of moments ago at full throttle.

They both stood up, and Archbishop Anarch said, "Finalize matters with Himmel and Black yourself. I have something more pressing to attend to. Do not disappoint me."

Reverentially, Father Gall bowed his head, and the archbishop walked out.

11

S lowly Claire awakened. The sweet scent of drying cilantro hanging from the kitchen vigas in Francesca's home drifted into the guest room, where she was tucked in bed. The atmosphere surrounding her made her remember the experiences of her youth, of being loved and cared for, guided with firmness and compassion.

Francesca often had the severely ill stay here so she could immediately treat any relapses in life-threatening situations, as Claire's situation had been. Claire knew that what had brought her into this room was nothing short of life threatening. This was a realm in which healing spirits warded away demons of death. Not always did the light overcome darkness; often, after weeks of travail, death staked its claim. Yet Francesca never gave up, tirelessly battling to save lives and defeat the workings of evil.

Groggy, Claire took comfort in the fragrant herbs festooned across the vigas in the bedroom. The herbs were Francesca's stock-in-trade to ease pain, restore health, and save lives. There was the minty smell of *yerba buena*. Dangling beside it was *berraza*, a water parsnip reputedly as good a remedy

as mint for stomach pains. Neatly laced in between was
poleo, pennyroyal—a potent fever reducer.

But, as Francesca always taught, the most important healing agent was the presence of the medicine woman, which
awakened healing in the patient. Francesca loathed false medicine women; charlatans engaged in far-flung rituals with
tricks culled from the Far East to seduce needy souls into pay-
ing for services that were no more healing than petting poisonous toads along the Aztlan River Valley. "Real medicine
women keep things simple. They need no gimmicks, just the
stuff of everyday life—good, down-to-earth talk to set the patient's thinking straight and teach how dreams and intuitions
heal, and herbs to soothe the spirit and heal the body," Francesca explained.

Francesca walked into the room, sat next to Claire on the
bed, stroked Claire's sweaty forehead, and whispered, "The
bite was bad." Claire flinched at the thought of the rattler. Her
left calf still throbbed and burned. Cold then hot flashes made
her want blankets one second and an ice bath the next.

Francesca wiped Claire's brow with a soft cotton cloth
and continued, "Raphael got me to the hospital after my accident, then we hightailed it back here and found you pretty
down and out. Raphael is in town getting bags of ice to bring
down your bad fever."

Claire squeezed her hand and whispered, "Did you spot
the man with the knife?" Her throat was parched, and the
room seemed swirling in fog.

Alarmed, Francesca asked, "Someone attacked you?"

As best as she could, Claire related the facts, then ended
by saying, "After everything, I popped him in the head with
Officer Yellowhorse's ring, the one that slipped off his finger
the other night."

"Really?" Francesca chuckled. "Maybe it lodged between his eyes. It'd serve him right."

"Yeah. A turquoise crucifix beats a scarlet letter," Claire quipped. Francesca looked stunned, not sure if Claire knew what she had actually said.

Once Claire had finished, Francesca reached toward the blue ceramic bowl on the nightstand, got an ice flake, and tenderly slipped it between Claire's lips. "The snake was his messenger. He wanted you out cold to do his evil deed," Francesca remarked.

"Thank you for coming in time, Francesca," said Claire.

Francesca affirmed, "You took care of yourself."

Claire knew what she meant. Unless they'd given up, or their time had come, medicine women summoned their own protective forces. "Quitters lose out in the battles that *make* the soul. Once the soul is *made*, then it is time to move on to the next level," Claire remembered Francesca instructing.

"You're no quitter. You exorcized that demon the other night," Francesca announced proudly. Claire remembered the knife on the kitchen counter and the pull toward suicide.

"And if it returns?" Claire asked.

"When it knocks on the door of your mind, it's you who decides whether to let it in or not," said Francesca. "True death only comes when we've finished our task here and are ready to move into a higher realm."

Francesca gently removed the cover from Claire's left leg and said, "As for this nasty bite, I made an incision at the wound and sucked out a mouthful of poison." She reached for a satchel from the nightstand and opened it. "Chew this snakeroot. I've already applied some to the incision." Long sweats and nightmares were side effects of snakeroot. Recovery, if possible, meant sweating out the toxins in the nervous system and purging the soul through frightening visions and dreams. If one lived after such a spiritual battle without loss of sanity, then the soul was stronger for having prevailed; death, on the other hand, brought a loss of soul, an eternal lingering in a psychic realm of confusion where everything was gray, bleak, lifeless like a dead man in a noose.

Claire chewed the bitter pulp, its juices slipping down her throat, perspiration soon rolling down her face and chest.

Francesca remarked, "Hopefully, the venom will pass within the next twenty-four hours. The poison injected into your soul will take longer."

Then Francesca opened a small drawer on the nightstand and took out a wide rubber band, tightly securing it above the wound to stop poisonous residue from traveling to Claire's heart. She would release it for ninety seconds every ten minutes for the next two hours. "You've seen me treat patients for the rattler bites. You know what's coming. I can only do so much," she told Claire. Nausea rolled through Claire's stomach, up to her throat and mouth. A metallic taste spurted over her tongue and the insides of her cheeks. She threw the blankets off, the bedroom turning from icy cold to sweaty hot.

Medicine women taught that a rattler bite signaled a spiritual contagion and could end in something worse than death—spiritual decay, the loss of one's mind. It could set loose any disease latent in the personality. The mind could shatter, the soul depart. During such a struggle, people often gave up and died, if not physically then psychically.

As a young child, Claire had heard the old medicine women saying that one patient or another had succumbed to the dark forces. These lost souls were no longer able to tell good from bad, right from wrong, and went through life muttering and smiling blankly.

"They'd have been better off choosing evil outright rather than meekly giving up life's struggles," Claire's mother had told Elizabeth and Francesca one bitter cold winter night. "Insanity happens when people give up. As long as there's fight left, there's hope."

Stomach churning, Claire clenched her teeth, clearly realizing that because he hadn't been able to kill her, Archbishop Anarch's intention had been to drive her mad since no one would believe the ranting of a lunatic.

Claire swept her hair out of her face, ran her tongue over her parched lips, determination breaking past her discomfort. At that moment, Claire saw something near the closet, in back of Francesca. Psychiatric experience told her she was hallucinating, the poison traveling into the parietal and occipital lobes of her cortex. But if the thing wasn't there, it may as well have been as hallucinating affected a person just as much as real experience. She knew that if she looked at it, it could get bigger, stretching out its arms into the wings of a monstrous bat before lunging at her. It would take her deep into the woods, gash her over and over with razor-sharp teeth, rip her to pieces so tiny that ants would carry her into the bowels of the earth—where her mother lay.

Scene after scene flew out of what felt like a hollowed recess in the back of her head, a spot that was so poison-filled that gray and green gunk oozed up into the soft convolutions of her brain. And she couldn't do anything about it. Archbishop Anarch had set loose in her something worse than venom—the pent-up fears of a five-year-old girl.

Claire's head shook feverishly. Hot, hot, hot, then cold, cold, cold beat a path out of caverns in her brain to her mouth and down her throat and chest and into her groin, where everything went dead as little clumps of flesh and hair and labia and clitoris and pelvis fell off and onto the bedsheets and dis-integrated—maggots vanishing into thin air. Emptiness yawned and a dark god stepped forth to take her to where bodies putrefied and souls died and were sloughed off into cosmic heaps. Tightly she clung to the fringes of sanity.

Everything was skewed and distorted. Fears of hanging somewhere between life and death were part of the sickness, which made the bad worse.

Freezing cold now, Claire shook so hard that every bone in her body seemed as if it were grinding against the one next to it. Her teeth chattered so loudly she was sure they'd soon be whittled down to stumps. Goose bumps ran up and down her flesh—a million minuscule ants on their way to driving off what tiny bits of reality she had left in her dazed mind. Nerves frayed, emotions high-pitched, she closed her eyes, hoping to find solace.

The poison forced her back to the past. A five-year-old girl cried; her head buried in her hands. The frigid forest air hurt her lungs. Startled by a woman wailing, she looked up to see a monster hovering over her fallen mother.

Then whipping winds broke the spell, propelling Claire back through time into the present. Gasping for breath, she opened her eyes. The black thing drew closer to the bed. Tears streamed down Claire's face, as she again became a young girl frozen with fear, screaming.

Evil had come.

While its lines were indistinct, its presence was not. It was hungry and tired of waiting.

Strands of her sanity continued to unravel.

The now gelatinous-faced creature screeched, touched her neck with a cold blade, and then quivered.

Next it morphed into a woman-creature-man—Lucia's

high cheekbones and brown eyes switched to a yellowed, weather-beaten skeleton with steel-blue eye sockets, then to a man, Archbishop Anarch with his sandy-blond hair and blood-red tongue that curled like a venom-spitting viper.

The pus-oozing head tilted sideways as the creature slid the razor-sharp blade across Claire's neck, but it didn't cut.

Claire sighed, tension pounding in waves over her head. She had the impulse to let her mind fracture. It would be as simple as standing on the rim of the Aztlan Gorge and dropping.

Anxiety gripped her, making her want to gash every bit of flesh she could dig into, letting her blood out to let the pain out. Then everything quit, as though she had partly emerged from a nightmare to find Francesca gone. She pulled the warm cotton sheets close, the scents of fresh herbs helping her drop back into mere panic.

Claire had always feared being nothing more than a weak imitation of her mother, a woman who had made her mistakes but had died fighting; now she hated this self-inflicted fate just as she hated the evil man of the night.

An invisible voice read Claire's thoughts. It vibrated through the room as if coming from inside a giant tin can. *Francesca's not here anymore. You're all alone, little Claire. Huerfana, huerfana! Orphan girl. You're all alone.*

Claire despised those words. Kindergarten and grade school children used to say them while cornering her between the trash dumpster and the back corner of the old adobe schoolhouse, their faces curled into gargoyles and gigantic rats.

Claire tried to steady her nerves, thinking that the voices came from the poison, that she was awake, alive, and going to get through this.

"You're not awake—not anymore," a voice squealed. A roar of foreign tongues broke in like a chorus of demons.

Claire was aware that auditory hallucinations, more than visual, were a key symptom of schizophrenia. But she knew this was not her fate. She had no family history of schizophrenia. Lucia and Francesca had loved her, helped form a solid emotional foundation, so she knew she would not go crazy in the usual way. Fear didn't cause her to crumble; it pissed her off. Psychically sensitive women like herself became healers or witches, directing spiritual energy for good or evil.

For a moment, cold rage and destructive hate burned through Claire like dry ice on skin. Feeling a new power, she knew that invoking the primal energies of earth, air, fire, and water could outdo the measly incantations of institutional religion. Foul spirits, older than the earth itself, would deposit Archbishop Anarch's psychic carnage in their wake, his body left as feed for desert vultures.

Shocked by her malevolent attitude, Claire realized that black magic would make her no better than Archbishop Anarch. Loss of soul wouldn't be worth the short-lived thrill. Rather, wits, the natural magic, were her key to survival.

Claire lifted her weighty arms to cover her ears while evil claimed the shadowy atmosphere as monstrous black wings flapped noisily against the walls. A sudden flash of a foul person stalking the home chilled Claire's core.

Involuntarily, as though pressed down by a devilish prankster, her eyes closed. Frightening images came—the lunge of the snake, Elizabeth's corpse strewn in the desert, the black-robed man, his face cowled, lifting a bronze crook high above his head then slamming it toward Claire.

Claire's eyes bolted open. The man sat next to her on the bed, wearing black coveralls and a silk ski mask, and pressed a blade against her throbbing carotid artery.

Claire was feeling again like a little girl hiding behind Francesca's skirt from every dark-clothed man she saw in the plaza, the grocery store, the highways and byways, wanted to scream out. *Not gonna cave. Not gonna die. Not yet anyway.*

He read her thoughts and responded, *I'm going to honor you with another extension. It's more exciting that way. But it'll cost you. Too bad, little* huerfana. *Too bad.*

Her mouth flooded with the taste of bile. She kept telling herself that the hallucination would pass, that it was coming from the snakebite, then chanting over and over, "It's coming from the bite... my mind's all right." From inside a zippered compartment of his black nylon vest the figure withdrew a loaded syringe, uncapped it, and shot a short stream of clear fluid into the air.

Claire strained but couldn't budge.

He noticed and said flatly, *Now, now. Sit still. Without this you die. With it, you live to see the left hand of the Almighty at work.* Skillfully, he drew Claire's left arm toward him and injected her then returned the needle to his vest. *You and I will meet again. For now, marinate in the tragedy of loss,* huerfana.

An empty hurting space deep inside Claire opened up. Flashing bright lights scattered across her field of vision as she lost consciousness. Anthony's smile, Lucia's loving gaze, and Francesca's warm and strong face died away—beacons lost during a dark night.

Crowing roosters startled Claire out of a dead sleep. Gazing toward the bedroom window, she saw the morning sun shielded behind black rain clouds.

Remarkably, her head was clear, telling her that the sense-warping viper's poison was gone. She wanted to get up. Her feet touched the red brick floor. She tugged the blanket off the bed and wrapped it around her.

She was eager to tell Francesca that she felt better. Francesca would probably already be up. She routinely rose at 4:00 am, bundled kindling for the iron stove in the kitchen, and started a blaze that warmed the three-bedroom adobe home quicker than a roadrunner's dash.

As she remembered the night's travail, Claire looked at the place where the dark-clothed apparition had sat and had to steady herself against the bedpost as she saw something that turned her stomach—a liquid stain that had dried.

Spurting the potion in the air, the man had given her an extension of life, threatening that it would cost her. Perhaps the spot was something else—snakeroot and saliva—she thought, trying to reassure herself. Then withdrawing her left arm from under the blanket, she saw a tiny puncture on her forearm just below the elbow. Swollen and pink, the wound was surrounded by a brown crust, which could have been a remnant of a dried herbal paste Francesca had applied earlier. Quickly, she walked to the bathroom, turned on the faucet, and waited for the water to warm up. When it did, she gently washed the area with soap. To her surprise, the tiny wound and inflammation disappeared.

A cold breeze rattled the old, single-paned bathroom window. The bathroom door slammed shut, startling Claire. A black shadow flew past the corrugated pane, a crow on a morning hunt.

Now she thought that, due to lack of food, low blood sugar and exhaustion were playing havoc with her reasoning and judgment. After splashing some warm water on her face, she would let Francesca know she was all right. Then she'd call Anthony, whom she missed badly. After that, she'd get on with her investigation.

There were no sounds coming from the house. She grabbed a face towel and dried her cheeks then reached for the doorknob. The old knob spun loosely. Francesca had said it needed fixing. When it stuck, only a hard push from the outside could force it open.

"Francesca, the door's stuck," she yelled. No one answered.

Heart thumping, Claire looked around. The only other way out was through the porthole-sized window. Wrapping a towel around her fist, she smashed the glass. She rubbed the edges of the pane free of shards and stood on tiptoe to see out.

She was clothed except for shoes. Her thick wool socks would be enough for a quick walk to the front door. Closing the toilet lid, she stood on it, stretched her left leg to the sink, then levered herself up. Thrusting her right leg and torso past the windowsill, she pulled herself through.

The drop to the ground hurt. Every joint and muscle ached, as though she'd survived a beating. But she had to persist in finding Francesca.

Twigs snapping in the distance caused Claire to glance into the piñon forest. She cautiously walked toward the sound, her breaths short and shallow, her heart beating in her ears.

When she got to the forest's edge, a blackbird flew at her. Stumbling back, she struck out at it, her fingers grazing its feathers. Cawing, it flew away. Walking further into the forest, she froze. Raphael lay gagged and spiked through the heart to a charred tree trunk. He looked lifelessly heavenward, his hands taped together as though praying for heaven's help. Claire ran to him and cried out, her rage echoing through forest and canyon. Trembling, she gently closed his eyes, thoughts riveted on Archbishop Anarch.

Quickly she dashed up to Francesca's front door and reached for the doorknob. Claire pushed the heavy door open and went in. Francesca was seated in her favorite chair near the fireplace, wrapped up to her neck in her favorite crocheted blanket. But the room was frigid.

"Francesca!" exclaimed Claire, running to her. The instant Claire touched her, Francesca slumped to the side, her right carotid cut.

Claire wailed.

12

Sirens blared, and tires spun in the loosely packed gravel drive as Claire watched the two ambulances speed away carrying the corpses of Francesca and Raphael. The early morning sky was lusterless with still-white clouds turning gray, then black. Charged with static electricity, long strands of Claire's auburn hair wildly lifted then descended about her shoulders. And thunder rumbled, first in the distance then closer, like the pounding fist of an unseen deity.

Officer Yellowhorse stood beside Claire while four other police roped off the grounds. "When they're done, we're going to search the house top to bottom," he said. There was no feeling in his voice. He chewed and cracked his gum loudly, spitting on the dirt.

"Why?" Claire asked, turning to face him.

A smirk rippled over Officer Yellowhorse's face. He cleared his throat, coughed up something, and spit again. He stared at Claire, enjoying making her wait, then replied, "Because she could have killed him and then herself."

Outraged as she had never before imagined, Claire thought

that if she could she would leave Officer Yellowhorse with a loss more permanent than his last. Incredulous, she asked, "You believe that?"

"Gotta check out all possibilities," he replied, aiming his gum with a curled tongue and spitting it out of his mouth, then chuckling when he noticed Claire's disgust. After a few seconds, he continued, "We might find something inside that'll help us in our investigation."

When the men had tied the last rope cordoning off the house, Officer Yellowhorse gave them a nod to enter it and begin the search.

Claire had a mental flash of one of his men checking a closet in Francesca's home, having been told what to look for. She wished she could get inside this guy's head, see who had put what in there.

For a second she thought of darting into the house, locking the door before anyone could get in, calling someone—the governor or one of the state senators she had served with on any number of state-funded mental health panels—and demanding that witnesses be present for the investigation. But she knew Officer Yellowhorse would like nothing more than for her to give him a reason to arrest her for obstruction of justice. That shifty look in his eyes and still bare right ring finger told her he'd take great pleasure in jailing anyone unsympathetic to matters of ecclesiastical concern.

Officer Yellowhorse looped his fingers through the thick black belt that held his holster and tugged his pants up. The second he let go, his doughy belly drove his frayed black polyester slacks back down. "Time to get to work," he said, like a man who was up to no good.

"Mind if I go in and sit quietly in the dining room? I need some time to think," Claire suggested. Under the circumstances,

Claire decided cooperation would be best.

He hesitated, then grimaced and replied, "I need to keep an eye on you. That's as good a place as any. Just don't get in our way."

Sadness descended on her the instant she stepped inside. Years of motherly devotion, love, and friendship seemed to breathe through the walls of the house. Officer Yellowhorse watched as she walked into the dining room, instructing her, "Stay in here. Nowhere else." Then he went to the back of the house.

In the dining room, she pulled out a book from the old pine bookcase. Francesca often sat in the chair in the corner and spent long hours reading to clear her mind. Claire touched the chair's headrest, a lump in her throat, then sat down, opened the book at random, and read:

Since our apparitions, the part of us which appears, are so momentary compared with the other, unseen part of us, which spreads wide, the unseen might survive somehow attached to this person or that, or even haunting certain places after death.

She closed the leather-bound volume, stroking its spine as she reflected on the speaker, Mrs. Dalloway, and the book's author, Virginia Woolf, turning Claire's thoughts to Francesca's presence and to love, death, and rage.

All grief was gone as Francesca's warmth and strength cloaked itself over her. She said softly, "Be well, Francesca."

"You talking to someone out there, Ms. Sanchez?" asked Officer Yellowhorse, walking in from the back bedroom, his surly voice stoking Claire's growing annoyance and anger.

She stayed quiet and left him guessing.

Kitchen cabinets were being opened and slammed shut, contents of bathroom drawers spilled out on the floor, and the huge cedar storage chest in the master bedroom shoved across uneven bricks as somebody prepared to jimmy it open.

Claire hated this insensitive searching of Francesca's life. Book in hand, she stood up and started to leave.

"Oh no. You're not going anywhere. I have more questions for you. You can't leave the crime scene just yet... medicine woman," demanded Officer Yellowhorse, saying the last words with particular relish.

Claire asked, "I've gone over everything with you. What more is there?" Earlier, once they had answered her call, Claire had described every event to the five officers—the assault, the snakebite, Raphael and Francesca rushing to her aid, and her discovery of their corpses after she had come to.

"If what you say is true, it sure does surprise me that you're up and around like you are. Like nothing ever happened," he chided.

Francesca's chair suddenly moved—its wood grating against brick flooring.

Officer Yellowhorse's eyes grew wide as he said, "Is there a cat in here or something?" Claire smiled.

"This is a damn strange house. Still haven't found my ring, have you?" he added.

The chair moved again. Magical energy pervaded the house.

"Something's happening here," he said, moving closer to the chair, looking around it.

"Yes, something is," Claire replied, barely above a whisper.

"Soon as we find what we're looking for..." Officer Yellowhorse said, stopping in mid-sentence with surprise at what had tumbled out of his mouth. "I mean, soon as we make sure everything's in order we're leaving. Damn medicine woman's house gives me the creeps."

A clanging, like metal instruments against brick, came from one of the back rooms. "Found something here, sir. Think you better take a look," said an officer. Claire followed Officer Yellowhorse into the small pantry at the back of the kitchen, where the four other officers were peering down at a gunnysack, its drawstring open.

Looking in, Yellowhorse remarked, "Well, well. Look at what we have here. Don't that beat all—a bag full of spikes. Just like the one through poor Raphael's heart." He stepped aside and motioned Claire forward.

"I say the old woman might have had something against him, did him in, then couldn't live with herself afterward. Her fingerprints are probably on the spike she nailed him with and all over these here. She was a tough old gal, strong as a trucker, wouldn't have had any problem doing it," he insisted.

Claire looked at him in disbelief.

"Open and shut case. Makes my work easy," he added, beaming. "We'll see," Claire said, moving quickly out the open back door and slamming it shut.

"What the hell! Get back here," Officer Yellowhorse yelled futilely. He stumbled past the other four officers who looked at him dumbly, waiting to be told what to do.

Claire quickly made it to her car, parked to the side of the driveway and hidden by four sprawling piñons. The officers' voices trailed off in the opposite direction, around the front of the house, where visitors usually parked. Claire started the engine and took a back road to the highway, dead set on what she was about to do.

꙳꙳꙳

An unsettling racket came from Anthony's studio. It was more like rats eating through wallboard than the familiar scratching of raccoons on the door or tree branches grating against windowpanes. He tried to ignore it. Once in a while odd sounds came from the thick adobe walls. Over a hundred and fifty years old, the five-hundred-square-foot room was thought to have been a turn-of-the-century jailhouse for northern Aztlan ruffians.

Allegedly, many a terrified person had been hooded, handcuffed, and led out to a nearby hanging tree. Terror was locked in the walls, village people claimed. He was not one to dismiss local lore, as he knew that old stories inspired the creation of art. Although the eeriness had never put him off, at times like the full moon or the witching hour (around three in the morning) he swore that reflections of light and dark were like people huddled and pointing upward and that nighttime breezes were similar to the murmuring of crowds.

He looked up from his sketchbook, peering out the small window and seeing nothing but a windless, grayish morning. Rubbing his fingertips against the rustic, oak drafting table handed down to him by his recently deceased mentor in Italy, he tried to find inspiration but couldn't. Throughout the night he had tossed and turned. Haunting images of monstrous, screeching blackbirds, Francesca's home surrounded by legions of long-tailed demons on black horses, and Claire clawing her way up a steep slope kept him from drifting to sleep.

Frustrated, he paced in his studio, looking at old sketches and clay maquettes of human and animal sculptures that often inspired him to make art. Letting his mind wander freely, he listened to the feelings and images that rose from his soul's troubled depths, seeing a spike. Blood dripping. Police cars at Francesca's. Two corpses belted to stretchers. Ambulances driving off. Stunned at these images, he closed his sketchpad and reached for his jean jacket. He needed to get his phone and call Francesca.

A big boom, like a large rock hurled against the front door of the studio, stopped him. He froze, then went to the door, grabbed the handle, and gave it an angry twist. But it stuck. Puzzled, he yanked on the handle, but nothing happened. Anthony wondered about village pranksters, but he didn't think anyone around there would mess with him. The local kids called him superman because of his well-developed chest and heavily muscled arms and hands. Gripping hard, he tried to force the knob, muscles and veins bulging, to no avail.

Infuriated, he went to the window, a small, four-paned, steel sash relic at least fifty years old. There was no way he would fit through it.

A visual impression of two black-garbed, hooded figures standing on either side of the door rushed through his mind. The longer he'd been around Francesca and Claire, the more he paid attention to psychic data. Slamming the palms of his hands on the twelve-foot-long pine table under the window in frustration, he hollered, "When I get outta here, I'm gonna get you and tie you into a pretzel."

Now he heard the sound of people running through fallen leaves and broken branches. Then something hard, like a rock or a chunk of metal, crashed through one of the small rectangular panes, and a piece of board was shoved up against the window, blocking both light and air. Smoke came out of a canister of tear gas, quickly filling up the small quarters.

Anthony dropped to the floor and used his shirtsleeve to filter the fumes from his nose and mouth. Frantically, he crawled toward the storage shelves where he kept clean cotton towels for polishing stone. The room thickened with smoke. His eyes teared. He couldn't see. Soon his head was spinning, his muscles went limp, and his face hit the cold concrete floor.

⟨⟨⟨

Archbishop Anarch consoled himself, thinking that wine from the gold chalice would have to do for now, though the consecrated blood of the Almighty was a distant second to Claire Sanchez's own body fluid. Sacred vessels were in the center of the main altar, and from the most ornate one he would soon drink in celebrating mass.

He sat piously on a bronze-crested, marble-inlaid throne while a thirty-person choir in the balcony facing him chanted:

Kyrie eléison, Christe eléison, Kyrie eléison, Christe eléison

Archbishop Anarch prayerfully folded his hands and touched the tips of his fingers to his lips. For the next five minutes, the Latin intonation would continue, but his mind was on Claire Sanchez's soft neck glistening under the night stars and the much-anticipated first taste of her blood. Claire's young moist flesh had to be his before tomorrow night, before the rising of the full moon; otherwise, her powers would be too great. He pressed his hands harder against his lips, as though intensifying his prayers, to keep from drooling.

It was the monthly first Friday morning High Mass offered for the repose of the souls of Ecclesia Dei's most generous, deceased benefactors. The special collection typically brought in well over one hundred thousand dollars. All the three hundred members in attendance were men and women of means who hoped to one day also be noted on the meticulously printed, gold foil card ceremoniously presented to each congregant upon entering since having their names appear on the card guaranteed eternal salvation, as Archbishop Anarch had declared.

The faithful present had been invited to this monthly event because they had so willingly provided copies of their wills to the Ecclesia Dei. The Ecclesia Dei's lawyers had notarized willed amounts in excess of $100,000, which was the minimum acceptable gift—a little fire insurance for the soul. Even their gifts to the Ecclesia Dei's coffers, though, did not earn them the archbishop's respect. He loathed all the men in their black, Italian tailored suits and the women in their black silk dresses and black mantillas laid so precisely on their dyed black, beehive hairdos. They were damnable people. How he stooped to have anything to do with such placating, ass-kissing dregs of humanity he didn't know. Only their cold hard cash, saintly generosity given to the kingdom of heaven on earth—the Ecclesia Dei—would save their contemptible little souls. However, he never revealed his true feelings about the people but instead warmly blessed and thanked them for their charity.

The choir tapered to a close. Everyone stood. One of the twelve altar boys went for the thurible, a solid silver censer, and brought it to Archbishop Anarch. Spooning the myrrh over the lighted wafer of incense, his mind lit on the rolling, spontaneously combusting tumbleweeds that frequently blew in and surrounded his desert altar during the secret rites. They were the Almighty's way of willingly and graciously accepting the flesh and blood of tainted women.

Anarch incensed the bread and wine on the altar, the crucifix, and the altar itself; then returned the thurible to the server, who incensed the archbishop, the clergy, and the people. Thick smoke enshrouded the sanctuary. Archbishop Anarch smiled and breathed the vapors deeply.

The server took the censer away as the archbishop moved to the Epistle side of the altar, where he washed his fingers while reciting Psalm 25: 6–12:

Lavábo inter innocéntes manus meas...

Ne perdas cum ímpiis, Deus: ánimam meam, et cum viris sánguinum vitam meam...

"I will wash my hands among the innocent. Take not away my soul, O God, with the wicked, nor my life with the men of blood." The words troubled him because they would come into his head at the most inopportune times and he could not banish them. They troubled him because they had a life of their own, a life he knew was no more than the faint glow of an ember that had once been a blaze—the remnant of an old conscience that would die when she died. As unleavened bread and common wine were finally being transformed into the body and blood of Christ, Archbishop Anarch thought of Claire and was transported to spiritual ecstasy. He genuflected, elevated the host, and turned toward the people saying, *"Ecce Agnus Dei, ecce qui tollit peccáta mundi."* He instead heard: The Lamb of God—Archbishop Anarch of the Ecclesia Dei—takes away the sins of the world, the screwed-up, woman-infested world that none of those looking up at him take as seriously as he because they are who they are and he is the chosen.

Suddenly, there was screaming from somewhere in back of the cathedral. A woman with long, matted bright red hair came out of one of the four confessionals near the baptismal font—the one in which he had heard Lucia's last confession—and walked like a ghostly incarnation of Lucia, a woman who had been willing to give her very life for the man she loved.

She'd been hiding there all night, as she always did when he offered sacrifice or killed just because it suited him, but she didn't scare him. Not anymore.

No one else saw her. The faithful were used to their arch-bishop's spiritual ecstasies, similar to St. Ignatius, who had cast his gaze upward, lost in heavenly rapture for minutes on end. Archbishop Anarch was a saint, and things like this always happened to saints.

He stood still, not afraid like he had been twenty years ago when the apparition had first appeared. Archbishop Anarch never showed fear, came across as above it all and so heavenly that he was sure his face glowed with holiness, his head surrounded by a golden halo.

Wild-eyed, the woman pointed at him, screeching like a lunatic Old Testament prophet ready to pronounce the Word of the Almighty to the spiritually corrupt, except that she was no more prophet than Satan was a good angel. She was a demon, sent from hell to distract him during mass.

Hissing and moving to the center of the main aisle, she screamed, *Beware of the man of secrets, the man of deceit.*

During his ecstasies, people often heard something like whisperings. It was the Holy Spirit, they said.

Archbishop Anarch's blood boiled. If he could, he would destroy Lucia all over again, right here, right now.

The woman screeched on, *Let those who have ears, hear. Hear me this day.* She moved at lightning speed to the front of the congregation.

Archbishop Anarch tilted his head a bit higher, toward the heavens.

He wanted their complete attention.

She raged: *For the foul deed that has been done, powers from the north, south, east, and west have been unleashed on this land and its people. Baptized infants will die tragic deaths—run over by cars, strangled by mothers seized by inexplicable fury, shot by*

drunken fathers. Lands blessed by the Ecclesia Dei will cease to pro-
duce—locusts will eat crops, hail destroy trees, drought wither all
that is green. She stopped and eyed the congregants, each un-
knowingly wincing.

Before the moon ends its cycle, the forces of light will battle the
forces of darkness. Do not interfere, or all that I have said will come
to pass—before the moon ends its cycle. Then flicking her up-
raised fingers high in the air, sparks and smoke enveloping
her, she disappeared.

Coughing rang throughout the congregation. Some always claimed to smell sweet incense. Others, roses. All believed.

Archbishop Anarch pretended to snap out of the trance,
and as he did the front doors opened wide and three state police officers walked in.

13

The Devil's Throne jutted over the horizon, easily seen from the road. The sight of its forty-foot-high sandstone spikes and deeply tufted basin made Claire nauseous and panicky as she imagined its form depicting the creature for whom it was named, although invisible, as physically present as the vultures that constantly circled overhead.

Claire slowed her driving as she maneuvered the twists and turns of the two-lane Turquoise Trail. She was alone on this deserted stretch of highway, which surprised her. It seemed as if Officer Yellowhorse would have put an all-points bulletin out on her by now. That's why she had taken the old highway and not the interstate, and why she'd found a pay phone and finally been able to get through to her old friend Manny Ortiz, the State Police chief.

Claire and Chief Ortiz had served on a panel together for the governor's task force on mental health and crime. He was a hard-nosed native of Aztlan who shot straight, didn't mess with anybody and didn't let anybody mess with him. He had immediately understood what she'd done and why. The State Police had for some time been keeping tabs on the Ecclesia

Dei, especially Archbishop Anarch. More than once the arch-bishop's black Mercedes sedan had been spotted doing some off-road driving on old roads not on current maps in the vicinity of the Devil's Throne. Chief Ortiz had also spotted Archbishop Anarch at least half a dozen times after midnight disappearing into the ink-black desert. In the morning when Chief Ortiz went back, there weren't even tire tracks, as if an unseen hand had wiped away any trace of the archbishop. Chief Ortiz knew the area well. Over the years, clues about mysterious disappearances and murders in Aztlan inevitably led there. He told Claire to be careful and that he was going to pay Archbishop Anarch a visit that morning.

Claire drove off-road to a spot behind an outcrop of granite boulders where no one would see her car parked. She needed plenty of time to investigate then tell Chief Ortiz what she'd discovered.

Hopefully, Anthony was all right. He hadn't answered his phone all morning, which wasn't unusual since he rose early, worked late, and didn't keep a telephone out in the studio. She and Chief Ortiz would check on him later.

Locking her car, she set out under the rising sun, her canteen of water. It was cooler than summer, although the heat of the high mountain desert always took its toll. But if she could find what she thought was out here, any discomfort would have been well worth it. Archbishop Anarch would be history.

Soon she had walked so far that she lost sight of her car and was suddenly gripped by the reality of being alone wandering through a psychic wasteland. Without any warning, blinding winds whipped out of the north, causing giant sand funnels to dance around her. She squinted then covered her eyes with her hands. The desert had its dangers, including unexpected windstorms.

When the winds stopped, Claire heard a sound like a woman in travail running toward the first human she'd seen for days in this desert of despair. Then she heard her own name riding the desert winds followed by a dirge sung in a ghostly tone, like a miserable departed being wailing from a tomb: *Claire. Land of the forsaken, land of the lost, hear me now and bring her to me. Land of the forsaken, land of the lost, hear me now and bring her to me. Land... bring her to me... Claire.*

Claire walked in the direction of the moaning, her spirit resolute at the memory of her mother and Francesca. Then dark thoughts flew at her, an unexpected mental hailstorm. *Francesca is dead is dead. All is meaningless... for nothing.* Anguish seized her. She looked around and saw a big crow sitting on a sandstone ledge staring at her.

Claire forced herself to gaze confidently at the crow, and soon it flew away.

The land stretched into a limitless brown sea. Hills and sky-towering cliffs were now well behind her. The morning air turned frigid, and she wrapped her arms around herself. The land seemed cold with fright.

Undeterred, Claire knew that sudden changes in atmosphere could be provoked by the presence of evil, according to the old ones. Medicine women said that the land cried out and recoiled, as if in shock, when a woman of the earth died tragically. On the night of her mother's death, it shook. And now scathing winds and bone-chilling cold told of the presence of evil and its deeds, making Claire anxious to get to the evil place and discover evidence of foul dealings.

As high noon approached, the desert began to heat up. Heat waves rolled along the desert floor like ocean swells, and the soles of her feet began to burn. Soon she came to a shady spot under a clump of yuccas and rested for a few moments.

After another ten minutes the nature of the isolated wasteland began to change. Blackness covered the parched earth, coal dust that was testament to mining days when the hills were populated by fast-talking snake oil salesmen who preyed on the coughing denizens who went underground clean-faced at the break of day and came out soot-ridden and spitting as coyotes howled at the moon.

As a child, Claire had heard about those days from nearly everyone she'd known in northern Aztlan, especially when late-night conversations turned to stories of witches, curses, and murders. The magic arts were said to have been a favorite pastime of folks in this area a hundred years back, many a man trading his soul to the devil for a curse to gain power over his enemies. Bodies were found with rib bones broken out of the chest cavity and arranged in weird patterns around the head. It was the devil's way of claiming his own, towns-folk said.

Claire squinted hard and spotted something about a hundred yards away. There, in the middle of a mesa blockaded by a few sandstone hills with a series of caves carved into them, stood a desert altar. She had heard legends about such a place—back country caves where demons dwelt and appeared as giant blackbirds that would attack anyone who dared enter their domain. She jogged toward the stone edifice, knowing she had finally reached the place she had been looking for, the place that would prove Archbishop Anarch's evil deeds. Finally, she could remove evil's mask to expose the truth.

Two crows were perched on the altar. She ran straight toward them, hands ready to grab them, but they flew away. Claire slammed her fists on the altar's wind-blasted top, then raised them to the sky and yelled with rage and grief for those whose lives had been cut short for having trusted a corrupt illusion of the spiritual dimension.

Her yelling was soon joined by the screaming of a multitude of medicine women warriors of the past—Lozen, Gouyen, Dahteste, and dozens of others. The earth quaked as she walked toward the surrounding caves, their black mouths gaping. She entered the first of what appeared to be six caves, which was eerie but empty. The others were the same.

Puzzled by their emptiness, Claire walked back toward the altar, where she noticed stray pieces of wind-ripped scrub oak and other desert debris clustered in the center of the six caves. Then it dawned on her that there was a seventh cave, one so well camouflaged that it blended into the surrounding sandstone formations.

Her breaths were short, quick. Energy went up from her lower spine to the center of her forehead. As she walked forward, her second sight opened, and she saw herself in the mouth of the seventh cave, which exuded a stench of human blood and rotting flesh.

She heard a voice whispering, *Land of the forsaken, land of the lost... bring her to me... Claire.*

As she ran forward, out of nowhere the two crows flew at her, scraping the air near her face with their sharp talons. Fists clenched, she struck out at one and grabbed at the other. They flew up, circled overhead, then dove, talons flaring. Unmoving, Claire placed her hands by her side and held their gaze. They fluttered above her head for a minute, then left. Claire turned and saw an eagle soaring—a healer's spirit manifestation. Medicine women said it came only when needed, when danger lurked.

Frantically tugging away bush, bramble, and cacti, she

uncovered the mouth of the seventh cave and stepped in. She had the feeling somebody was watching.

Her eyes adjusted and she made out the contour of something. Squinting, she stooped and touched what seemed to be a circle of stones and charred, cold logs. She stood up and pulled back. A bat flew at her. She waved it away.

She stopped, waited for her breathing to slow, and, stepping sideways, touched the walls of the cave. They were damp and the stink of blood and guts was everywhere. Using the hard surfaces as a guide, her fingertips suddenly brushed through a hollow space roughly the size of a human body.

14

Archbishop Anarch, I'm Chief Ortiz of the State Police. I'd appreciate a few moments of your time," said the officer.

Archbishop Anarch was in the cherry-paneled sacristy, facing a wall-to-wall dressing credenza into which his solemn-faced assistant carefully placed each individual garment the archbishop was removing. The large mirror in the center gave the archbishop a full view of the room.

Chief Ortiz had been led into the sacristy by a pimply faced altar boy who was now scurrying off. Archbishop Anarch's displeasure permeated the atmosphere like the stench of cow manure on an otherwise crystal-clear morning. An interminable silence hung in the air, radiating a tension somewhat like that produced by walking barefoot on broken glass.

Sighing, Archbishop Anarch slipped off the last vestment and asked in a disgusted tone, "Have you no respect?" Chief Ortiz didn't answer, trying to contain his immediate dislike for the man.

"You're not a religious man, I take it?" Archbishop Anarch asked, wheeling around, and boring into Chief Ortiz with cold blue eyes.

"No need for it," Chief Ortiz answered flatly, holding the archbishop's gaze. "Now I have some questions for you."

"I'm a busy man, Chief," Archbishop Anarch said, starting to leave. "I have an officer outside who would be glad to escort you to my office if you'd prefer to talk there," replied Chief Ortiz.

"Is it that important?" asked the archbishop.

"Here or there?" asked Chief Ortiz, becoming impatient.

Finally, Archbishop Anarch went to the end of the long, dimly lit hallway and opened one of the double doors, waving Chief Ortiz forward as if he were a minion. Dimly lit hallways lined with closets made Chief Ortiz uncomfortable, especially when investigating murders. He had been down one too many in his law enforcement career. The fact that it was a church didn't make a difference. An old uncle had always told him that men of the cloth weren't to be trusted, that priests came from the runts or rascals of families and were often useless, cagey, or self-seeking.

"We can't talk across the hall, Chief. Come on," said Archbishop Anarch, waving Chief Ortiz forward.

Chief Ortiz, still uneasy, began questioning him, "There's been a couple of murders. We need to talk. We'll talk down here," said Ortiz, remaining at the farthest end of the corridor, where large windows and a sliding glass door opened to a brick-lined patio.

Archbishop Anarch stiffened and walked back toward Chief Ortiz, stopping partway down the hall. "Murders?" he asked. His raised eyebrows weren't convincing.

"Out here, Archbishop," directed Chief Ortiz as he stepped outside to the center of the large patio. Off to the side, atop a lone branch on a lightning-charred tree trunk, a large crow was perched. Chief Ortiz noticed that the drifting mountain breezes did not cause it to move, and its gaze remained unflinchingly directed toward the police chief.

Archbishop Anarch approached, looking every bit the self-assured, composed cleric. Except for the most minuscule quiver of his right upper lip, nothing betrayed the tension that consumed him, but Chief Ortiz felt it. He had learned to take the measure of a man—his life, at times, literally depending on it.

"Two people were brutally murdered before dawn," Chief Ortiz said. "One was a hospital employee, the other the stepmother of Ms. Claire Sanchez, director of natural therapy and mental health for the hospital. Ms. Sanchez and I have served together on the governor's mental health board."

"I'm shocked. Two of our employees, killed?" replied Archbishop Anarch. The archbishop blessed himself, closing his eyes as his lips moved with whispered prayers. After a few moments, he reverentially stopped, slowly opened his eyes, and asked in a silky smooth voice, "And you've made a special trip to inform me of our loss. How kind." He had a look of feigned gratitude.

Chief Ortiz wanted to be done with this slick, seedy man. There was nothing quite like the feeling of emotional grime that came with standing in the presence of a compromised man.

"I'll make sure to mention them in my prayers tonight. Thank you for coming, Chief. Anything we can do to help, just let us know," said Archbishop Anarch, moving toward the sliding door and motioning Ortiz out.

"Not so quickly, Your Highness," Chief Ortiz replied sarcastically. "Excellency is the proper ecclesiastical designation," Anarch retorted, head held high, gaze officious.

"I have some questions for you," Chief Ortiz insisted.

Chief Ortiz felt the hair on his arm curl. He didn't like being alone with the archbishop, not for concern about potential physical harm—the archbishop was no match for him—but because the archbishop's mind was as dangerous as any he had ever encountered, including those of the criminally insane. He could get people to think and act in any way just by looking at them. He could talk people dizzy with half-truths made to look like whole truths. It was by what he left out more than what he said that he did his conjuring. And obviously he was on to Chief Ortiz. Psychopathic minds picked up on everything—details, shifts of mood, alterations of attitude. Quicker than a rabid coyote attacking its prey, a psychopath pounced, tore into, and devoured, without warning, without conscience.

Chief Ortiz looked Archbishop Anarch straight in the eye and asked, "Have you heard of a place called the Devil's Throne?"

Anarch laughed and replied, "You came here to ask me about a silly superstition?"

"You've heard of it?" Chief Ortiz continued.

"I've been in Aztlan a long time. Myths and legends abound. If memory serves, it's reputedly the seat of Satan," remarked the archbishop.

Chief Ortiz persisted, "Ever drive out there?"

Archbishop Anarch sighed condescendingly and asked, "What does this have to with the murders, might I ask?"

"A black Mercedes has been seen numerous times in the area. Over the years, it's been the spot of police investigations into human sacrifice and cult activity," replied Chief Ortiz.

"There are a lot of black Mercedes's in Aztlan, Chief," responded the archbishop.

"The night of the most recent death of a hospital patient, I spotted a black Mercedes going over a hundred miles an hour. I tried to follow it, but it was way ahead of me then turned off-road near the Devil's Throne. I lost it. And a black Mercedes may have been spotted this morning near the most recent crime scene about the time the murders would've happened," continued Chief Ortiz. He paused then asked, "Does the Ecclesia Dei have a black Mercedes, Archbishop?"

Archbishop Anarch didn't answer.

"Ever been to the Devil's Throne, archbishop?" Chief Ortiz persisted.

Archbishop Anarch twisted his head slightly, looking at Chief Ortiz through the corner of his eye, then answered sharply, "No."

Hearing someone clear their throat from behind the sliding door, Archbishop Anarch, concerned that their conversation had been overheard, turned to look behind him, the smiled and said, "Father Gall, join us."

The priest bowed his head, came in, and whispered something in the archbishop's ear.

Archbishop Anarch lost his color and asked aloud, "When?"

"Early this morning, Excellency," replied Father Gall.

Archbishop Anarch turned to Chief Ortiz with a troubled look on his face and announced, "My mother is ill. A stroke, the doctors say. I need to be by her side."

"You must leave, Chief. You bring bad with you." The arrogant man of moments ago was reduced, withered.

Chief Ortiz held the archbishop's gaze and said, "We'll talk more when you return."

"Archbishop, the Mercedes is waiting to take you to your private plane," Father Gall stated.

The archbishop left, hoping his future held rapid liberation, that he would never have to encounter Chief Ortiz's questioning again, that Claire would promptly be out of the picture, killed so the medicine women were obliterated, and that this would be his final meeting with his mother.

15

Anthony remembered passing out, coming to outside his studio where he'd been dragged, and being punctured with a needle. He was bound and gagged, having been thrown like a side of beef into the back of a van. Despite his lack of mobility, he desperately tried to keep his mind clear because of his pressing need to protect Claire, to stop what seemed like a slide into a realm of danger and destruction from which there would be no return.

Voices came from behind the grated window separating the front seats from the cargo area. He strained to hear the conversation but could only make out the words. "Easy enough... the drug will keep him out."

A gray mist fogged Anthony's eyesight. Fear rose in him, not for himself but for Claire. He knew if it weren't for the drug, he could snap out of the ropes binding him and kick the back door out. He needed to get to her, but his eyelids were becoming heavier and heavier. He tried to whisper Claire's name but couldn't move his lips, and soon consciousness slipped away.

⚡⚡⚡

Claire waited by her car, which she had now parked in the shadow of the Devil's Throne in a location visible from the Turquoise Trail. The sun was high overhead, and the throne cast an ominous shadow across the desert floor as though it came from someone holding a pickax. Despite the blood-curdling effect of its darkly majestic presence, Claire preferred to stand as near to it as possible because she had been taught by the medicine women that one is always best advised to remain conscious of the potential of darkness, to take in its scope, so as to have clarity in the midst of the obscurity that evil deems its hiding ground.

An hour earlier she had driven to a gas station in the middle of nowhere, where she used a pay phone to call Chief Ortiz. He had just walked into his office from having seen Archbishop Anarch, and after what Claire told him said he'd meet her at the Devil's Throne right away and bring some other men with him. She had also tried calling Anthony, with no luck. After a while, she saw two police cars approaching, slowing down as they spotted the hulking red rock. The white vehicles went off-road through waves of desert heat, the glare of the sun off glass and chrome making them disappear now and then. It was as though they were driving in slow motion when their trail of dust was abruptly whipped up by a harsh wind into funnel clouds that seemed targeted right at them.

Claire drummed her fingers on the hood of the car, hoping the vehicles would hurry as her anxiety felt like a circling pack of ravenous coyotes. A few seconds later the cars swerved here and there through a sandstorm until they cut out of it like machetes through brush. Claire pointed her thumbs up as they drove to where she was parked.

Chief Ortiz stepped out of the first car, looked at her, and commented, "Thought that dust storm was going to blow us away." His tough, gravelly voice matched his sturdy, five-foot-ten, middle-aged frame.

Claire went up to him and said, "Thanks for coming. We're gonna have to walk from here. There's no other way. It's a good two miles or more into the desert."

"We could drive in. There's an obscure road that'll take us, if I can find it again. It's the one the archbishop uses. It loops around from the back. But by the time we figure out where it is, we probably coulda walked there and back a couple of times," said Chief Ortiz.

He took a deep breath, his barrel chest expanding, then slapped his hands together, and ordered, "Everybody out. Time for a little trek through hell."

"It's this way," Claire pointed, starting to walk.

They walked at a fast clip, as she briefed him on the history behind her investigation into the archbishop and the Ecclesia Dei.

"You should have called me earlier," Chief Ortiz said after listening to the whole story.

"And tell you what?" Claire asked.

"Your suspicions," he replied.

"I had nothing firm to go on until now," answered Claire.

Minutes later, as Ortiz looked up at the sheer walls of a narrow canyon, he snorted. Dark clouds bundled together and blocked out the sun, the high sandstone canyon looking like a black chute into a malevolent underworld. "Let's sit a minute," suggested Ortiz as he got his handkerchief out again and wiped his heavily beaded forehead. Claire remained standing as the men all sat on the nearest low, flat boulder.

"Ever felt anything like this, boys?" Chief Ortiz asked.

Claire knew the place was permeated with psychic energy.

The men shook their heads no.

"I have once, not too far from here while investigating a missing person's case about twenty years ago when I was a young lieutenant," Chief Ortiz said, surprising Claire. Aware that few people were sensitive enough to pick up the vibrations that could be tuned in to the way an audio receiver picks up radio waves, she was glad he had told her that.

Wind whistled through the canyon, blowing man-sized tumbleweeds through. They grazed the sandstones sides, smoke curling from their edges, then passed out the ages-old fissure and burst into flames, looking like devils dancing as they went across the shadowy landscape.

Ortiz stood up, cocked his arms at his sides, and asked his men, "Your grandmothers ever tell you about *el diablo*?" Their eyes became wide, their faces pale. "The devil's real, and we're trespassing on his property. He just told us to get out and never come back, or else," continued Chief Ortiz.

"Or else what, Chief?" asked the youngest officer, a little weak-kneed as he got up.

"We'll have to see, won't we?" Chief Ortiz replied, drawing a deep breath. As they resumed their trek, he and Claire walked together, the other men some ways behind. Near the canyon's end they saw an expanse of gloomy terrain with puffs of sand crisscrossing maniacally across it and into the horizon, as though rushing to a secret haunt.

"Bad spirits," Claire commented, her eyes surveying the dark landscape.

"You believe in that stuff?" Chief Ortiz asked.

"The wind isn't letting up," was all she said.

Claire walked past the canyon mouth and stepped out into what had been a raging windstorm just as everything lulled to a hush.

Suddenly the sun came out, and a dazzling sweep of blue arched overhead. One after the other they cleared their throats, spit, and wiped their lips and nostrils free of grime. Then they started walking again, briskly.

A bad smell came up, making everyone cough and try to block it out by covering their noses with their hands as the odor hovered around them like flies in a manure patch. "It's the smell of the dead. Evil leaves a stench," Claire commented. They were all wide-eyed. "Psychic rot. Rotted flesh, spilled blood," Claire emphasized.

"You've smelled it before?" Chief Ortiz asked.

"It's in the corridors of the Ecclesia Dei. Incense covers it up," she replied. The four officers stood stone still.

"The closer we get, the worse it'll be," warned Claire, staring off in the direction they had to go. She grew quiet, hearing something like the far-off rumble of a stampede.

After a while, she said, "Gonna have to be careful. We passed through hell's gate when we set foot on this land. Something's coming our way, and I'm not sure what it is. Different rules apply here. Keep listening to me and do what I say."

Claire stepped off the trail and listened again. Then she turned, looked each one in the eye, and advised, "Evil works through thoughts. Keep a good attitude. Don't let fear in."

"Nothing can happen that this baby can't handle," Chief Ortiz said, patting the gun in his hip holster.

Minutes later Chief Ortiz, obviously tired, asked, "From what you told me on the phone it shouldn't be too far off now?"

"Time and distance can be deceptive out here," Claire stressed.

Straight ahead there was nothing but dirt and sky and heat waves rolling over the ground.

"I need to stop and drink some water," one of the men said anxiously, coughing, his throat rattling, dry as desert dirt.

Claire heard fear in his voice.

"Just take a sip from your canteens. Conserve your water. No telling how long we'll be out here," ordered Ortiz as he unhooked his canteen from his thick leather belt and opened it.

Claire opened hers, wet her lips and tongue a little, and waited for them to catch their breath.

A couple of the men started to groan. The sun glared harshly on the desert floor like light off a mirror. The hike in the strong sun was taking its toll, making a bad situation worse. Claire felt a bit light-headed and weak-kneed herself.

A little later one of the officers cried out, "What the hell is that?" as they had come up to a group of small hills. A couple of buzzards stretched out their wings tip to tip, appearing as one unearthly raptor eyeing its prey.

The officer drew his gun.

Chief Ortiz broke in, "There's no cause for that. It's just a couple of funeral directors prospecting for business." He laughed uneasily.

A curious twilight was falling over the isolated mesas as thunderheads rolled rapidly over the mountain ranges, the men commenting about how the desert looked like a no-man's-land in a bad dream.

"We should be able to see the altar after that next bend," Claire said, pointing to a grouping of boulders in the distance.

Finally, they reached the boulders that marked the entrance to where the ritual sacrifices had been performed. A sense of ominousness pervaded the spot. Hordes of huge black crows dropped out the sky quick as a cloudburst and surrounded Chief Ortiz and his men.

Claire called out, "Don't look at them. Get over here by me."

No one responded. They had been sucked into the spell of the black guardians, minds numbed by shock at the suddenness of the occurrence.

Francesca had always said, "Force is the antidote to lethargy."

Now was the time to test it, Claire realized. She went up to the men, screamed, "Look at me!" then slapped each one.

Jerking back to awareness like puppets on strings, they fixed their eyes on Claire and shook their heads in disbelief.

"They're the guardians of the altar, black birds of despair. They do to the soul what spikes do to tires," explained Claire. She was relieved that the awakening, Aztlan style, had worked. Bewitchment set loose a despair that could make the hardiest soul want to lay down and die.

"Let's get to the cave, take care of business, and hightail it back home," Claire said, walking briskly, hoping their spirits stayed buoyed. The sun had returned and shadows cast themselves on a nearby mesa like grotesque gargoyles hunched over and asleep.

Soon Claire pointed and said, "Those are the hills with the caves. You'll see the altar once we're closer. It's hidden in the shadows now."

The next second Claire's breath caught in her throat as two crisp rifle shots hummed through the air. Everyone dropped to the ground. From the corner of her eye, Claire saw that blood was pooling around the heads of two of the officers. *Went past me for them. Wants me alone,* she thought.

Chief Ortiz was on the ground directly behind Claire, his

pistol drawn and aimed upward.

Claire's heart beat like a stampede of wild horses. They were both sitting ducks out here, and at this distance Chief Ortiz's pistol was no better than a pea shooter used to down a wild boar.

"He's up there," said Chief Ortiz, pointing up ahead with his gun barrel. "Faraway but close enough to get us."

Officer Yellowhorse streaked across Claire's mind, and she asked, "Is it Yellowhorse?"

"Could be, from what you told me… lots of kill-for-god psychos on the loose," replied Chief Ortiz.

Claire knew that sometimes people came out here and were never heard from again—assumed to have died from exhaustion, dehydration, or worse. "If he kills us, this varmint-infested desert will clean up after him," Ortiz said, as if he'd heard her thoughts.

"I'm sure it's him," Claire said, rising to her knees.

"Get down," Ortiz said, groaning.

Without responding, she crawled to the two officers and found they'd each been shot through the back of the head so that the bullet went out between their eyes. Then she heard another bullet whistling through the air. In front of her Claire saw Chief Ortiz, face to the ground, blood and gray matter spewing out the back of his head.

16

rchbishop Anarch's flight to the southeastern Aztlan home of his childhood had ended in a blink. His mind had been obsessed with thoughts of his mother and the way in which she had molded him during his childhood. There was no doubt that he was his mother's son. And this, he knew, was not good.

After landing at his mother's private airstrip, he had been picked up and taken to the family estate. The chauffeur had said that his mother had come out of the coma, taking a turn for the better. He felt sick at the thought, for it meant that the bond between them would remain, at least for a while, tight and thick when he wanted freedom from her chastisement and tyrannical ways. She was like a steamroller ready to crush, grind down, and destroy. It was time for it to be over. He knew his mother would be deathbed ornery. Her resolve was second only to his own. Life meant everything to her because in life she could control him, her psychic plaything.

But nothing in heaven or on earth would stand between him and that for which he had sacrificed everything: the fulfillment of his vow to obliterate medicine women and assume the office of patriarch. Dealing with his mother was just part of his path to freedom and more power. His time had come. And his mother's time and the medicine woman's time were over.

Tingles went up his spine, which meant that his wish would be granted. It always worked that way—the tingling as a message from the Great Beyond to the mortal great Archbishop Anarch. He had no reason to think otherwise. After all, Officer Yellowhorse had never failed to do what Archbishop Anarch commanded. Father Gall never fell short. Hosts of mortals did his bidding. No one suspected the secret violence that stormed within him. He loved it! Confident and grinning, he got out of the Mercedes and leaned against the cold, black metal. It was nearing evening, the air chilly. Acres and acres of gray, grim Aztlan flatlands appeared deserted. Everybody around here, wetbacks, feared him, their eyes bulging whenever he walked through the garage or kitchen or laundry. It gave him a rush. The bosomy *mamacitas*, he thought, should make penance for stirring his manhood in an unholy way.

Closed-door priest talk with Father Gall had made it clear to him that hooking a piece of their Grade A brown meat would do them a favor. It would be the closest the dirt-skinned fools would ever get to heaven. After all, the archbishop was the intermediary of salvation, and he never failed or hesitated to insist that lowly ones take what they were offered and be grateful for the opportunity. Cain's cousins of the desert Southwest, they weren't bound for paradise—maybe some bean picking in the sweet bye and bye, but not the sacred sanctuary of the pure and the white. They couldn't possibly fathom the totality of the idea in their tiny brown brains that heaven was ruled by a white deity. A modern-day slave wiggling on his celestial pole would suit Archbishop

Anarch just fine, especially since it would be his mother's property. There were a few things to take care of, and then he would reward himself. He had mighty stirrings at the thought of a little post–mother-son jubilation. The best part of such shenanigans was that none of it constituted sin. Moral theology made the distinction between private and public conscience. Sin for one person was not necessarily sin for another. And priests did have human needs, those meant by the Almighty to be satisfied with already soiled fleshpots.

His mother, like all the rich and white true believers, didn't really care what priests did as long as they did it secretly and were never caught. It was the getting caught that brought scandal and could spell the end of their religious office. At the same time, she had always told him that he should live his life as if it were an open book, which meant keeping two sets of books. When she said to be faithful, it meant boys will be boys and I don't want to hear about it and I don't want anyone else hearing about it either. She let him know that he had to be true to what she had taught him so that she would never be embarrassed in front of her friends and he would never lose his inheritance.

It was uncanny how his mother saw right through him and, because of his philandering, made him feel under her thumb and cringe with a kind of mother-son how-could-you-be-untrue-to-me guilt. No amount of behind-the-scenes priest talk with Father Gall or any other high-ranking cleric could absolve Archbishop Anarch's pangs of conscience forever thinking of any woman other than his mother, whose manipulative behavior was coldly calculated. But once she was dead, things would be different. He would no longer have a mother who scouted out and zeroed in on every entry in his personal ledger.

He walked toward the mansion, contemplating his mother's death and his freedom. His head began to hurt directly between the eyes, where an image of his mother flared like a flaming rocket, and at the base of his skull, where sharp red nails clawed. The doctors had always said that his headaches were due to strain because he had too much on his mind. But he knew they were linked to his mother's abusive accusations and manipulations. Staying strong, composed, he kept walking.

The house now looked huge, hungry, evil. The winding porch seemed like a big black mouth with red lips opened wide. He forced one foot in front of the other, knowing that strange things always happened when he was home. Confusion, like crazed bugs fluttering in his head, usually stopped if he told himself that things would be okay in the end, and he did this now. But blackness like a starless night sky fell over him. Flashes of sharp white lightning bolts flew out of the corners of his eyes. Pinpricks jabbed behind eyeballs. Dropping to his knees by the side of the house where no one could see him, he hit his head with the heels of his hands, knowing that sometimes body pain made mind pain stop. Rocking back and forth now, hunched over and clutching his knees, he groaned. Palms pressed against his temples like a vice on steel, he pushed hard, the way he'd done as a kid when the headaches and the zigzag lights and the red-hot lap rocket had made his mind crackle and smolder like tin foil in an oven.

Then came the sad, mad voices, saying: *Shoulda killed her already already already already. Shoulda killed her already. Bad bad bad to hell to hell bad. Shoulda killed her already.*

His skull pain pounding like a hammer in a steel drum, shooting sparks of reds and yellows and greens through the midnight black canvas of his mind, made him feel like a fetus writhing in the womb of a dead woman. Then his spirit took leave of his flesh, as had happened so often before, just as it had for other men of the Almighty who had been sent on similar missions.

The first time he had experienced bilocation, he had gone to a twenty-five-year-old woman. That night she had seduced his most recent ordainee, Father Albert—a twenty-six-year-old priest, whom Archbishop Anarch had considered a son. Days later, when Archbishop Anarch returned to Aztlan from an apostolic visit to a mission in Mexico, Father Gall told him that Father Albert had been found dead, castrated in the arms of a loose woman, Juanita Dominguez. To this day, Juanita ranted and raved up in the psychiatric hospital's locked ward for the criminally insane, crying out about a black beast, the left hand of the Almighty, that had reached into her lover's chest and squeezed his heart until it had stopped, then sliced off her lover's member and presented it to her with the words "Behold, cunt, the cock." Then the beast dipped his hand into her head and twisted her brains. Now she scarcely ever slept and, if given the chance, would cut at her breasts with the razor she claimed the beast provided as a means of atoning for the most grievous of sins, causing a priest to fall from grace.

This time as the archbishop's spirit took leave of his flesh, it soared over mesas and mountains to the place where it could find Claire Sanchez and deal with her.

17

Anthony's heart tightened as he awakened and saw gray concrete block stretched fifteen feet high and floor-to-ceiling jail bars locking him in. He was strapped to a wooden table in a medieval-like dungeon that was frigid as an ice box and cluttered with antique torture devices—a machine used to stretch a man limb from limb, iron pokers meant to be heated white hot and burn flesh, and, in the middle of the room, a body-sized metal table with leather wrist and ankle straps.

In colonized Aztlan, the Spanish Inquisition had tortured numerous Indians and local settlers for the sake of the cross and the crown, and been directly responsible for wanton killings. Charges were heresy, immorality, and unholy religious practices of indigenous people, ranging from the pueblos of Isleta, Sandía, Cochiti, and Santo Domingo to the furthest reaches of Aztlan. This dark marriage of the church and the crown had led to horrific displays of power, such as when Acoma Pueblo males over twenty-five years of age had suffered the amputation of one foot and, along with males twelve to twenty-five, all females had been forced into twenty years of servitude. Ghosts of the long gone breathed through the dank chambers now preserved by the Ecclesia Dei.

Chills crept through him like frenzied fire ants. Nauseated and achy, he couldn't budge. The leather straps were tight, and he was weak. He thought of Claire, knowing she had to be in danger, but all he could do was remain still so his body could fight off the poisons it had absorbed. Hopefully, he'd soon regain his strength.

A door slammed. The thud came from the top of wrought-iron stairs that led up and out. Anthony closed his eyes and feigned sleep while he strained to listen. The door at the top creaked open, and someone called out in a tough voice, "If he is not awake, wait." Anthony heard the door close and the shuffle of leather flats on steel, like the shoes worn by brown-robed monks near the plaza.

A black-hooded figure approached his cell with six-foot-long chains hanging from each hand. Cowled by shadows and cloth, he was faceless.

Anthony became increasingly worried not for himself but for Claire. The maleficent dark being seemed capable of inflicting any manner of cruelty and prolonged torture. The footsteps finally stopped, as chains dropped to the cement floor. Eyes closed, Anthony waited.

18

A pair of eyes peeked over the edge of the barely discernible arroyo. "Pssst. Over here to the arroyo," the youngest of the officers called out to Claire. "Stay low. Crawl."

Three dead bodies provided some camouflage for the lone killer, his rifle still reflecting glints of sunlight from over the distant hilltop. Claire pictured him perched there, his telescopic sighting perfectly adjusted, waiting to plug her between the eyes. Only ten yards away, the long arroyo might as well have been in another world. The gunman could get Claire anywhere along the way. Fingers digging into dirt, knees scraping against sandstone shards and broken off cacti, Claire crawled toward the arroyo, hoping the assassin couldn't get the angle he needed.

Once at the edge of the arroyo, she rolled on her side and slid into the crevice. Spitting out dirt and wiping her brow and eyes free of grit, Claire looked into the youthful face crouched beside her.

"When that first shot was fired, I dove for cover, ending up down here," he said.

"Everybody's dead but us," Claire said, swallowing hard. "Any ideas?" He was wide-eyed with a trembling lower lip.

Clarity slowly came to Claire like quiet after a storm. "He can't see us down here. My guess is that he'll figure we're running back to the cars and that's where he'll go," she said.

"And if not?" asked the officer.

Claire didn't answer.

She walked a ways through the narrow arroyo, kicking bramble and debris out of the way, thinking. Then she came back and said, "Looks like this arroyo goes up pretty close to the caves."

He shook his head, understanding what she was driving at. "Still wanna go for it, huh?" he said.

"That's why we came out. Let's wait a few minutes before starting off, to make sure he doesn't see movement out here," Claire replied.

Five minutes later, she heard rumbling in the distance. Catching a foothold on a piece of granite jutting out from the arroyo's side, Claire looked in the direction of the rumbling. A trail of dust spread out from somewhere behind the hills and curved toward what Claire guessed was a confusing mess of back roads.

"He's gone. Let's go," she said, propelling herself out of the arroyo before the young man answered.

"Wait," he called out, sounding distressed.

"What is it?" Claire asked, already a little ways off.

When he didn't answer, she turned around, only to see a gun inches from her forehead.

19

You gonna shoot me?" Claire asked in a derisive tone. She hated the son-of-a-bitch for setting her up and was pissed that she hadn't seen through him. She wasn't about to die at this point.

Despite the fact that he now wore a black suit and gun, she wasn't scared. She didn't fear men dressed in black anymore.

"You gonna shoot me or not?" she demanded again. Then she added,

"'Cuz if you don't, I'm outta here."

He laughed and said, "I'd shoot you, but..." He stopped short, not wanting to say anything more.

Claire had visions of Archbishop Anarch directing that nothing go wrong, that no one go near the cave, that Claire be taken alive and uninjured so as not to ruin his sacrifice and blood-fest, that this runt avoid killing or he would be filleted alive himself.

Meanness was written all over the guy's snarling face. He had it in him to pull the trigger, without blinking an eye. But the archbishop wouldn't tolerate it.

Heat from the center of Claire's chest and forehead began to rise. She was perfectly collected, eyes welded on the gunman. Stroking the bottom of its pearly handle with grimy fourth and fifth fingers, his trigger finger seemed itchy to end her life.

Concentrating, Claire sensed the heat becoming a bright white-hot that was matched only by the intensity of the blazing afternoon sun. The perfectly polished stainless-steel gun seemed to absorb sunlight like a magnifying glass, beginning to glow as in a forge. Beads of perspiration formed on Claire's brow. She remained silent and motionless, her gaze riveted on the gun.

Nervous, uncertain about what was happening, the gunman shifted his eyes back and forth from the gun handle to Claire. Relaxing then tightening the grip a couple of times, he squinted. Sweat rolled into his eyes. He didn't wipe it away since doing so would have made him appear weak. His shooting hand trembled a little.

Claire concentrated even harder.

He moved his feet, gripping and re-gripping the gun handle. Sweat rolled down his temples and cheeks.

Wildfire from the center of Claire's being became visible, jumping right where she told it to.

"Son of a bitch," said the guy, jerking three feet back and dropping the gun.

Quick as a bolt of high desert lightning, Claire slammed her right foot into his groin. His howl could have been heard throughout northern Aztlan. From the corner of her eye, she saw the guy bend over in pain, falling backward into the arroyo.

Claire grabbed the gun, cool to the touch, threw it farther than the sun-strained eye could see, and left him squirming, then ran off through the desert like a wolf set on course. Running with ease and speed, Claire spotted a trail of dust. The lone van from near the cave was winding toward the downed officer. Its driver had probably been hiding, waiting on a secluded ridge, needle in hand.

The driver wouldn't have a chance of following her through these boulder-strewn badlands, as it was impassable terrain for a car. By the time she'd get to her vehicle, the young officer would be barely limping the quarter mile to the location of the driver. The road was a good four miles from the highway. Claire could beat them there.

Father Gall's name rang through Claire's head like Angelus bells in the plaza, and she realized he was probably the one driving the van. She'd like to deal with him the way she had dealt with the young officer, but Archbishop Anarch was her biggest concern.

She continued running as though flying, intent on getting back and breaking the news to the *Aztlan Crier*. The editor-in-chief, known for a hard-hitting, nonpartisan style, would jump on this case, exposing Archbishop Anarch's wheeling and dealing, plotting and conniving. She had to expose the hard evidence she had discovered in the cave, aware of its significance. She knew that corpses instantly captured the media's attention. The press would have a field day with the body, which was identifiable despite lacerations to both carotids, a double mastectomy, and vaginal gashing.

Archbishop Anarch had left her face intact while excising what he considered evil, sinful. The victim was a member of the Ecclesia Dei and a recently deceased patient of the Ecclesia Dei Psychiatric Hospital. Swallowing hard, Claire momentarily stopped running while traversing a narrow canyon, overwhelmed by grief and rage at the thought of the mutilated corpse of her patient Elizabeth.

Suddenly, a high-pitched whistling pierced the air, sounding like a screaming child. Looking in the direction of the caves, Claire saw swirling dust clouds resembling small tornadoes headed her way. She tried to run again but had pinpricks of pain shooting from groin to lungs, possibly from dehydration, exhaustion, or heat stroke she thought.

Whipping winds tore through the canyon, spitting dirt at her; then, as if caused by some quickly moving phantom, the ear-splitting whistling ceased. She felt a cunning presence lurking in the stillness, taunting her. Atoms split, sparks of light moving outward from an undefined center of whirling energy and coalescing into the shape of an ominous being.

Crouching on the ground, her head spinning and eyes aching from the dazzling display of electricity, Claire watched as a hole opened in the dirt directly below where the display had been. Black smoke trailed out of the hole like an antediluvian serpent. Gagging from a smell of raw eggs and sulfur, she cupped her hands over her mouth and waited.

She felt no fear but thought that desert energy was playing havoc with her mind, which had already been stressed by the unrelenting sun, evidence of cold-blooded murder, and the necessity to outmaneuver a maniac intent on killing her. Stink and smoke spread to infect the land. Then the contamination was blown away by a breeze, refreshing the atmosphere and lending a seductive tranquility to what she felt was a lurking subterranean terror.

On edge, Claire heard a voice say tauntingly, "Be afraid, little Claire."

Claire turned in the direction of the voice that sounded like Archbishop Anarch in a twenty-foot-high pulpit staring down on her. She saw nothing but knew that even if the voice were only some kind of badland auditory illusion due to dehydration or exhaustion, it was a reminder that Archbishop Anarch was, in fact, on the prowl, determined to kill her. She further realized that Archbishop Anarch's spirit could have left his body with the aim of causing her harm, something black magicians often did. This was a practice medicine women also employed but only for protection in times of crisis. Adepts in black magic, however, bilocated especially when they had lost their mental equilibrium, like a house with electrical wiring shorting out, causing crackling and flying sparks. Claire realized that Archbishop Anarch's mind must have snapped and, if so, he was desperate and deadly.

"Over heeeeeeere, Claire," the voice now called.

Archbishop Anarch's voice bounced from one spot to another, an evil trickster playing hide and seek.

Gritting her teeth, Claire tried not to react emotionally or think too much, not wanting to give him an edge or allow him to read her mind. She knew that bad spirits did bad things when not bound by earthly limitations. Psychologically troubled people or scoffers at the supernatural were a favorite prey. Unsuspecting people could die in their sleep, eyes open, mouths agape with horror. It was best not to deny the energy operating in such a way, Claire had told her patients. Now, she was face to face with it herself. If Archbishop Anarch was in such a state, he could conjure the power to step inside her soul, bang around her mind, or even make her heart stop, causing her enormous harm or death.

Memories of how she had seen Lucia battered and killed in the forest flooded her mind. She wasn't going to let that happen to her. Then an image of gray wolves suddenly appeared in her mind. With her renewed determination, power shot through her, catapulting her body into motion.

20

rchbishop Anarch opened his eyes, head groggy as from a bad dream. He was flat on the ground, grit cutting into his cheek, nerves tingling fingertips to toes. Women were loathsome—the thought hummed through his mind in high C, as if ready to shatter glass. Claire Sanchez had escaped, and that meant he had to physically do what he could otherwise have done psychically with dream hate.

The process was the reverse of the way husbands and wives and closest friends could be in each other's dreams and wake up feeling better and loved; but instead, feelings of hate were used to hurt or kill others. He had intended to kill Claire this way with a fatal injection of fright, causing her heart to stop when he materialized before her sun-weary eyes as a play of light and shadow. He had believed that because of her weakened condition—due to desert heat, grief over finding Elizabeth's body, self-doubt and terror from the killing of her comrades, assault by the young officer shoving the pistol in her face, and finally experiencing his own voice and apparition—Claire Sanchez's mind would disintegrate like the brittle bones of a dead prairie dog in the desert. Then his spirit hand could have entered her mouth smooth as a knife through butter, gone down her throat, then twisted and pulled her esophagus and entrails up and out like fish guts. To others, it would have seemed like a young woman had been lost in the Aztlan desert, hallucinating then dying from dehydration, convulsive fits, or both.

Writhing in the sand, Claire Sanchez would have seen a gentleman who, weeks earlier, had stopped and offered a helping hand during a rainstorm as he had checked out a potential sacrificial offering to assure the best for the Almighty. An acute cardiac hemorrhage would have left Claire Sanchez's choice morsels and tangy blood fresh for the Almighty, stored in the cave until his return to Aztlan in the evening, when he would have offered her succulent flesh to the Almighty with no one the wiser and him a free man.

But now that Claire Sanchez had escaped, he was at risk. He feared she was going to discover a talisman that he hoped either no longer existed or she would never find. First, however, he needed to be at his mother's bedside, to send her to paradise. He knew that her death would finally sever their bond and allow him to retrieve what she had in her keeping. It was only right to get back what was his, for what soon would be required of him demanded that he have the totality of his inborn powers.

Squinting, he suddenly sensed an old urge. Smiling widely, his body tingled so much that his fingertips, eyeballs, and teeth all but sparked. He reached across the sand to the old, tired white-and-gray-striped cat, which didn't even squirm as it surrendered to the inevitable.

⚡⚡⚡

The harsh fluorescent lights in his mother's laundry room illuminated clumps of white and gray cat fur and specks of dry blood clinging to Archbishop Anarch's black cashmere blazer. Quickly, he brushed off the fur and scraped off the blood with his sharp fingernails. Twisting easily, snapping with the crack of a dried-out twig, the old cat's head had flopped round and round, making Archbishop Anarch laugh harder than at any time since he had last visited the site of his boyhood altar.

Sentimentally, he whispered the Aspérges, *"Aspérges me, Dómine, hyssópo, et mundábor: lavábis me, et super nivem dealbábor."* Then, after drying his hands with the white Egyptian cotton towels on the brass rack next to the industrial-sized porcelain sink, he repeated this affirmation to the Almighty in English: "Thou shalt sprinkle me, O Lord, with hyssop, and I shall be cleansed; thou shalt wash me, and I shall become whiter than snow." Feeling better, he had an intense desire to go upstairs and see his beloved mother.

Less than ten miles from the nearest large city in the southeast corner of Aztlan, his mother's estate provided jobs for scores of grateful members of the Ecclesia Dei. She required that all employees be members in good standing, feeling that the Almighty's chosen must work together, the high and mighty charitably assisting the weak and lowly.

Accolades from Patriarch Peter Kulten streamed her way. "We all know that those uneducated, untrained Mexicans owe her so much. The Good Lord has a special throne in heaven for your mother," he would tell the archbishop at their quarterly meetings.

Patriarch Kulten treated the archbishop like a son, but Archbishop Anarch loathed him. Kulten interfered. A mother and son belonged together, especially once the father was dead. For years, his mother and the patriarch had been friends, even before her marriage. And now the patriarch made too many visits, spending long hours praying with her into the night in her private chapel, according to the archbishop's well-paid informants.

Balling up three wet cotton towels, Archbishop Anarch stuffed them angrily into a five-foot-deep trash compactor. It was already a quarter filled with newspapers and yesterday's leftovers—two blood-red half-eaten pieces of cherry pie. Oddly, they resembled the profiles of his mother and Peter Kulten. The archbishop recoiled. Banging down the stainless-steel lid, he turned on the compactor. Its loud crunching lit his nerves on fire. Then it ground to a stop.

At that moment, somebody knocked on the locked laundry room door, irritating him.

"Yes. What is it?" he asked, his hands trembling. He needed to get rid of whoever was there and check inside the compactor to make sure the cat had been ground up sufficiently to be disguised, since bloody things could spoil twenty years of his work for the Almighty.

"Archbishop?" said a teasing voice he recognized. It was the Mexican maid who had soft curves and a shapely tush.

The archbishop ignored her and turned the compactor on again.

But she knocked louder, calling out like a cat in heat,

"Arrrrch biiiiiishoooooooop!"

How dare the fucking bitch distract him. His blood boiled, his skin started tingling again, and soon every square inch of flesh on him wanted to bite, especially his red, hot member, hard as steel. It wanted what it wanted. It couldn't help that. She had brought it on herself. Toying with the only begotten son made bad things happen. Bitches like the one at the door, Claire Sanchez that day on the road in the rain with her wet blouse, and seductive Lucia needed to pay, as did every woman who had ever dared tempt a priest.

Archbishop Anarch opened the door. Pearly white teeth, a taunting bosom, and insolent eyes betrayed a damned being asking to be put out of her misery.

"Archbishop," she coyly said in Mexican, "your mother needs to see you." Ten minutes later, the petite bitch was history, and his red, hot member had cooled. He had enjoyed twisting and cracking her little neck and the brown head, which had swung limply like a Mexican Raggedy Ann doll, and the way the industrial-sized trash compactor had gobbled her up with five gallons of acid and Clorox added so no one would smell anything, and knowing that the trash man would take away the canister just as was done at the end of every day, leaving him free of suspicion.

⚡⚡⚡

Now Archbishop Anarch needed to see his mother. Gazing up the sweeping staircase, he was exhilarated at the thought of seeing his mother on her deathbed, like experiencing the Fourth of July and Christmas bundled into one mind-dazzling package.

Immediately he was at his mother's bedside, smiling, calm. *Wonderful to be alone with her.* The thought struck sharp as a pick through ice. "Mother, I've ached to see you," he said. In minutes it would be over, his mother no longer sucking air through tubes, sent to the Almighty, and the archbishop restored.

"I'm so glad to see you, William," said his mother in a harsh voice that caught him off guard. Until the instant he had stood beside her, her eyes had been shut tight. Now they were open.

The room was rank with decay and death, light sealed off by squarely drawn floor-to-ceiling red velvet curtains. His mother lay in her eighteenth-century canopied bed, covered with a red silk blanket over Sea Island cotton sheeting, oxygen streaming into her nostrils. She was ashen and thin, with tiny purple veins streaking the backs of her hands, temples, and neck. Unblinking, her eyes bore into him. *Those damn eyes. Crawling into me.*

"Mother, I came as soon as I heard," he emphasized. He fidgeted, looking at his watch. At the airport, he had told the driver to pick him up at 6:00 pm. It was 5:05.

"In a hurry, dear?" she asked, her thin lips curling up maliciously. It meant she was going to tell him something, for his own good.

Stomach roiling and neck hairs on end, he didn't answer.

Waiting a few moments, she sucked in a deep breath and said, "Doesn't matter. What I have to say will be brief."

He swallowed then interrupted, "Don't waste your energy, Mother. Sleep. I'll stay as long as the Almighty's work permits."

Lips curling again, she furrowed her brow, not about to drift off to sleep while he was there. "Open the center cabinet," she ordered, gritting her discolored teeth like a female Satan.

Under her spell, he walked to the turn-of-the-century, wall-to-wall étagère. He could finish her right now and not have to endure even one last reprimand or command. He had spent years obeying her directives.

"Tonight I will die," she said, smiling. "Your life has been a tangle. Before I die, I will untie the knots."

The world dropped away. He floated in black empty space,

nothing inside holding him down, everything disintegrating, molecule by molecule.

⚡⚡⚡

"Mother, there's no need," he said, his voice trembling slightly.

"Listen to what I tell you, *boy*," she went on.

He had endured insult after insult for a lifetime, and now she slashed at him again. She hadn't called him that in as long as he could remember, except in her own mind. When she put her thoughts into his brain, in the ghastly way she had of getting under his skin and scratching, making him hurt on the inside. Needle pricks as sharp as his mother's fingernails clawed at his testicles. It wasn't what she said that made him retreat into coldness, but the way she said it—smooth as a butcher's blade slitting a lamb's neck. He closed his eyes for a split-second and willed the pain away. Then he opened the cabinet.

"William, stop there," said the puppet master, jerking the string.

He didn't respond.

"I have sinned," she hissed.

He did not want to hear. She had her own confessor, Peter Kulten, who forgave her, scrubbed her vicious little soul clean.

Seeing right through him, his mother scolded, "Listen!" Rage welled in him.

She continued, "Your beginnings..." Her voice turned into the screams and shouts of the damned. Calm shattered to porcelain pieces as her face imposed itself in the center of his forehead—inescapable.

For a few seconds, William stood paralyzed by her grip, then turning on his heel he flung the cabinet's double doors open, the heavy mahogany nearly ripping off its hinges, and reached inside.

On the uppermost ledge lay a lone object. He touched it with his fingertips, then recoiled as if burned.

"No. Not until I say what I have to say," his mother reprimanded. But he grabbed the object, opened the gold-leafed glass case, and stared at the contents. He was shocked but not surprised. He had guessed as much. Moving toward her, he cradled in his hands the framed photograph of two lovers embracing.

"Your father refused to acknowledge the truth," his mother said, gasping.

"Mother, you're irredeemable," he uttered coldly. He had never spoken truer feelings to her. "There is no hope for one who steals another's life." He had been used, a sin offering.

A flick of a finger and the oxygen tubes would fall out, and she would gasp and struggle and cast her cloudy eyes one last time at him but they would not get inside because he knew now. He inched closer, flush with the bed. He had done everything for her, and now he had to focus on himself.

Lips barely moving, he whispered the words, *Lavábo inter innocéntes manu meas… Lavábo inter…*

"No, my son. No salvation. Hell's fires will be our bed," she muttered, sighing and reaching for his hand.

Violent trembling shook him as he flashed back to images of blood and screaming and father red-faced and mother limp on the floor. Dry-mouthed, he whispered, "I think not, Mother."

Ice-cold blue flickered through the slits of her serpent eyes.

He would waste no more energy. "This means nothing to me," he said, raising the picture, preparing to let it shatter.

"Foolish boy," she chided. "It means more than you know," she said, guttural sounds forming the barely discernible words.

"Goodbye, Mother," he said, turning to leave with the picture poised on his fingertips, eager to hear the glass break and his mother moan. Photos of himself as a young boy, and of mother, father, and son, were nonexistent. Glass encased, gold bedecked, this was where her heart lay.

"Peter Kulten..." she muttered.

"Is nothing," he interrupted. Through the corner of his eye, he saw her flinch, then shake a crooked finger.

"You, William Anarch, are his seed," she confessed. There was nothing more she could say to him, do to him, steal from him.

William laughed and tossed the picture in the air.

As glass shattered, she lunged toward the shards, her bones snapping like lightning-charred twigs as she hit the floor and turned from purple to ashen gray to white, and cold.

He left.

22

F ists flexed, drenched with sweat, Anthony strained a final time. Immediately the last of the tarnished brass rivets popped off the leather straps, and he tugged his legs free.

A short time later, the door upstairs creaked open. Flopping the straps back in place, Anthony lay down, closed his eyes to slits, and quieted his breathing. Soon a hooded monk, rattling chains, turned the key to enter the cell. For what felt like forever, Anthony feigned unconsciousness. If it seemed he was out cold long enough, he knew the kidnappers would grow worried. They wouldn't want something unexpected happening to their catch. They needed him.

The monk entered. Claire's face flashed into Anthony's mind. A lover's protectiveness was all it took for him to spring out of bed, grab the chains, and squeeze the flabbergasted monk's neck. Anthony knew that if he applied enough pressure to the neck it would crack, but he refrained, deciding that it was enough to knock the monk out.

Anthony laid him on the floor, then picked up a sealed plastic bag the monk had dropped containing a chloroform-drenched rag and put it under the man's nose as an extra precaution. Taking a good look at him, Anthony saw it was Mr. Himmel, the hospital administrator, whom Claire had pointed out to him at a staff Christmas party. Anthony wrapped the chains around Himmel's torso and legs then hooked them to a wooden plank. Himmel wouldn't wake up for an hour, and when he did, he'd only be able to grunt and wiggle a little.

Enormously satisfied to have defrocked a friar on the prowl, Anthony felt clear-headed and energized. Slipping the key ring off Himmel's thick leather belt, he locked the cell then made his way up the shadowy wrought-iron stairs.

Getting to the top, he clicked the door open and dodged a fist. As her black hood fell off, Anthony saw it was Wardene Black.

"Medicine woman lover," she shrieked, lunging for Anthony's throat. He pushed her away. Wooden floorboards creaked as she crumpled to the floor, hitting her knees hard.

"Jesus, Mary, and Joseph," echoed Wardene Black's voice through the sconce-lit narrow central corridor, quickly trailing off into the darkness.

Disgusted, Anthony watched Wardene Black writhe like the snake she was and waited for her next move.

Mean as a crazed bull, she came at him with a shoulder-to-thigh tackle. Anthony didn't budge. He then cupped his hands on her face and jerked her upright.

As her lower back popped, she yelled, "Do not touch me. I am a consecrated virgin."

Anthony boomed out a belly laugh. Hands under her armpits, he lifted up the chunky woman, saying, "I'm going to pack you up for the Almighty, sweetheart."

Wardene Black gasped and froze.

Flipping her around, he cupped his hand over her mouth and carried her, squirming, to a small chapel at the end of the hall, with rows of pews, a gold tabernacle on the altar with a bloody crucified divinity above it, and red votive candles flickering. With one arm, he pulled down a veil of gauze covering the entrance and held Wardene Black with the other. Quickly he ripped the gauze in two and gagged and bound her, then dragged her to a closet that contained white robes hanging hunched like spiritless monks. Seeing a wooden chest behind them, Anthony pushed the robes apart, then flipped the chest's lid open, forced Wardene Black inside, and closed it.

Finally, Anthony looped the chain of a silver censer through the chest's handle, wrapping the excess chain around the censer. Uneven wooden slats would let enough air in for Wardene Black to breathe. Anthony left the closet door open, knowing that someone would find her later that evening.

After a few minutes, Anthony went outside and discovered that he was at the archbishop's hacienda high in the Sagrado Mountains, about twenty miles, a four-hour hike, from Francesca's home. He didn't want to be spotted on the highway since too many of Archbishop Anarch's cronies were out and about, so, with the sun setting, he took off into the hills.

22

S mooth until now, Archbishop Anarch's flight took a turn for the worse, the plane rocking through the dark sky like an out-of-control kite, as lightning zigzagged, electric fingers lighting up the horizon. He gripped the leather armrest hard and tried to focus on how he would soon be back in northern Aztlan and able to finish off the medicine woman so he would be freed from the twenty-year-old vow.

In the darkness, he heard a demanding voice say, *Your will for mine. Mine, William. Your will. Now mine.* He lurched forward, like waking from a bad dream, half expecting to see the Almighty appear, reminding him of the agreement—years of power, wealth, and fame in exchange for the final sacrifice.

Teeth clenched, Archbishop Anarch gripped the armrest tighter, knowing that nature's whims revealed the hand of the Almighty at work, and tonight the Almighty howled with white-hot rage reflecting the craving for sacrifice—that which had been vowed. Soon he would be able to satisfy that craving, dispatching the last medicine woman likely to challenge the Ecclesia Dei and his authority.

23

The cave near where her mother had died had called Claire back. She didn't know how she had gotten to the Place of the Granite Boulder. Time had stood still and moved backward. Ominous and dark and red, the moon was centered at the top of the mouth of the cave, wolves howled in the distance, and the little girl within her moved into a trance as her mother had taught her, watching and listening.

Now seeing through the eyes of Lucia, she could perceive a black-hooded evil man with a crook, caped and howling, drawing close. She experienced terror—not for herself but for her child.

Gripping her wooden staff, she readied herself. Moments earlier he had not believed her, but she knew he already suspected the truth. Vicious rumors had flown through the Ecclesia Dei.

His tormented face shaking with denial, the black-hooded man shouted,

"Father Gall would not do such a thing."

"He is your Judas. If he can topple you, the power is his,"

claimed Lucia.

"He has no motive," continued the black-hooded man.

"Come away with us. The man I have loved is still in you. And once Claire knows you are her father, she too will love you," pleaded Lucia.

He raised the crook.

"Noooooooooo," screamed Lucia, stepping back—the blow fatal, the staff flying out of her hand.

⚡⚡⚡

"Child," a harsh voice whispered from the mouth of the cave.

Claire opened her eyes and saw a black cape fluttering in the howling wind, blocking the sight of the red moon. Unafraid, she seized the staff next to her, which Francesca had returned to her years ago when Claire had refused her calling, and stood up.

From beneath his cape, Archbishop Anarch flashed his bronze serpent-headed crook high overhead then vanished.

Claire stepped out of the cave to see where he had gone, whereupon a blow to the back of the head sent her to the ground, her staff still in her hand. Anarch hit her again, in the side. Blistering pain momentarily paralyzed her, but then Lucia's presence, the chanting of past medicine women, and the howling of three gray wolves propelled Claire back to her feet.

Claire concentrated then struck out with her staff, causing Archbishop Anarch to double over and moan.

Three wolves, moonlight glistening on their fur, emerged from the forest. Archbishop Anarch cringed at the sight, and with the pain of broken ribs. Pitifully, the archbishop gazed into Claire's eyes, his thoughts becoming hers. She had spent years never knowing her true father, and now he was before her, weak, injured, at her mercy.

With his left hand, the archbishop reached out, groaning, "Daughter." Stunned, Claire hesitated, almost drawn into his ruse.

Taking advantage of her bewilderment, he instantly bolted upright and swung his crook high to crush her skull.

She fought to regain her balance, stepped aside, leveled her staff, and then hurled it at the bridge of his nose. Immediately, lightning struck the bronze crook, and the staff hit its mark. Blue and white electric fingers flicked Archbishop Anarch to the ground. Three wolves drew near as Claire's auburn hair stood on end, and she screamed like an Aztlan medicine woman at the blood-red moon.

Moments later Anthony arrived at the Place of the Granite Boulder with the State Police. They found Claire encircled by three gray wolves that quickly withdrew into the forest.

24

Claire gazed at the sparks and flames from Francesca's funeral pyre leaping into the night sky at the Place of the Granite Boulder. Anthony stood beside her. Finally, the elevated bed of branches illuminated by the crackling cedar and piñon fire crashed to the ground, Francesca's corpse no longer discernible amidst the charred wood. Spirits of Lucia, Lozen, Dahteste, and Gouyen cried out the sounds of the medicine women as fierce mountain winds echoed through the canyon and Francesca's departed soul made its way into the spirit world.

It had been seven days since Archbishop Anarch had been killed. Earlier that week headlines of the *Aztlan Crier* had read, *Evil Archbishop Dead.*

Page after page had detailed the uncovering of the archbishop's blood sacrifices by state and federal authorities. Emboldened by news releases, woman after woman, all patients of the Ecclesia Dei Psychiatric Hospital, had broken down and admitted how Archbishop Anarch had used them, threatening eternal damnation for breaching secrecy. Father Gall, on behalf of the patriarch of the Ecclesia Dei, had at first decried

Archbishop Anarch's actions as "the obscene and evil behavior of a demented man who fooled so well those who trusted him so much." But later he too had been investigated, and named an accomplice. An international television news magazine had run a special weekly feature entitled "Religion Kills," with revelations about the lunacy, carnage, and religious fervor being broadcast to millions worldwide. Cameras had zoomed in on the towering red sandstone peaks of the Devil's Throne. Archbishop Anarch had been exposed as a man who had once been revered but who had ultimately been exposed and was now reviled.

After days of depositions that would clarify charges, Claire had remained in seclusion, reflecting on what had happened. She had fought for her life and won. And she had faced her past as the last of a lineage of strong medicine women and claimed her role in that lineage.

Wolves howled in the moonlit night. Anthony wrapped his arm around Claire, who looked at him as he spoke of the past, present, and future, of losses gone by and intimacy to be forged. With her left arm, Claire drew Anthony to her, and with her right hand, she clutched the staff of the medicine woman.

CONNECT WITH PAUL DEBLASSIE III:

www.pauldeblassieiii.com

Twitter: @pdeblassieiii
Facebook: @pdeblassieiii